More praise for *Marching to Valhalla*

"Blake has Custer's journal touch on everything, from his triumphs to his political naiveté, and makes the closing chapters a matter-of-fact ride to storied glory."

—*New York Daily News*

"Blake merges his imagination with Custer's journals to weave a colorful novel."

—*St. Louis Post–Dispatch*

"A richly textured tale."

—*The Wichita Eagle*

Other books by Michael Blake

DANCES WITH WOLVES

AIRMAN MORTENSEN

Marching
to Valhalla

Marching to Valhalla

A Novel of Custer's Last Days

MICHAEL BLAKE

Fawcett Columbine
The Ballantine Publishing Group
New York

A Fawcett Columbine Book
Published by The Ballantine Publishing Group

http://www.randomhouse.com

Library of Congress Catalog Card Number: 97-90870

ISBN: 0-449-00044-3

This edition published by arrangement with Villard
Books, a division of Random House, Inc.

Cover design by Ruth Ross
Cover illustration by Jim Carson

Manufactured in the United States of America

First Ballantine Books Trade Edition: October 1997

10 9 8 7 6 5 4 3 2 1

For an unflagging student of life,

my father,

JAMES LENNOX WEBB

ACKNOWLEDGMENTS

I wish to acknowledge the hundreds of Custer scholars, known and unknown, who have made such a large contribution to our knowledge of Custer and the times in which he lived.

Specifically, I wish to acknowledge the contribution of my wife, Marianne Blake, who stood at my shoulder during the writing of this book.

Marching
to Valhalla

MAY 18,

1876

I am as compelled to write as I am to take breath. There is so much in my heart—anger and the deepest pain and love for so many things. Yet it all remains unspoken because emotionally I am mute. I have been as a muzzled dog all my life.

But I can write. I feel I can write all the way through till morning, stopping only at the waking of camp. There is something afoot in me tonight that tells me I am finally writing with my true heart. Not a chatty letter, nor a calculated article, nor a carefully worded report. The constant compulsion to write is now wedded to an impulse to tell all, to tell it simply and without embellishment. To tell the truth.

I will lay this down when we meet the enemy, if we meet him at all, but until that time I will make these nights after tattoo my own—a stool and a tiny desk, a candle and a pen. And I, of course, my brow fully knitted as I try to squeeze something out in ink that I cannot say through the hole in my face. Me. The man from Monroe, the Boy General, Son of the Morning Star, Iron Butt, Old Curly, Long Hair, Fanny and Cinnamon and Autie and Bo. And so much more. And so much less. And like all the great and small of this constantly convulsing world, so alone.

It is terrible to be alone. It leaves a certain part of the human appetite forever unfed. But sitting here by myself in the night, still in my boots, the only sound the mechanical scratching of the pen, makes me feel a king. Strangely, being alone has always filled me with courage, too. Perhaps that is why I have always done so well in battle. I have always felt as alone in the chaos of battle as I do here tonight.

Libbie is gone now. She has been my other life. In lives I have always had two. Life with myself and life with Libbie. I can still feel her breath on my shoulder. It cut through this morning as it always does, cut through the tunic and shirt straight to the skin. Her breath has always burned straight into my flesh.

For a long time we have been experts at separation. She shed no tears as I helped her into the paymaster's wagon. She smiled her brave smile and said she would listen each night for my step on the stair or the clank of my saber in the hall. She knows that I will come back to her as soon as I can. I have always come to her. She knows I will pay any price to be with her because I have done so many times before. And so has she. We have never been content to be devoted in mind or spirit alone for our marriage has been a marriage of action. We have thrived on demonstrating our devotion and our love has never been at rest.

When the column moved out, I cantered far ahead on Dandy,

ascending a ridge from which I hoped I could see the wagon. It was there, far below me like some lonesome ship at sea, rolling over the landscape on a course for Fort Lincoln and home. I lifted my hat and waved it back and forth over my head. And there was her tiny hand, sticking through the canvas doors at the rear of the wagon, waving some piece of fabric back at me.

We have been married for twelve years and yet it seems to me only a blink in time, for Libbie has remained the girl who captured my heart. She said then that her only wish in life was to be with me and that conviction has remained constant through time. It is popularly believed that a woman's function is to provide a moral foundation for a man, and if that is so, she is a master builder by any standard and I am the luckiest of husbands.

There is business at hand, hard and ugly business that must be completed. How long we must march before engaging the enemy I do not know. I only know I shall miss her little body lying next to mine in this tent. I will miss the rise and fall of her breath at night, the touch of her hand in mine, the perfume of her skin. I will miss her smartness and her readiness and I shall miss the light that shines so brightly in her eyes. But I shall not pine for her. I know she is with me at every moment. She is with me now, even as she sleeps somewhere on the trail back to Fort Lincoln.

MAY 19,

1876

Never could I have imagined all that would happen to me in this life. I have been both king and beggar and all that lies between and I often take solace in the knowledge that few men in history have walked in my shoes.

Few men on earth have dined on the antelope that nourished me this evening. The meat is exceedingly lean—not my favorite. Buffalo is my favorite. I believe I could eat buffalo forever and never tire of its taste. Antelope is far gamier, much like the land it roams, I suppose. I too am roaming this land, headed for a rendezvous with

Colonel Gibbon's column and the steamer *Far West* on the Yellowstone River.

It is a cold, damp camp tonight with little progress made today. I detest the wagons trailing behind with their loads of rations and ammunition. I wish I could live without food and still spit fire in battle. I wish I could live without sleep. I wish that every day were without impediment and every horse under me without need of rest. But with a force this large there is no escaping the tedium of the march and its many details. Each man must eat, each man must drink, each man must evacuate his waste and be clothed and mounted and spend a third of his every day unconscious. The column moves with the sloth of some monstrous snake that has swallowed some monstrous egg.

As a boy I used to dream of being conscious every minute of every hour of every day. I would lie in my bed, wide awake, wishing I could keep my eyes open till dawn, then to bound from the covers as fresh as if I had slept. To be awake my whole life. The memory drives me still. I have always shunned sleep, always been a slave to a boy's dream. How grand it would be to miss nothing.

I have feasted on life and feasted on death, yet I have never been full. My blessing and my curse all in one. When I am finished here I shall close my eyes for two or three hours with a single expectation—that of getting up and out. In the morning I will outline the day's march with the wing commanders and throw down breakfast as fast as I can. Then I shall climb onto Dandy's back and scout ahead with a small escort, leaving the elephantine mass of wagons and baggage and troops far behind. That is when the joy of my day begins. We will be exploring ahead of the column and I cannot wait to see what tomorrow may bring.

I have been through this country before but I will relish every step that Dandy takes. There is something new to be found each day and it is sure that my restless eyes, which I sometime think have a life of their own, will search out every wood and stream and ridge and ravine for any interesting sign. Perhaps we will find a layer of ancient fossils jutting from the strata along a bluff. Perhaps in a grove of aspens, leaves quaking in the breeze, we will see the flash of a living hide and the chase will begin. If we are determined, the game will be run to its death and there will be fresh meat over the fires tomorrow night. Perhaps, in some glade or coulee, at some unknown distance to our front, the enemy will conceal himself until the desired moment and then we will engage in the point of this campaign, far from home and family. We will lock then in mortal combat, testing the strength of each other's arms and wills in a fight to the death.

I must laugh at myself. I love moments of discovery and I love combat, but even as I write I know the enemy will not be discovered tomorrow, nor for many more days, I think. The enemy has little interest in our activities and we will not meet him except by some happy accident. The free roamers have gone west, following the buffalo, which is their lifeline. Some of the men are already joking about the prospects for a long summer picnic, saying that it is likely we will trek the whole summer without seeing a single Indian. That is possible. Our foe is the most elusive imaginable. Whole villages can disappear in a single night, large war parties can splinter and vanish almost in a wink. This foe can conceal himself in plain view and is loath to fight unless cornered or given a superior advantage.

But it is I who will eventually find their trail, and once I strike their scent I will be on their track to the very end. I am a hound in uniform the likes of which they have not known before. And I am not the type of hound who wearies of the chase. Once loosed, nothing short of being called off by my masters will induce me to give up. And when I am finally free in the field I will course far beyond earshot of my masters. I have always found the enemy and I will do so this summer.

My scout Bloody Knife will be with me tomorrow as he was today. I will have him with me every day possible, though I'm sure his services will be needed elsewhere from time to time, particularly if the action gets heavy. Like all aborigines he reads the country as well as an architect reads a blueprint at a glance. It is a pleasure to have an expert reader of the land on this march. In essence he has been teaching me to read as well, and such endeavors not only enlighten but ease the labor of establishing the route, finding proper fords, and selecting suitable camping spots.

He is even more important in a larger military sense, having, I am certain, saved lives on more than one occasion with a warning that could only come from his special gifts.

He was with me three years ago on the Yellowstone Expedition, and I shall never forget one afternoon in particular. The column was charged with protecting surveying parties of the Northern Pacific Railroad. While the main force was engaged at a difficult ford I grew restless and rode forward with a company to have a look at the country ahead. By one or two o'clock in the afternoon it was sweltering and I ordered a halt in a pleasant stand of trees near a cool, high-banked stream. I was dozing in my underwear when someone softly called my name and I awoke to find Bloody Knife and our interpreter squatting at my side. His face was as pale as any Red Indian's can be and I was soon made to understand that pony tracks belonging to fifty or sixty Sioux warriors had crossed the stream above our camp.

Thinking only of pursuit I got to my feet and started to dress, asking which direction the enemy had taken.

"They have not taken a direction," he replied solemnly. "They are here."

He then explained that the tracks had been made only moments before.

The horses grazing a hundred yards off were our first concern. Brother Tom was with me then as he is now, and together with a half dozen members of his troop we dashed to where the horses were gathered, crept to the edge of the cut bank, and peered over the edge. We found ourselves gazing down on the heads of a line of warriors, walking in a crouch below us. I remember the sunlight shimmering on their oiled hair.

They were completely unaware of our presence and the thought of the terror we were about to subject them to produced a giggle in my throat which I was barely able to suppress.

Tom fired the first shot. Our adversaries jumped as one and were in full flight while still in the air. It was as if we had dropped a snarling fox into a coop of roosting chickens. The Sioux ran for their lives, losing two killed and at least one wounded as they sped back up the stream. The whole company went to horse but we were unable to catch them and broke off the chase after several miles.

The Indian is always eager to boast of his exploits in war—I am eager for the same, I must confess—but I doubt if this foray was often recounted by them. For us it had turned out as nothing more than a lark. But it could have been much different if those warriors had killed the pickets and gotten off with the horses.

That evening I asked Bloody Knife what he had seen in the pony prints that made him think the war party was upon us. He said the prints were deep and when he found them grains of sand were still tumbling down the walls of the impressions.

Since then I have always looked for the same in fresh prints but have yet to find any with grains of sand still falling along the walls.

There is more to Bloody Knife than the admirable outdoor traits he shares with his brethren. He is stolid and firm with the other scouts, his fellow Rees. His voice is deep and authoritative and they listen to him with respect. He follows instructions well and his reports never fail to contain information that is useful. In another time he and I might discuss everyday matters of mutual interest in good comradeship. He possesses a certain merriment of eye that I think lends itself to appreciation of fun as well. But that is not to be. I am a part of the engine that powers the wheels of progress, progress that will eventually destroy his way of life. For now I believe he knows my wild heart better than many of those close to me. And I know that, given the choice, he would no doubt kill a Sioux before turning his knife on me. He and I are after the same game. I feel secure with Bloody Knife.

In fact, I would feel even more secure if I had several Bloody Knives on this campaign. If that were the case I would replace some senior officers with the spare Bloody Knives. Captain Benteen, who I'm sure will be commanding one of my wings, would be the first to go. Benteen is an individual I will never understand. There is a bitterness in him toward everybody and everything and particularly toward myself. Captain Benteen could be placed amidst the fairest company, at the prettiest picnic table, on the sunniest June day and, to me, he would still appear as a man sunk in shadow. His bulging eyes seem fixed, as if in a state of constant obsession, and though his seeming malevolence for all things is constant, I believe he regards me with a special acidity. On more than one occasion he has tried to draw me into settling our disputes by fighting one another. Our disputes have been legitimate and deep, but on reflection I have come to believe that Captain Benteen's chief goal at these times has been to put himself in position to kill me legally. He has so far drawn the line at murder, but it has often crossed my mind on a march that if conditions were right he would seize the opportunity to put a ball between my shoulders and say afterward that his horse had stepped in a hole. I have known a number of officers who have detested me, not for what I have done, but rather for who I am. Men who hate without knowing precisely why are men to be feared and of them all I fear Benteen the most.

The second to go would be Major Reno. If Captain Benteen were to reside on one side of the moon I'm certain Major Reno would be in residence on the other. He is a quiet man—unless drunk, at which time he is loud and boorish—and largely keeps his own counsel. What manner of counsel this may be brings eerie bumps to the surface of my skin, for there is something perverted about Major Reno. He is naturally heavy and clumsy, yet he affects a military bearing. The overall impression reminds one of a boy who, under the threat of severe penalty, has had his face spit-washed, his hair oiled, and his body stuffed into an ill-fitting suit for attendance at Sunday worship. There is a softness about him, too, and his eyes often have the limpid look of a man who can be broken. He is extremely awkward in the presence of women and no one seeks his company. He always seems to be thinking of something else and I have never been able to deduce whether he is merely slow of wit or if he is constantly haunted by secrets and bizarre thoughts, circulating endlessly through his brain.

Both Benteen and Reno have been good career soldiers. Each was outstanding in the Great War, having distinguished themselves in battle on many occasions. They have never disobeyed my orders, nor have I had to reprimand either since the initiation of their service in the Seventh Cavalry almost ten years ago. They are experienced soldiers but unbearable men—typical ironies of military life. They are excellent testimony to the democratic nature of military life, and in the end, they are what I have drawn, nothing more, nothing less. My one overwhelming hope is that both of them have good days when we meet the enemy.

There are some officers on this campaign, mostly company commanders, in whom I have the utmost confidence. I have family with me also, and I know I can depend on them. I love these men dearly, but, reaching back through time, I know it would be impossible to love men more than I did those of the Michigan Brigade . . . my Wolverines. At first they rejected me and I suppose rightfully so. They had no reason to love me in the beginning and I had no good reason to love them. We were all so young then and the violent convulsions of war impel the soldier to shift allegiances on the run, often in the inferno of battle itself. But an unseen force had been driving me toward the Michiganders long before I reached them. Perhaps it was the force of the Creator. I do not know. I only know that the mysterious currents of destiny, which seem to have ruled my life, brought us together. We were meant to achieve glory over and over again, and how it came to be surpasses the imagination.

If I was born to anything it was to be a commander of men and from the onset of the war my every step seemed guided toward that end. Command was not something I wanted in the way an amateur painter dreams of composing perfect pictures or an amateur vocalist dreams of singing thrilling arias. I hungered for command with a raw instinct I could neither understand nor plan. I didn't want to command, I *had* to command. These feelings were never fully articulated in my mind. They were not manifested in words or dreams, only in action. Action attracted my instinct as surely as a blade of grass is attracted to the power of the sun. And I have grown.

Much of my military ascension has been ascribed to the whims of fortune—"Custer's luck" I believe is the phrase—but, while I have often been in the advantageous setting at the advantageous moment, it is evident to me that a single condition has been constant throughout my army career, a condition that overrides all else. In every case it was owing to my own initiative that I found myself in favorable circumstances. One can backtrack the trail that led me to command the Michigan Cavalry and find that without fail it was the action of an individual that tripped the mechanism which propelled him to the heights.

The cosmos may have played a role in my appointment to West Point in June 1857, but it was I who long before that date picked up a pen and wrote to my home congressman, this in spite of coming from a family without influence who had loudly and for many years proclaimed its opposition to the political ideals of the same congressman's party. More than any other single factor I believe it was that letter, the honest, unabashed request of a sincere boy, which eventually made the appointment possible.

I was not in the least interested in school and never had been. In that sense I was eminently unqualified to attend an academy of such prestige. For the duration of my previous education I had ventured as little as possible to get by and the energy I expended in passing the Academy entrance examinations was probably in excess of all I had expended before.

Scholarship and study held no appeal to me in those days and the long winters bent over books of philosophy and mathematics were agonizing torture which could only be relieved by bouts of unbridled fun, fun which resulted in a steady parade of demerits. When these black marks brought me to the brink of expulsion I pulled back, transforming myself into a model cadet for the balance of the term, at which time the cycle of study and fun and punishment began all over again.

My long pattern of disinterest in the study of most subjects repeated itself as well. I graduated last in a class of forty. But I graduated. So many more never made it that far. I saw those who were insufficiently quick of mind or character slip solemnly out of their rooms, a bag or two in hand, to begin the long journey home, each mile of which must have been clouded by defeat.

It is a matter of public record that I was detained for court-martial on the eve of graduation because of one final, trivial infraction. I was designated officer of the guard on a day when two underclassmen who disliked each other vehemently could restrain themselves no longer and began a fistfight. As officer of the guard I was charged with keeping peace and order but when I saw who was engaged I threw aside my responsibility in that regard. The two adversaries would come to blows eventually, of that I was certain. On this day they had bloodied themselves already but no victor had been decided. If necessary they would resume their fight on some dark night out on the grounds. I could have ordered them placed under arrest at that moment and no one would have opposed it, but something told me that the least harm would come if the hostile parties had it out then and there. Perhaps I was so relieved at the conclusion of four years of unrelenting labor that I wanted to vent my own frustration through theirs. I don't know.

I bade the onlookers step back. I too moved aside, looked at the two combatants, and said, "Let's have a fair fight."

Given my sanction the two boys attacked each other with renewed fury, attracting a larger and larger crowd, among them one of my superiors.

I explained, then pleaded, then begged, all to no avail. While my fellow graduates boarded trains for the capital I was left behind, awaiting justice.

The board decided at last to give me a simple reprimand and that action is one I have often heard referred to as a piece of "Custer's luck." It is said that the Great War interceded on my behalf but to my mind the greatest human conflict in our history interceded in the lives of everyone and I was but one of millions whose fate was altered by an all-consuming national calamity. All I know is that I was anxious to be part of it.

I stopped in New York City for I was now a soldier, a tardy soldier who possessed neither a sword, nor sidearm, nor even spurs. All of these things I purchased at a military supplier, and though I was still a soldier in name only, at least I now had the required raw materials to present myself as one. The pride that went with being free of academia and being in uniform and under arms on the eve of a great conflict was unbearable. I had to share it with someone and had a picture of myself made in a studio on Fifty-seventh Street. I posted it immediately to my sister and she still has it.

I cannot help laughing each time I see it. It is a picture of the rankest boy, a child ready to play at war. In times past I would beg Lydia to pack that silly image away but I do not mind it so much now. When looking back on the years of a life bursting with meaningful events large and small, it becomes difficult to separate the sum from its parts. After so many years it is difficult to perceive the growth which was constantly occurring. But frozen in that aging ambrotype is a vision which never fails to give me pleasure, for what is frozen there is a vision rarely seen. The boy in the picture is in the last moments of true youth, about to leave behind all he knows of naïveté and irresponsibility and boyish dreams. I've had many pictures taken since then but the boy of that time has never reappeared. I believe he was gone the moment the shutter snapped.

None of this was known to me as I arrived in Washington. I was much more concerned with having been left behind, for the city was largely devoid of military activity, most of the men and materials having been moved forward, massing for the first great battle of the war.

I presented myself at headquarters; a staff officer took notice of my West Point uniform and ushered me into a large room, where I was introduced to the supreme commander, General Scott. I was too stunned to feel any trivial emotion like embarrassment. I thought not of low stature or innocence. I was paralyzed at the mere sight of a great general, so great that he seemed to outsize the room even while sitting. His face was still as a stone but there was nothing brusque about his expression. His eyes were so open and calm that I was put at immediate ease. Though I was still uncertain whether I could move my lips words somehow issued freely from my mouth.

The general welcomed me and asked if I was in need of an assignment. I told him that I was and the general asked what my specialty had been at school.

He asked this with such sincere interest, with the same enthusiasm a father might use with a son, that I felt compelled to answer him from my heart.

"Matriculating, sir," I said.

The general laughed without taking his eyes from me and I laughed with him.

"I daresay that must be the specialty of every cadet," he continued. "Let me put it another way. Where would you like to apply your skills?"

"On horseback, sir."

"Cavalry?"

"Yes, sir. I believe I am more at home on a horse than I am on the ground."

"Well, I should like you to feel at home," he said, "I'll assign you to a cavalry unit. And I think your first act of duty will be to carry forward some dispatches of mine."

"Yes, sir, thank you, sir."

"You're welcome, Lieutenant. I want you to leave by eight o'clock this evening. In the meantime, you will have to find yourself a horse."

My boyish heart danced along the cloud tops for some time after that interview, but the longer I searched for a horse the more desperate I became. There was not one horse in all of Washington, and my ecstasy at the prospect of serving my country through its supreme commander faded with the passing of each frantic, futile hour of my search. I had exhausted virtually all hope and was sitting in despair on a city street, feeling certain I would be denied a great chance, when I saw a soldier whom I had known at West Point riding down the middle of the avenue. He remembered me as well and I asked what had brought him into the city. When he said he had come to fetch a spare battery horse that had been left behind I felt as if I was listening to a pronouncement of Providence.

I was amazed to discover that the spare horse was one that I had ridden often and well at West Point. As my friend and I left Washington that evening I was well mounted but somewhat lighter, now lacking my pistol and spurs, which had become the property of my acquaintance. While many able-bodied men throughout the country were scrambling to buy their way out of the war, I bought myself into it. Call it Custer's Luck!

It was difficult to find General McDowell's headquarters, for the army was so large that it seemed I was searching for an address in a modern city I did not know. Never had I seen so many men and horses concentrated in one place, all of it sprawling before me in flickering darkness at three A.M. Some men had already breakfasted and were forming columns for the morning's march. But because of various delays thousands were still upon the ground, some smoking, many still sleeping. I was forced to use care to keep my horse from walking over them.

At last I found General McDowell's headquarters and handed my dispatches to a white-haired major. I had been awake for nearly two days and was faint with hunger but wanted my assignment and waited for the major to return. He asked for news of the capital and I replied that everyone seemed to be waiting for news from this quarter. The major laughed and said that the news should be out soon. The whole army was going to attack the enemy on this very morning and all believed the outcome would be decisive. There had been light skirmishing for the last two days, but this morning's contest would probably end the war. No one dreamed it would take more than one battle.

I had made many friends from the South and no small number of my sympathies lay there. But on entering the academy at West Point I had given my word before God to uphold the Union. This was a vow I could not break, and like the rest of the country I imagined the power of the Union to be absolute. Defeat was something that simply did not occupy our thoughts on the eve of Bull Run.

The battle was barely begun before our army went mad. Suddenly, everyone, so far as my eyes could see, was running. I was commanding a company and had no chance even for a view of the enemy before we were overrun by our own soldiers, eighteen thousand wild-eyed men throwing their weapons aside in a titanic scramble for their lives. Only through vigilance and firmness and constant cajoling was I able to keep my sixty men from doing the same. Some had to be threatened at sword point to maintain ranks. It was a lengthy retreat but I was able to reach the point where the army was regrouping with my first command intact. For this I was cited for bravery but I took no pride in it. The inconceivable had happened. The Union had been routed and this first clash was to birth a thousand more. By the conclusion of the war I felt as if I had ridden in them all.

That I survived the war is thought by many to be a miracle. It didn't feel like a miracle, it felt like the natural result of surrendering one's life to a cause, that of victory over the enemy. To prevail, I knew of but one way to proceed: to give my all. I accepted every assignment. I volunteered whenever possible. I threw myself gladly in the path of danger and built my reputation on a certain lack of fear, which came to be greatly appreciated by my superior officers. I was blessed in being able to serve on the staffs of men like Kearny and McClellan and Pleasanton. General Kearny taught me the value of discipline and McClellan taught me generalship. It was Pleasanton who taught me cavalry and then put me in a position of command.

I had performed well under all of them, having been cited for bravery or gallantry on many occasions and advanced quickly to the rank of captain. I had fought and killed the enemy but I was still a staff officer with no real command of my own.

So great was my desire that I went to the trouble of seeking out the Michigan Brigade in the spring of 1863 and asked the officers to sign petitions which would let me lead them. I had captured the enemy, destroyed his railroads, confiscated his money, faced the mouth of his cannon, outwitted him time after time and sent many of his number to wander the halls of Valhalla. These deeds were well known throughout the army and I suppose that is why the officers of the Michigan Brigade did not laugh in my face. They politely declined my offer and I left that afternoon feeling so foolish that my only relief was the thought that I might never encounter them again.

One week, the week of June 26th to July 3rd, 1863, proved that hope wrong. In the span of those few long summer days of death and glory I became what I wanted to be.

✧

I've been asleep, for how long I'm not sure. It is still raining and seems likely that the going will be muddy tomorrow. The wagons will be up to their axles the whole day long and there will be much complaining all around. But we will be moving forward. I shall see to that.

MAY 20-22,

1876

Tonight my body cannot make quick, physical movements, yet my eyes and mind are fully awake. It is as if I am two people, one made of pure flesh and bone, prey to the dissipation that stalks every man, the other composed entirely of spirit, immune to the rigors that wrack the human form.

It is curious to be two beings at once, but comfortable, too, for I have lived in such a state for weeks at a time throughout my life. What drives me so? I have never enquired very deeply into such subtle thinking, but if pressed I could only surmise that my drive is part of a single ambition I have held for as long as memory can serve. I have always aspired to greatness. Dwelling in the midlands of human endeavor is one of the conditions of existence I truly fear. The fear is so great it has placed the mundane beyond my reach, like some far-off country I shall never see. Greatness has been my aim, and though the personal rewards are so attractive as to make one hunger constantly for more, I believe that to be able simply to stand in the glory of greatness is a reward which cannot be exceeded. To see and feel and taste and hear greatness is the single, most wonderful achievement a human can reach. Even if it is reached for but one tiny moment the participant cannot help but carry such a moment to the end of time. Greatness stands above all else.

I was poised for greatness in that late June of 1863 but I had as yet failed to possess the instrument that would carry me into such lonely but ecstatic territory. It was waiting for me at a small table in the officers' common tent when I returned one night after helping secure the perimeter of our large camp during a lull in hostilities.

✌

A momentary interruption I cannot resist. A vision of Libbie, years ago in Kansas. I, lolling in the shade of a monstrous tree, watching her gambol with one of the dogs on an unusually warm and sunny winter day. I can see her in a light cotton dress, the sunlight passing through, transforming her slim, small body into a dancing silhouette. I particularly remember her strong, vital legs, so full of life. I wish they were dancing before me now in this candlelight.

✌

On the table was a large envelope. Before I could see to whom it was addressed, my fellow officers besieged me with a familiar greeting that had begun as a good-natured tease but had lately grown tiresome.

"Hello, General"; "Good evening, General"; "Welcome home, General."

I had made no secret of my desire for command, as did many of my brother officers. With few exceptions we sought the same prize. I was only a captain but I had been influencing command decisions for some time. I had distinguished myself in combat almost routinely. Combined with my avowed intent to command, I suppose these elements prompted greater teasing than I was willing to absorb. Especially on that night.

The day had been a difficult one. A horse I admired greatly and had hoped would last through many engagements had been severely wounded in the flanks by shrapnel and I'd been forced to abandon him for a comparatively inferior mount. Securing pickets is critical but time-consuming work and I had endured a long ride back to headquarters without enjoying one step of my new charger's gait.

After hearing several of these unwanted greetings I fixed my flintiest expression on the nearest tease and said curtly, "I believe that will suffice. I've had enough. You may laugh as long as you like but I *will* be a general."

The officer who was the object of my heat only smiled as I spoke, increasing my frustration. The blood went to my face and in moments I knew I would have to leave the tent. But one of the snickering officers pointed to the little table upon which sat the envelope. The mystery of all this held me at a loss but I took a step or two toward the table and cast my eyes upon it. Could it be part of the joke? I glanced up at the others and was convinced that the congratulations on their faces was sincere. The inscription on the envelope was addressed to Brigadier General George A. Custer, U.S. Vols., and inside were formal documents from the secretary of war confirming my commission.

I rushed from the tent in search of General Pleasanton and found him drinking coffee at a fire in front of his tent. He was a hard man, made harder by the weight of command, and I had never seen him smile before that night.

"I see you have received a communication," he said, nodding at the envelope. "Good news, I presume?"

Then his upper lip rose, revealing a line of jagged, darkened teeth, a feature that must have played a role in his aversion to smiling.

He told me I had been nominated some weeks before but he had kept his actions to himself in the event the nomination failed to go through.

"In the main," he continued, "I wanted to see your satisfaction at the very instant of your joy. I had no doubt you would have your star."

"Why were you so sure?" I asked.

"Because I was not going to be denied," he said, "because I need you and others of your ilk to command something we as yet do not have . . . an attacking cavalry. I am promoting fighters. I must have men who are willing to lead and fight. And I think it is clear to all that General Custer . . . General Custer loves battle like few others."

I told him I would like to assume command immediately and enquired which regiment he had in mind. Off-handedly he told me I would be commanding the Second Brigade of the Third Cavalry Division, a group consisting of the First, Fifth, Sixth, and Seventh Michigan Cavalries. To hear this after beseeching politicians and other officials, after my appeals to the same units had been rejected, was a dream come true. Now I was to lead the same men as the wearer of a star. It made me light-headed.

General Pleasanton rose, said "Good luck, General," and left me sitting at his fire.

My orderly dashed into a nearby town and after a long search was at last able to find two cloth stars. These were hastily sewn on the collars of my blue navy shirt. Together with my Negro cook we set off at dawn, riding the road north, following the thunder of guns, searching for the brigade that was destined to become my vaunted Wolverines.

Along the way I constantly considered my appearance. All the effective generals I had known looked the part and I believed a distinctive and authoritative appearance would give my men a clear idea of whom they were following. I wanted to leave an indelible impression on whoever saw me. And my newly-won status gave me free rein in selecting my costume, particularly because I would be commanding volunteer units. I suppose it would be fair to say that I pushed the limits of what was considered acceptable wear. But I was only twenty-three years old, the youngest general in the Army, and could not help but show my age.

We were still upon the road when passersby began to turn their heads. No one dared to mock me, for the general's stars were conspicuous on my collar points. Soldiers saluted as I passed, then stood watching my back. Some men in small groups raised a cheer as I went by. Several women in a hamlet we rode through chased me down with a basket of blueberry muffins.

My appearance was an oddity—and would be until the end of the war—but I believe it was remarkable in ways that lifted the spirits of many who viewed it. And I felt fine, as fine as any boy of twenty-three has ever felt on this earth.

I had ridden through wave after wave of risk in battle and risk had infected the whole of me. Over mile after mile of roadway I thought, "To live is to risk, to live is to risk. To risk all is to live at the fullest." A Secessionist ball might find my brain, a saber might pierce my heart and lungs, a whirling, ragged scrap of shell might sever my legs, but by those means only would I fail and then I would not be failing. I would be dying and nothing would matter after that. I was euphoric with all I had to risk, and the spirits of the people on the road apparently responded to something of the same at the sight of me.

I was "complete" by the time I reported to General Kilpatrick at division headquarters. Over my torso I wore a black velveteen jacket, a twin row of gold buttons on its front. On each arm were sewn five loops of gold braid. My black pants were trimmed in gold stripe and each leg was tucked deep into black cavalry boots, the heel of each bearing a golden spur. At my throat was a sash tie of the deepest crimson that could be found. On my head was a wide-brimmed felt hat that I had liberated in battle from a Confederate officer. On this I had sewn the single silver star of my rank. After talking over military matters for a time, General Kilpatrick asked me rather dryly if the blue in my eyes and the flaxen curls hanging past my collar were aspects of the uniform.

"They are probably the most vital aspects," I answered.

I never found out whether he approved or disapproved, but we worked well together after that interview. Kilpatrick was a vicious fighter and a shrewd commander. In all the time I served under him I was never able to ascertain how he regarded me personally, but in the end it mattered little. I would have continued to wear my "uniform" regardless.

The Wolverine brass did not treat me kindly on arrival. I have labored under factionalism and jealousy and hate and envy on the part of subordinate officers many times since, but I have never seen such bold disappointment on the faces of staff officers as I saw the day I took command of the Second Brigade. I suppose "disappointment" is an improper word to describe their reaction. No single word is adequate. As I shook hands with each of them I could not fail to glance at the others standing by. All of them were staring at me with open disbelief, as if I were a grotesque and disagreeable object.

I realized they did not want me and for a few seconds my youthful heart sank and I wondered privately whether I had taken on responsibilities that human nature would never allow me to execute. For those few seconds, after I had shaken many hands, there was silence as I stood watching them and they me. The only sound amongst us was the clear boom of cannon at the front, and as the concussion of the guns shook the ground underfoot I reminded myself that I had been given the responsibility of leadership. It was my duty to lead, not to be liked. The war raining all around us made no exceptions: it killed the good and the bad, the gentle and the brutish, the young and the old without prejudice. I was now a child to the mother of war. I would show no prejudice either.

I broke the silence with words of my own, telling them what I expected of each regiment and its various companies. I told them that I expected everyone to be in a state of complete readiness at any time an engagement with our enemy was imminent. I told them that the men could drink all they desired so long as no one became drunk. In that event, any drunken soldier would be placed under arrest and court-martialed, the punishment to be death unless I decided otherwise. I told them simply that drunken soldiers do not fight as well as sober ones.

I told of changes that were coming in the conduct of the war. There was a new resolve on the part of the Union to utterly destroy the enemy. There could be no more thought of spanking the enemy. Total war was coming and the cavalry would have a different role to play. We would no longer be a cavalry of reconnaissance and escort. Henceforth we would be a fighting cavalry, charging the enemy whenever the opportunity arose. We were to be a cavalry of destruction. Our primary goal, aside from winning battles, was to make the enemy fear us absolutely.

At last I told them I would not be commanding from a tent or hilltop. I would be riding to battle with them.

A few of the officers nodded as I spoke but the majority kept their eyes averted. Some looked into their hands. Some looked away arrogantly. One or two on the fringes of my little audience spoke to their subordinates while I was speaking.

Looking at it fairly, I have no doubt that each listener had perfect reason to be sour. I'd been promoted over others who felt cheated. Two majors were well past thirty and one colonel was past forty. Others were undoubtedly devoted to former commanders. And here, standing before them, was a boy with a star, a boy with a red tie and gilded spurs, a boy into whose hands they were to deliver the lives of thousands of men as well as their own.

But fairness was of no import in the present situation. I was their commander and I decided that the best way to make that point clear was to act the part. For the rest of that day I conducted a minute inspection of our camp. There was plenty to fault and I found it all. By tattoo that evening I felt sure the lips of every soldier had blasphemed my name. That knowledge wounded me not at all. To the contrary, it made me feel secure for I wanted all to know who was in command. And by tattoo they did.

Our armies of the Great War were massive and cumbersome. They were moved into fields of combat with meticulous and lengthy care, and, as is well documented, large engagements were similar to the wrestling of two leviathans. Merely moving the armies into positions that both felt was suitable for attack involved titanic effort. It was almost ironic, then, that once in position, the slightest spark could ignite a firestorm of hellish proportion.

No one knew whence the spark might come, but on the eve of battle the very air was so charged with volatility that no soldier could fail to smell it.

Such was the atmosphere on the second morning of my tenure with the Michigan Brigade. The day before we had skirmished with the enemy's lower flank without achieving a satisfactory result for either side. But now the time had come for the armies massed around Gettysburg to seize each other by the throat.

At noon my division was ordered closer to the center of the fighting and, after an interminable wait, was ordered to protect the army's lower flank once again. It was anticipated that enemy cavalry would try to get around this particular flank and strike our army from the rear. Shadows were beginning to fall when we were finally ordered back down the road to our new position. A ragged civilian had appeared and to my irritation acted mad with fright as he told of J.E.B. Stuart's Invincibles, having been sighted in the vicinity of the flank we were to protect. The "invincibles" had served the Southern cause with spectacular success. No single unit struck more terror into our soldiers. To have a hysterical civilian screaming out his fear of them provided me and my unit commanders with an unwanted complication.

For me personally it was a happy development. I had day-dreamed about a chance to meet the Invincibles in combat many times, and my heart jumped when General Kilpatrick directed me to lead the division back down the road to find them.

We had not gone far when a sudden heavy fire forced us to halt and deploy. The rifle fire was coming from a nearby ridge; a few glances told me there were perhaps two hundred guns firing at us. I dismounted three of the regiments and had them take defensive positions. I directed several companies of the remaining regiment to assemble for a charge. This they did in perfect order.

As I rode up and down the rapidly forming line I could not mistake the curious expressions some of the soldiers evinced on seeing their leader for the first time.

These expressions had no effect on me, as I was entirely consumed with the fight about to begin. To describe the special qualities that overtake me in the moments before an armed fight is difficult for they are not common. It is as though the whole of me is suddenly a filter; my eyes see only what needs to be seen and my body assumes instincts it does not usually possess. It is as if my eyes have suddenly become wedded with every movement of my form. At any other time I might stumble over the smallest pebble in my path but when in this state such a thing seems impossible. I am somehow most completely coordinated when facing death.

I saw a company captain raise his sword as his bugler raised a horn. Before they had time to sound a charge I spurred into their midst, commanding the bugler to wait. My horse at that time was Roanoke and he was as prepared for battle as I. He pawed the ground anxiously as I tightened my flop hat and surveyed my troops.

"I'll lead you this time, boys," I cried. "Come on."

I laid rein on Roanoke's neck and his front feet lifted off the ground as he spun toward the enemy, who were still firing at us from the ridge. His back feet dug deep into the ground and in one great bound we were away. The voices of the men rose behind me as we shot forward, racing for the ridge. I looked back once and saw a vision that is as unforgettable at this moment as it was that day, almost thirteen years ago. A solid line of horsemen, each voice uttering the charge, each saber lifted to strike a blow, the sparkle of steel lighting the afternoon, the pounding of hundreds of shod hooves rolling over the earth. No man could but feel a surge of courage with a driving force of cavalry at his back.

On this occasion all my expectations dissolved as Roanoke and I flew over the ridge. A much greater number of Confederate riflemen were concealed there than I had thought. They rose as one, hundreds upon hundreds of men in butternut. And they fired as one, obscuring themselves for a moment behind the smoke of their rifles. Roanoke's front legs buckled and I took flight as his head dove toward the earth. Before I struck the ground I caught sight of him rolling past me, head over heels.

I jumped to my feet and grabbed for the pistol on my hip but it was gone. With the exception of my saber, which had somehow stayed in my hand, I was weaponless. Seeing me fall had inspired the rebels to mount a counter charge, which was now robbing our own attack of its potency. I glanced to the right and saw the enemy crash into my horsemen after shooting many out of their saddles. When I looked to the left I found myself staring down the barrel of a Confederate rifle not six feet away that was aimed directly at my head. My gaze lasted only a moment but that was sufficient to imagine the ball that would cause my own destruction rushing out of that dark hole. In the same instant there was an explosion in the face of the enemy rifleman and I watched stupefied as the man dropped onto his back, clutching at his eyes as he fell.

At the same moment I turned and saw the source of my deliverance. It was a young Union soldier surrounded by the enemy. The private's horse plunged up and down as he struggled to pull away from his attackers. He slashed madly with his saber but it was not until he drove a boot heel into the face of an enemy that he was able to break free.

He came for me, his arm outstretched. I grasped it and pulled myself up behind him. The private kicked his horse furiously, trying to hasten our escape. I felt a strong tug on my sleeve and looked down to see that one of the enemy had grabbed hold of me as we tried to pull away. Though my saber was in my left hand I swept it down with all of my might and relieved the rebel of his lower arm. For one fleeting second the severed limb clung to my sleeve; then it fell away as we caught up with our troops, now withdrawing in disarray.

I leaped onto a loose horse and was able to exercise some control over the withdrawal. The men stood and fought when I ordered them to and kept the superior Confederate force from overwhelming us. By the time we reached the defensive perimeter I had deployed earlier, the retreat had slowed to a walk and we had inflicted as much harm on the enemy as he had on us.

Scenting blood, the Confederates had rushed more of their legions forward, but General Kilpatrick had also arrived and they were unable to penetrate our rear. By nightfall the firing had slowed to nothing and our position had been reinforced.

I and the brigade were formally praised for our action, but I took no pleasure from it. I had underestimated the enemy and led my men into a trap. On seeing the leader of their attackers fall, the enemy had mounted its own charge and pushed us back.

I sat humiliated in my tent. How I now appeared to my men after what had happened I did not know. Surely they were talking about our failed charge. To the soldier, victory is a magic elixir. It fires a fighting man's courage, enabling him to fight again and again. I had not brought them a severe defeat but I had not produced the victory that every commander seeks to bestow on his men. The band played a number of sentimental tunes that night, but I would rather they had not played at all. I had nothing to celebrate.

Roanoke was much in my mind. I had captured him on a raid behind enemy lines that previous spring and he was so magnificent that I had for some time held him in reserve, not wanting to risk a dream horse. The blackness of him was so deep and his condition so superb. His coat shimmered like sun on water. He wasn't tall for a stallion, but was perfectly proportioned. His muscle was dense as steel and the power he generated had seemed unconquerable. To be astride him was like having my legs around a bomb; unlike others of his race, who might be given to panic as the battle commences, Roanoke knew instinctively how to behave. I had made several prior charges on him and he always maintained perfect control, no matter how much lead whistled in the air about his head. Now he lay still, somewhere out in the blackness, dead flesh waiting to bloat in the next day's sun.

But taking the best is at the soul of war. War is a last resort, to which the opposing parties never fail to commit the best of their ranks, man and beast alike. It is only through risking the best that victory can be achieved and so the best must die . . . the ugliness and beauty of war all in one.

I pushed such thoughts from my mind by composing letters to my family long into the night. In these missives I tried to put a positive face on my activities. A general cannot expose his true heart, that is, his fears and misgivings and perhaps even feelings of shame when a deadly contest is being fought. To expose his true heart at these times only serves to reduce his power, in his own eyes most of all.

I wrote of my promotion, of my assumption of command, and of the critical battle that would soon commence in full. I have no doubt that those letters glowed with pride. I was not disgraced, only discouraged, and as the wheel of night crept toward dawn my feelings of well-being gradually returned. I had learned valuable lessons on my first day of combat as commander of the Michigan Brigade. Of greatest importance was the fact of my survival. I had lived to fight again and I could barely wait to do so.

I was sitting straight up when my orderly woke me before

reveille. He said I had been dead asleep, a cup of coffee in my hand.

The men were silent that morning as we were ordered north to join General Kilpatrick. I took no comfort in that particular silence for I knew that these soldiers had not yet made up their minds about me. It was obvious that I could fight but not so obvious as to how I would respond to yesterday's debacle, and I believe the volunteers were reserving judgment. I believe they were curious about my next move. They had surrendered their lives to a stranger and now they were in doubt. Doubt circled and surrounded me as well. All along the road I was burdened with a floating, indecisive doubt that would come near then fall back, never mounting a frontal assault on my senses but rather holding off at a distance nagging me with its presence.

My immature mind decided at last to seek the shelter of its strongest asset: my commitment to fight. No matter the situation, I resolved to fight that day with greater energy than I had ever expended before, to fight with a fury unknown to me previously, a fury whose existence would be discovered anew in battle. I would not meet the enemy, nor stand before him. I would hurl myself against him. It was the only way I knew to attain full control over my command.

As we neared our rendezvous with General Kilpatrick my misgivings disappeared. I said little and remained somber as we waited hour after hour for specific orders. Through each tedious minute of our wait a single litany repeated itself in my head. I wanted the enemy to come near. I wanted him to come near with the bravest, strongest, meanest-spirited fighters he possessed. Then I wanted to cut them as I rode over them, trampling the finest, chopping through the strongest, mashing their blood and their pride into oblivion.

Before reaching General Kilpatrick, however, we were intercepted by a courier on a foamy mount. General Gregg, commander of the Second Division, had only two exhausted regiments with which to defend a sensitive section of the army's flank and required the Michigan Brigade's immediate presence at a place called Runnel's Farm three miles distant. I swung the men around and we hurried down the road, two thousand soldiers going at a gallop. The boys of the two worn-out regiments cheered mightily when they caught sight of us, lifting my already rising spirits. With the addition of my own regiments we now had a total force of between three and four thousand with which to oppose the enemy.

I dispatched several scouting parties with orders to locate any enemy units lurking in the vicinity and to pay special attention to precise numbers. While these small groups dispersed into the surrounding countryside the brigade settled into the cover of a long line of trees, there to await developments.

Runnel's Farm spread before us as a wide pool of quiet, undulating green a thousand yards long, its perimeter guarded by thick copses of trees in full summer leaf. From where I stood facing the farm, it ran flat for most of its length. At the far end was a gentle rise that disappeared momentarily, then sloped up again rather steeply for thirty or forty yards before reaching a narrow ledge of green. The farmhouse stood on this ledge, slightly to the right. Behind it rose another line of dense trees that marked the farm's distant border.

The lay of this land was common to the area: a checkerboard of fields and trees well suited to cavalry, the trees affording cover for clandestine maneuvers, the fields providing the ideal arena for mounted combat.

From time to time as we waited I looked out at the baking field of green before me and felt certain that we would be battling here. I had served with some of the ablest military minds of the age. From them I had learned the necessity of reconnaissance and strategy and defense—but every time I looked across that field my thoughts inevitably returned to a single, simple conclusion. The clash to come would be a contest of will. The men with the strongest will would likely be victorious and I repeated this to my inner self in the hope that I would do all in my power to bolster the resolve of my men. Armed with a superior will we would be able to roll the enemy back across that field.

About midday the last of my scouting parties sped into camp. A dark-faced lieutenant about my age leaped down, pointed to the trees behind the farmhouse, and said: "They're coming."

"How many?" I asked.

"I couldn't say sir."

"I specifically instructed you to be precise," I said.

"Yes sir," he replied, "but I didn't have time to make a count. There are thousands of them, sir."

Two Confederate brigades and at least one battery of cannon had been discovered in our front. I hurried to General Gregg and found him occupied with two new couriers, one from General Kilpatrick, the other from General Pleasanton. Each was ordering the Michigan Brigade to present itself at two new locations, but General Gregg, on hearing my report, courageously countermanded both of his superiors' orders and instructed me to ready the Michiganders for battle. To my delight, he selected the Michigan Brigade to engage the enemy in the open at a time of my own choosing.

Minutes later, while I was laying plans with several line officers, the woods in the distance began to move and excitement broke over our troops as the Confederates rushed their cannon out of the trees and began firing. The men scrambled for cover and as enemy ordnance began to whistle overhead I leaped onto a horse I had acquired only hours before.

She was a sleek, dapple-gray thoroughbred, long, lean and well conditioned. Her feet were small but well rounded, characteristics I suspected would give her superior balance and agility. A horse with quick steps can be the difference on the battlefield, and my athletic mare was to serve me well on that 3rd day of July in 1863.

My sole worry was whether or not she would go wild in the midst of exploding shells, carbine fire, and the terrible screaming of killers and their victims. But as we raced to and fro showering line officers with orders, as streams of men coursed about us and cannonballs burst like lightning overhead, she kept her wits beautifully.

Through pure fate there were few gray horses in our command at the moment, and May's coat gave me an advantage beyond her amazing deftness and heart. Her gray color stood out in battle and together with the uniform I wore gave us a distinction in appearance that could be seen by everyone. For the men to see their commander at all times was most important, particularly so in the confusion of battle.

Of course the enemy would see me too, and this was pointed out as cause for concern on many occasions. Curiously, though, I never thought of myself as a target. On balance, I don't think the man who ignores death is more likely to be killed than the man who seeks to hide from it. Death's game, like all other true mysteries, cannot be understood. I have never been able to dwell long on the unknown, and on that day, as on all other battle days, I was simply too busy to bother with thoughts of death.

I believe May was of the same mind. I rode her almost daily for the next several months and cannot remember a time, no matter the situation, when she lost her head. Not even the awful screams of her own race's wounded deterred her. May was utterly fearless and incomparably beautiful and my only consolation after she was shot from under me at Culpepper was that she died instantly.

Our battery commander, the excellent Alexander Pennington, who served with me for the duration of the war, was already answering the enemy with his six cannon and we galloped past him without bothering to stop. I merely tipped my hat as we swept ahead to help deploy our defenses properly and organize fighters to meet the enemy when he attacked, which would surely happen soon.

In a very few minutes the men were well situated. The cannon were adequately defended, as were our flanks. The First Michigan, whom I selected because of their superior experience, were placed on horse behind a protective wall of dismounted skirmishers. There we waited as Pennington's sure shots poured fire on the Confederate batteries, at last forcing them back under the trees.

The withdrawal of the enemy cannon was followed by ten or fifteen minutes of strange silence, which I could only liken to the stillness in the air preceding a thunderstorm. Then, as I watched the woods, they came alive again. More than a thousand men on foot suddenly emerged from the trees and started toward us. I ordered Colonel Alger to take the Fifth Michigan forward to meet this initial advance, his regiment being equipped with new seven-shot Spencer carbines.

Colonel Alger hurried the regiment forward and succeeded in settling his men behind a fence. They held their fire until the Confederate line, coming faster now, had penetrated deep into the killing zone. Five hundred carbines spoke as one and the Confederate line staggered.

Thinking our regiment behind the fence would have to reload, the rebels kept on coming, only to be cut down again and again. But shortly the Fifth's ammunition dwindled and the Confederates, sensing the potential for a rout, came forward again. I could see them vaulting the fence as Colonel Alger and his men fell back.

Enemy artillery had commenced a new fire, and Pennington, brilliant as usual, was answering back perfectly, taking two of their guns into the hereafter with direct hits that blew men and pieces of cannon into the air like debris from a cyclone.

General Gregg had ordered the Seventh Brigade into action to support Colonel Alger, and as I watched them form for a charge, I could no longer contain myself. All that had come before amounted to a tuning of instruments. Now the orchestra was going to play and it was my right and responsibility to conduct. I laid a spur on May's flank and she jumped forward.

The Seventh Michigan saw us coming and I felt a jolt of electricity as hundreds of young faces, sitting atop their horses, watched us dash up and canter twenty or thirty yards onto the battlefield. As the first men of Alger's withdrawal stumbled past me I stood in the stirrups, shaded my eyes against the sun and surveyed the scene. As I watched, the oncoming enemy kept firing and the hiss of their balls began to rend the air about my head. May was dancing beneath me, and when I glanced down I could see the enemy's fire cutting the grass at her feet.

When I looked up again I realized several things at once. Far back near the tree line another large force of rebels was massing. The enemy already on the battlefield had drawn so near that I could see their faces. Some of them were smiling as they raised their weapons to shoot at me. I wheeled May and we galloped back to the waiting regiment. Some of the men cheered as I reached them, probably buoyed by the realization that I was not yet dead. As May pranced before them I yelled: "Those men on the hill are still getting into position. And this line coming behind me is spent. We'll have at them now."

In her excitement May reared and walked a few steps on her hind feet. While she was still in the air I screamed with all the power of heart and lungs: "Come on, you Wolverines."

I don't know why "Wolverines" leaped from my mouth but in that single moment it manufactured an identity the brigade would carry with pride to the conclusion of the war.

As May's front feet returned to earth a great cheer sounded and six hundred horsemen followed me at a run. We cut through the advancing Confederate line in the same manner an ill and powerful wind cuts all before it. Those we did not trample we killed and those left undead were captured. The remainder stumbled back the way they had come, unencumbered by packs or weapons.

I wanted to press our advantage, and after breaking their line we paused only briefly before reforming and continuing our charge toward the rise where I had seen the enemy massing.

As we closed on the rise I could see our foes streaming down the hill, but there they passed out of sight as if swallowed and I could not imagine what might have become of them.

The Confederates opened fire from the farmhouse at my right and the air was again filled with the peculiar whizzing of balls as May jumped a small ditch at the base of the rise and dug for the top. So great was her speed that we seemed to float over the tiny summit in front of the hill I had seen the enemy stream down.

Suddenly and before I or the regiment could pull up, the mystery was solved. A rock wall, perhaps one hundred yards in length, lay concealed in a declivity at the bottom of the hill. The rebels had thrown up a rail fence which now ran along the top of the wall, an obstacle nearly impossible to jump on horseback.

Riflemen rose before us as we crashed into the wall and their concentrated fire brought down half the horses and riders in the first ranks.

We might have stopped had we been able to but the force of the charge threw those of us who had survived the fusillade against the wall, causing the rest to pile up behind.

May's momentum sent her forelegs pawing over the wall and I vividly recall firing my revolver into the faces of men standing to my right while I raked at the heads on my left with my saber. For how many seconds we hung over the wall I do not know, but undoubtedly it seemed longer than it was. The close quarters made it difficult to move, much less fight. Several enemy soldiers tried to take hold of May's bridle and legs but I was able to drive them back with my sword and moments later May was able to free herself.

We retreated a few steps and while reloading my pistol I watched for an instant the intense panorama of the fighting along the wall: fifteen hundred men twisting and straining and lunging to kill one another, the crackle of their weapons, the screams of horses and men, those dying and those struggling to live, all of it sounding like the roar of a cataract.

The combat, so furious up and down the wall, was mindful of a molten river of violence that had somehow insinuated itself into a green, peaceful field in Pennsylvania. There can be no comprehension of such a spectacle.

May and I rode along the rear of our force for a few moments, during which time I perceived a thinning of Confederate ranks at a particular spot on the wall. It was imperative that we remove the rail fence at the top of the wall for it had compromised our mounted attack and we would surely be driven back unless the obstacle to our passage was breached.

Gathering all the men who could hear me we pressed in against the weak point. I dismounted a number of men and ordered them to tear the fence down while those still mounted covered their work. Too late the Confederates realized what we were doing. In one explosive burst the men on the ground had the rails down.

I beckoned fifty or sixty mounted fighters to fall back from the wall with me. Twenty yards away I wheeled May about and, facing the wall, dug my heels into her flanks. As she gathered herself to jump I could see enemy soldiers swarming in to fill the gap. I sailed over the wall with May's thousand pounds beneath me and we fell in their midst, landing squarely on those who had failed to scurry aside. May went to one knee as she stumbled on their bodies. As I fell with her, I drove my saber tip into the onrushing ground and was thus able to keep my seat until she righted herself. Looking over my shoulder I saw horses flowing over the wall as our men spread among the rebels like a bloody stain of spilled milk.

But the enemy was determined. As we fought on their side of the wall they gnawed viciously at our flanks, an action that eventually succeeded in stopping the flow of our cavalry.

All in all, the fighting, much of it hand to hand, lasted thirty or forty minutes; in an odd way it was reminiscent of two gangs of schoolboys fighting in a playground with weapons of destruction. We mangled them horribly but in the end we were too few and I took the troops back over the stone barricade. As we regrouped I noticed that many more of the wood rails topping the wall had fallen during the fight.

Immediately I ordered another charge and we took the wall again, this time with double our number, falling upon the rebels almost as they saw us coming. We fought another thirty minutes and had driven the opposing force to the brink of ruin when I was told that a regiment of five or six hundred Confederate infantry had been brought up behind the farmhouse and were now advancing at a run.

The speed and volume of decisions a general must make on a field of battle should make the head spin but my brain is somehow immune to confusion at these moments. As I saw fresh Confederate troops spilling down the little hill I knew we would have to withdraw. Back we went. The rebels, lifted by the appearance of screaming reinforcements, came after us. May and I were among the last to leave the fight. We cleared the wall with one of the enemy clinging to my stirrup leather.

We were fortunate to have Alexander Pennington that day. He is unusually alert, and moments after we left the wall shot from his cannon began to fly overhead, effectively keeping the Confederates from our heels. Losses might still have been heavy, were it not for Colonel Alger, who took the field with cavalry and met the enemy in our rear, holding him long enough to allow us to break clear.

For the next hour I saw to the task of reorganizing the remnants of the Seventh Michigan. They were green but had fought tremendously at the wall. A hundred men had been lost but the enemy dead and wounded were even greater than ours. We had halted the foe's advance but had not licked him and all knew that the peace settling on the battlefield was temporary. Each side was gathering its breath for the next and, as it proved to be, the final round of struggle.

Twenty minutes after being established the peace was broken by a commotion toward the front. I jumped on May and had not ridden far when I beheld a sight the memory of which sends a thrill up my spine even to this day. Thousands of Confederates on horseback, eight regiments of the South's finest cavalry, had emerged from the woods and were forming for a charge. Thousands of sabers glinting in the afternoon sun. Thousands of hooves swinging into line after solemn line. Scores of beautifully mounted officers trotting calmly back and forth, readying their men. I had never seen a like exhibition of power and confidence.

For a few moments they stood still and machinelike. Then, as if no force could oppose them, they started forward, aimed at our center.

The "invincibles" had arrived and they came now at an eerie trot, sure of their might.

I saw the First Michigan forming hastily into ranks and guessed correctly that General Gregg had ordered our most experienced regiment to do battle with the South's finest. I knew without doubt that their commander, Colonel Town, was unwell. He was so weakened by diseased lungs that he could not sit straight up.

I galloped over, gave the colonel my respects, and informed him that I was assuming command.

He gazed out at the oncoming Invincibles and looked back at me, his expression both baleful and courageous.

"This is suicide," he intoned.

"No, sir. This is our moment and we must make the most of it. Order the men to draw sabers."

Colonel Town did as instructed and I went to the front on May.

I called out the order to charge.

The men responded with a cheer and we bounded forward as one against the oncoming lines of the enemy.

The dependable Pennington was with us on this fateful charge. Looking back, I saw puffs of smoke from our cannon and heard the shells whistle above my head. Then I saw them explode along the length of the Invincibles' front ranks. As soon as a gap opened, the magnificent discipline of the enemy cavalry closed it and they came at ever greater speed. The famous rebel yell seemed to spiral into the air, and defying our relentless cannon they reached a gallop. When we were within a hundred yards of each other I could hear individual taunts. I could see individual horses and sabers raking the air above horses' ears. In moments the cannon would cease; as was my custom, I selected a single horseman in the enemy line to throw myself into.

In the next instant Pennington's last, desperate barrage reached their line. Canisters of double shot rained down on them like a lowering curtain. The fury of it caused me to pull up. The whole regiment slowed behind me as a vision of incredible carnage spread before us. From one end of the line to another men and horses went down like tenpins. The Confederate ranks shivered and paused. Raising my saber I stood in the stirrups and screamed over my shoulder: "Come on, boys."

We pounded in on them, instinctively sailing into every hole which was hemorrhaging. As we slammed into these open wounds we entered chambers of misery so ghastly as to make the grotesque seem routine. I was enclosed in a cocoon of human and animal catastrophe draped in floating blankets of dense smoke from which emerged images real and horrific; a horse circling insanely on what was left of its shattered front leg; another, its jaw gone, flailing blindly into all that surrounded it. A severed human head, which might have belonged to friend or foe, passed before my eyes, tumbling like an unbalanced cannonball. Blood exploded everywhere, in so constant a stream that it felt like a covering mist, drenching every combatant. The cries of the dying were pitiful beyond comprehension; cries of strong, brave men calling for mothers and lovers, begging anyone to end their misery.

Curiously, the tableau of mayhem, unforgettable as it may have been, moved me not at all, particularly in the first five or ten minutes. I considered nothing but the living foe. The human and animal wreckage all around me was only waste. As the enemy was being slain I called more and more men to my side and we grew stronger. The carnage itself seemed to make us stronger. Soon we were a united force and I realized that we had ripped a yawning cavity in the belly of the Invincibles.

Seeing our success, other regiments seized the moment and fell upon the Confederate flanks. Their lines wavered and broke and suddenly the enemy was running by the thousands, leaving hundreds of dead in their wake. We chased them for two or three miles before they were able to rally.

In the twilight our numbers returned from the killing field and went into camp with the knowledge that we had beaten back a savage charge, that we had held the enemy from the army's rear and that the Invincibles were no longer so. From that day on we fought them as equals.

I didn't know how many men I had killed that afternoon. I had killed my share was all that I knew, a share that combined with the others had been sufficient to make the enemy take flight. I was so thoroughly spent that I could eat only a mouthful of food. Then I lay down in the rain and fell asleep. The ground was muddy and wet but a princely bed could not have felt finer. The Michigan Brigade had fought and won and I had led them. The glory of victory surrounded my sleep and made it sweet.

In the morning I discarded the jacket of gold braid for it was ruined with the blood of yesterday's battle—I would use up many other velveteen jackets before the war was finally ended. I could not mourn the loss of my treasured coats or the dozen fine horses who were shot from under me. Nor could I mourn the thousands of brave men who fought and followed only to fall and never rise again. The ordinary and extraordinary alike, smiling over coffee in the morning, silent and stiff in the afternoon, their bodies gazing open-mouthed and mute at the Almighty, the true, dead orphans of war, no longer dreaming or dancing or loving but reduced now to simple compost on the battlefield. It is only the nature of war. The great mill of conflict reduces its living fuel to pulp and death and destruction is the price of victory.

When humankind determines to make no more war I shall lay down my sword and turn my energies to less violent pursuits. But so long as I remain a soldier and am called upon to do my duty I shall do so without grieving. Grieving is a useless distraction in the business of war, which is, in its most basic terms, the business of conquering through killing.

In the morning, as I made my rounds, I noticed that several soldiers had acquired red ties like my own. I allowed myself a smile, indulging their homage. That same smile was often on my face in months to come, because after each engagement more and more soldiers' necks were wrapped in crimson.

When the time came for us to part, the Michigan Brigade had come to be known throughout America. No other fighters had achieved more glory than my Wolverines. They vanquished the enemy whenever and wherever they found him. They were never defeated. On them were bestowed many nicknames, monikers that reflected the intense pride and respect in which they were held by civilian and soldier alike. The one most widely used and one of which I still think often, is "the Red Neckties," though in my secret heart they will always be simply my Wolverines.

MAY 23-26,

❧

1876

A short march today. General Terry is fearful of overextending the pack mules, so after only eight miles a place of profound beauty, so profound that it practically ordered us to halt, became our camp.

There is wood and grass in abundance and a small creek with cool sweet water. It is sheltered by sparkling cottonwoods, and the low hanging branches of one scratch gently at the ceiling of my tent with every lifting of the breeze. Prairie flowers are everywhere in bloom and everywhere one looks there is color from the fragile petals standing proudly at the tips of the stalks. The light descending from the limbs of the tree above me filters through the tent canvas immediately overhead and dances in mottled patches on this paper, on the toes on my boots, and on the earthen floor.

The men have found a bathing pool a few yards upstream and over the pleasant sounds of their splashing and shouting the regimental band is playing its repertoire of plaintive tunes. The dogs stretched out on the floor like carcasses are serenading me with snores. All in all it has been a matchless day, one that even the blind or deaf could not fail to appreciate. Even my restless drive has been quelled.

At first I was dismayed and grumpy over General Terry's desire for rest, but I too have fallen under the spell of this perfect May day, a perfection that reached its zenith with the arrival an hour ago of a courier, who brought among other things the soldier's most precious commodity . . . a bag of mail.

There were two letters from Libbie. They are sitting on my blankets unopened because I cannot bear to tear them apart, read what's inside, and have it gone. I will open them only when I can no longer resist.

With considerable certainty I can predict what will be in the letters. There will be no gossip, for she has never approved of it. There will be no complaining, for she has always sought to spare me worry on her account. If there is any news of home and family it will be recounted. Comings and goings at the post will be noted, as will the guests there have been and the talk between them. She will not fail to mention the health and spirits of the animals whom I left behind, paying special attention to their antics in and out of the house. The letters will be filled with light and longing.

I treasure them precisely because I know so well what is in them. That they come from her, from her thoughts and from her hand, is a thrill I still feel after being together all these years. If there is such a thing as perfection in love it is found in our union.

I knew that I loved her at our first, fleeting meeting when I happened past as she was swinging on the gate in front of her father's house and asking with a slight narrowing of her dark, fathomless eyes: "Aren't you that Custer boy?" Then she ran up the walkway and into the house. We spoke not another word until years afterward, but something about that moment while she hung on the gate staring at me with her siren's eyes penetrated and held me fast.

I have always been at ease with women and they with me. I have never been able to resist their charms. On several occasions I thought of marrying someone else but it was never to be. From the beginning it was always the judge's daughter with whom I was fated to make my bed for life and I shall be indebted to that fate through eternity.

Chance had driven us toward each other but there were many impediments that at the time seemed insurmountable. I suppose it is the same with all passion that is kindled between a man and a woman. The first flames are often snuffed but when the fire reaches a certain height nothing can douse it. The fire consumes all. So it was with me and Elizabeth Bacon . . . my Libbie.

Alcohol nearly killed our love before it began. I had begun to drink at the Point, where the only relief from discipline and drudgery were nocturnal forays to a nearby tavern, which I often led. What a time that was; gathered around a warm hearth in the early-morning hours with fellow cadets, quaffing rum and telling ribald stories, laughing so hard as to cause pain while Benny Haven's rum created oceans of smooth sailing in our young heads.

Rollicking in Benny's tavern made our strict lives bearable, and the intimacies we shared forged friendships that would last for life. The single drawback was the habit of the alcohol itself. I knew somehow it was wrong but youth made me unaware at the time that my energy is too great to be harnessed to the drag of a bottle.

I had not yet come to this realization while on leave in Monroe, Michigan, around October, 1861. I had contracted the grippe and it had laid me low. My health has always been robust, but there is something about a common case of the grippe that my body cannot tolerate. The congestion and sneezing and the fever seem to permeate the whole of me. When I am afflicted my spirits invariably sink, and while others may recover in a week or two it seems to take me twice as long. Yet my lungs remain as strong as any man's. It is a mystery.

My recovery in Monroe was quite rapid, and like anyone else escaping the sickbed, once well I could barely contain my exuberance. I always feel reprieved when emerging from an illness and on this occasion I remember being seized with particular joy. I was among family and friends, far away from the thump of cannon and the muddy filth of winter camp.

After several days of heavy snowfall the sun had broken through just as I was able to walk the streets again. I encountered an old friend and he suggested we repair to a rum room in back of a mercantile. We sat on sacks of grain until midafternoon and my giddiness at being well carried me far past the threshold of prudence. When I rose I found it hard to keep my feet. Neither could my friend. We staggered out the door and up the street in support of one another as we made a pathetic attempt to reach our respective homes. As we passed by Libbie's home I lost my feet altogether and fell into a berm of snow piled at the curb. I managed to gain my feet again only by way of a supreme physical effort. To my chagrin I tumbled again. The rum, which had rendered me happily useless, turned against me.

As I lay in the snow trying to regain my wits, sweat covered my face in large, cold drops. My brain began to spin with sickening speed and the drink sloshing in my stomach turned sour. My abdomen began to roll in a nauseating manner and a moment later I was vomiting violently into the snow.

When finally the retching stopped, I lifted myself up, and, wiping the spittle from my chin, I looked across the street. The image I beheld lasted but an instant, though its clarity and horror are burned forever in my memory. I was staring at the figure of Libbie, standing in a second-floor window. Suddenly, the stern image of her father, Judge Daniel Bacon, appeared behind her. He looked directly at me, I who was still on all fours drooling into the snow. I watched helplessly as he pulled Libbie aside and a curtain fell across the window.

I might as well have appeared naked in the street for the mortification it must have cost Libbie and especially her father to see me like that. In those few blundering seconds I had forfeited a dear dream. I felt forever stained, my character marked with a blemish that could not be removed.

Somehow I got to my feet and found, not surprisingly, that my friend had disappeared. I do not recall whether I crawled or walked but do know that I was able to reach my sister's home. There I suffered the further indignation of Lydia's reaction. She was neither angry nor icy but her remorse was complete. She was not shy in letting me know that I had failed her, failed my entire family, and, most tragically, failed myself.

These were words I could not bear to hear. I lay the remainder of the afternoon completely demoralized and despondent. But as my head cleared I stopped wishing that what was done could be undone and searched through all the things I could do to prevent my being in this situation ever again. There was but one thing to do.

I believe I apologized to Libbie some years later but the subject was never brought up with her father. Nor did Lydia and I speak of it again. In a few months it will be fifteen years since I lay vomiting in the snow for all to see and in those fifteen years not a single drop of alcohol has touched my tongue. The shame of public drunkenness could not be erased but it has never been repeated. Even my bitterest enemies will attest to that.

Aside from the incident in the street, there were other obstacles for Libbie and me to overcome. My family was of one denomination, hers of another. My father was a blacksmith, hers a judge. The judge was a pious man and though I always knew him to be kindhearted, like others of his class he was not inclined to trade down economically or socially.

But as it has been with all else in our lives, none of these obstacles was strong enough to stop us. I believe we are each formidable individuals; but together we have never been defeated and it occurs to me now that this quality of being unvanquished in the face of difficulties great and small has much to do with our longevity as a couple.

Our first formal meeting was on Thanksgiving night, 1862. We wed in early 1864 but have always regarded the moment of our meeting that November evening as our true anniversary. She bowed to me and I to her and while our eyes swept the floor we were seized with unknowable, uncontrollable desire to look at each other's faces again. One look spawned the need for a million more.

All that night, in a considerable crowd, her eyes were on mine when I looked her way and vice versa. Measured in time these looks would have meant nothing, for they were only flashes but for what I read from them; the sudden sparks of curiosity and risk and longing struck me as having a quality that could be sustained for a lifetime. What lurked behind her quicksilver glances made me feel as though I stood fully exposed and vulnerable before her, that I could hide nothing from her, that it would be useless to be anything other than exactly what I was. It frightened and excited me at once and as I lay in bed that night I could not keep her face from intruding on my thoughts.

In the following days I swallowed my fear and labored tirelessly to put myself in proximity to her. My efforts were rewarded and I was able to escort her here and there on a variety of errands. On several occasions we involuntarily reenacted our first meeting, an evening characterized by silent, penetrating stares. At these times I found myself on the streets, engaged in conversation or tighening a cinch, when I would experience the sensation of being watched. I would turn and she would be there, gazing at me from across the street or up the road. There were several instances when, feeling the identical sensation, she would turn to find me staring at her from afar.

Our meetings accelerated. Libbie could not stick a finger out of an open door without finding me standing at the ready. But as the weeks passed our visibility and the mounting gossip that went with it came to the attention of her father. I was never invited to their house and soon Libbie was refusing my offers of public company. Apparently the judge remembered the spectacle in the snow and did not want his daughter romantically absorbed with a young captain of common background . . . a captain who would return to the war at any moment, there most likely to have his brains blown to pieces. And no one could begrudge the judge this assessment. By the end of that year, 1863, many thousands of northern boys had returned home in boxes and it was rare to encounter a family that was not in mourning over someone.

I would have been glad to enlighten the judge as to my invincibility but I was not given the opportunity. Libbie made it clear without saying the words that she could see me no longer, nor was I allowed written communication with her.

We concluded it would be best for the time being to do what we could to deflect gossip in hope that the judge's preoccupation with extinguishing our infatuation would somehow disappear.

While Libbie accepted escorts from a long line of Monroe's eager swains I threw my attentions into the active pathways of the town's varied and well populated society of eligible young ladies. Whatever charms I possess have always worked to good effect on the opposite sex and I cannot say that I did not enjoy time spent in the company of other girls. There were some days when the pleasure of my company drove away all thoughts of Libbie. But I ached for her often. Always, I ached for her at night.

Our charade continued for several torturous weeks and had the desired effect of diverting gossip. But our separation was like a wound that refused to heal. It was especially painful when, out walking in the town, we passed without speaking, turning our heads away, thus depriving each other of our greatest joy . . . that of looking into each other's eyes.

On a snowy afternoon a few days before Christmas we passed on opposite sides of the street on the arms of other people and at that moment I judged the charade could go no further.

I employed an urchin to carry a message to her and to deliver it through his own lips. The message consisted of four words: "Grover's Mill, noon tomorrow."

When the boy returned and told me he had done as ordered, a wave of second thoughts passed through me and I wished desperately to have the message back.

It snowed heavily that evening and the next morning, as I procured a sleigh and team and set out for the mill, my heart was filled with despair. I had selected the place for its desolation and desolation was the emotion that filled me most as I sat shivering against a grist wheel and scraped my boots on the dusty floor, amazed at the folly of having concocted such a ludicrous scheme.

I cannot remember how many minutes I stared at my boot tops in self-pity but it was not too long before I felt like laughing. Imbecile! The word hammered out a soft, melodic tempo in my head and the only way to make it cease was to acknowledge its truth by laughing. A girl like Elizabeth Bacon was not the type to brave deep drifts alone, risking her good reputation in order to rendezvous with a man whom she loved without knowing.

I shook my head and laughed and brought my stiff body up from the floor. As I did, something crept into the corner of my eye and I looked out through the crumbling mill to observe the unmistakable dark speck of a rider approaching in a distance.

As the rider came nearer my uncertain heart suddenly commanded me to hide, and for several wild moments I searched the old mill for a place to secret myself. Of course there was none and I regained my senses sufficiently to stand in the doorway, watching with forced ease as she drew closer. But my heart was now flopping against my chest so insistently that I had to withdraw again, pacing the floor to the opposite end of the dilapidated structure in a vain attempt to calm myself.

I heard her horse's steps come to a halt outside and was taking deep breaths when she appeared from nowhere in the open wooden doorway. Looking utterly composed, she pushed back her hood and shuffled off her cloak. She wore a long black dress and her dark, wavy hair was braided in girlish pigtails.

For a few seconds we stared silently across the space between us. Then, though I didn't want to say it, I stuttered, "I . . . I didn't think you would come."

Her mouth twisted into a faintly sarcastic smile and she replied, "I didn't think I would either."

There was silence again and then we smiled simultaneously, laughing at ourselves and our foolish actions. Then we fell to talking.

We talked about our mothers and fathers, art and the theater, the war, our favorite foods and secret hopes and horses and snow. Many other subjects flew through the air about our heads but the one to which we constantly returned was ourselves. We made no declarations of love but it hardly mattered. The subtlest hints of affection had nearly as great an impact. Our meeting in the mill that winter day was so dominated by the promise of love to come that declarations would have been more than we could digest.

We must have talked for at least two hours before I was made aware that her time with me that day was running out. I so abhorred the idea of her leaving that I suggested taking a ride in the sleigh. I suppose in my addled state I hoped for some divine miracle that would keep her from going forever. Perhaps the team and sleigh, once started, would never stop.

There had been no intimacies of a physical nature all during our long talk, but once we were aboard the sleigh and I had clucked to the team I could feel the pressure of her shoulder against mine, a feeling that produced as much calm as it did excitement. No previous romantic encounter had been anything like this. The familiarity I felt in her presence was akin to the long-standing comfort one feels with family members or stalwart friends and the excitement was so complete as to convince me that the well of passion from which I was now drinking must be bottomless.

The storm of the night before had cleared completely, leaving a brilliant day behind. The bare branches of the trees passing overhead had begun to throw their shadows across the landscape but the sun was still shining and it seemed to focus all its glory on her face. It was as if the sun itself was serving her beauty, filling her hood-shrouded countenance with a radiance I could not look at squarely, lest I fall to pieces on the spot. I tried to concentrate on driving but I did not have much success.

We did not speak as I guided the team through one snow-covered field after another, searching for a backroad that would make for sure traveling. I was glad for the respite in speech for the sound of her voice and its many bright inflections had a power of seduction that made me altogether helpless. I do not remember the reins in my hands, nor the rush of the sleigh's runners, nor the exertions of the horses. Even as my eyes were fixed straight ahead they were busy with images of the girl sitting next to me; the straightness of her teeth, the squareness of her chin, the smoothness of her skin, and the clear light in her eyes. The whole effect of her was narcotic. My mind was no longer a private place.

Unable to think of anything else, I silently repeated her name over and over. Were it not for the slight pressure of her shoulder I could easily had believed that I was living a happy dream. But the arm against mine was a constant reminder of her mortal existence, proof that the girl sitting next to me was made of flesh and bone and blood. This knowledge only made my happiness greater and the memories of that December day constitute a treasure that can never be taken from me.

It was not many minutes before we struck a picturesque track that had been used heavily but was now empty. Rising at a gentle incline, the road wove through a thick wood and, because horses and curves and speed have always been a temptation too great for me to resist, I suggested that we see what the team could do.

Through a peaceful smile she said, "All right," and squeezed herself tighter into the seat, the pressure of her shoulder increasing.

Cracking the lines over their backs, I shouted encouragement to the horses and we were off. The team was as good as I had suspected when I picked them out, tall and strong and eager. I held them as we passed through the first curves but soon gave them their heads. The faster we went the louder we screamed as the sleigh whipped through the ever-tightening curves. The power of the team was such that I had to rise slightly off the seat as we entered the turns.

I was in this position when several deer bounded from cover and dashed directly across the road in front of us. The horses didn't stop but leaped sideways and scrambled up a small embankment on our left. The sleigh tipped to one side and rolled as it struck the roadside, launching both of us into open space which we navigated in free flight for several seconds before coming to earth almost side by side.

On hands and knees I asked if she was all right.

Libbie was just sitting up. She glanced about herself and looked at me with pride.

"I believe I had an excellent landing," she said.

I wanted to kiss her then but the horses were thrashing about after becoming stuck in the trees. The sleigh was still on its side and was too damaged to carry us back. There was nothing to do but unhitch the horses, and I was surprised to see that Libbie knew the procedure for doing so. She was wrapping one of the horse's lines into reins when her animal suddenly bolted again, jerking her off her feet and into the snow.

I reached her in a few, quick bounds and we were able to control the frightened creature as she regained her feet.

"You hold on tight!" I exclaimed.

"Well I wasn't going to walk home," she said, still breathless from being pulled through the snow. She looked at me solemnly and sincerely. "When I want to hold on, nothing can tear me off."

We stared into each other's eyes and I said, "I have to kiss you," as my mouth moved toward hers. Her short, warm breaths caressed me for an instant before our lips were together. Hers were the most giving and exciting I had ever felt; strong and soft and perfect. Our first kiss seemed to last forever but a moment later we were holding each other close, our bodies connected in the same way our lips had been.

I cannot remember how long we stood transfixed but I remember her humid breath against my cheek and the smallness of the back I held against my hand and the beautiful fit her thigh had against mine, but from then on, the afternoon's memory is as diffuse as that of a picture covered with a gossamer screen.

I boosted her onto one of the horses and we rode back to the mill without saying a word. When we alighted from the bare backs of the horses she turned to me quickly and said, "I don't want you to touch me now . . . I do but . . . I can't."

"Well," I replied, "I have to help you onto your horse."

I must have said these words in a way that showed not the least disappointment because she smiled as if relieved and said, "All right."

Her tiny elbow settled into the cup of my hand and she rose gently into the saddle. As my hand slipped away from her arm a flutter of panic seized me. I had not lived very long but my experience in war had taught me that life is the most delicate of flames and in one second can be snuffed out for eternity. I bid good-bye knowing I might never touch her elbow again. Then I watched her ride back the way she had come. I watched but I was numb for all emotion had been drained away and my heart was lost. It was now riding with hers.

❧

I have just returned from a commotion in camp. One of the sentries shot at what he thought was an Indian but was in fact an oddly shaped clump of sage bobbing in the night wind. A horse broke free and trampled some tents in which men were sleeping. No one was injured save the delicate ears of those who cannot tolerate profane howling in the middle of the night. It seems an appropriate end to a day filled with ludicrous mishaps.

One of the wagons caught fire before we began the march today, apparently ignited by a brand from a driver's pipe, the owner having thrown the pipe aside in a fit of temper at the disobedience of a mule.

One of the men, in a display that defied the laws of physics, managed to shoot himself in the heel while mounting his horse.

The first wagon crossing the day's first ford snapped an axle and held up the column for an hour. The same wagon lost a wheel at the instant it moved forward again, necessitating another delay.

And now a horse among the tents.

Despite all the bumbling we still managed twenty-one miles and I am heartened. The winnowing of mishap is a process that must be endured at the beginning of a campaign and it is my fervent hope that by the time we have located and are in pursuit of the enemy these silly disasters, many brought on by ourselves, will be at an end. I am guessing it will be at least two weeks before we can reach the free roamers and by that time the wheat should be separated from the chaff. That will be imperative.

These details of getting over rough country are nothing compared to the worries I have concerning the overall design of the campaign.

The caprices of politicians and deskbound military commanders are as a smothering smoke, constantly irritating my eyes. They want me to lead and fight and win victories yet they want to supervise all that I do by imposing trivial restrictions on my freedom to operate. When the time comes I will, of course, operate with the freedom of a fighting commander. The politicians and generals in Washington know that the commander they desire to restrain is at the same time their best chance for success. In the end it will be I who meets the enemy. I know that and so do they.

But these worries I cannot allow myself to dwell upon. At least not for now. It is a temptation to which I have too often succumbed in the past and every minute of life I have used in contemplation of the mysteries of politics has been a minute wasted.

I cannot influence the forces swirling about this campaign but I certainly do feel their presence. The recent shock concerning my return from Washington is a good example. I still do not know what has happened to me or will happen but I do know that those who characterize me as a marionette could not be more literally correct. I am not the Armstrong Custer of popular thought. Every arm and leg of me, even my head, has a string attached and the strings are often manipulated by powers whose very existence is unknown to me.

It is a lesson that has taken a lifetime to learn. How ironic that the lesson, once learned, can not be applied. The course of study involves nothing more than the discovery of truth. I have discovered more truth than I wish to know, particularly as concerns my future as a soldier, and it is a heavy, heavy weight. But all the weight on earth could not keep me from leading the Seventh Cavalry on this campaign.

⤝⤞

Libbie says that the magazines are asking for more articles from me. I wish I could comply. Perhaps I will invent a writer's life for myself. Nothing would suit me more. Saber or pen, it matters not, so long as I am standing in the action, the closer to the center the better.

She also reported in her wry way that there is little family news, "since most of our family is accompanying you." As always she said she missed her Autie and that she is constantly dreaming of the day when scouts will arrive at the fort to say we are coming. She dreams of hearing a jaunty melody from the band floating over the prairie as a column in blue gradually appears on the horizon.

We have been separated so often that dreaming of each other has come to be a common and strangely beneficial practice. It lessens the pain and keeps one alive in the other's mind at almost all times. It is a sweet and necessary practice we have cultivated through many years of marriage.

It was not so sweet when I left Monroe in the spring of 1863 to return to the war. It was a terrible agony. For all the winter months it was agony and I cannot recall a period of life during which my nerves were as frayed. To love someone so completely is to entertain constant thoughts of the beloved. I could not button my shirt without thinking of my girl.

Lovers need to reassure each other and since we could neither see nor write each other I fell prey to as many thoughts of doom as I did passion. Would she change her impression of me? Were her impressions as strong as I thought? Would we ever be together? These gloomy questions nagged at me with the same ferocity as did the dreams of our promised Nirvana.

I endured relentless frustration, which began before I left. The worst was glimpsing her on the street. There were secrets behind our eyes now and in the precious times I saw her walking outside I had no choice but to pass in silence. It made me feel as if the whole world was a cheat. I thought of elopement and though I think it would have suited our styles neither one of us could have abided the pain it would have cost our families.

Our love remained stillborn and there seemed to be nothing that I could do. My mind told me constantly that she was slipping away. I realized that my dream was obscured behind a single, imposing edifice that stood between us. It was Judge Bacon, who, to the depth of his character, was an unmovable man. Here was a tree that must be felled, and up to a week before my departure I had searched every inch of my brain for a plan, but to no avail. Even the employment of prayer, a weapon largely unknown to me, proved a failure.

Then one afternoon I happened to see Judge Bacon pass through the doors of the Governor's Club and realized that an opportunity might be presenting itself. I stood in the same place the next afternoon and was pleased to see a pattern of routine. Again the judge came and again he entered the club, precisely at five o'clock. Something tripped in my head and in no time a scheme was being constructed which I hoped would expose me to the judge in an irresistibly favorable light.

I purchased a blank sheet of paper, a plug of sealing wax, and a single envelope. I folded the paper, slipped it into the envelope, and sealed the flap. I then walked a block to the office of a prominent lawyer I knew. He was at work but not too busy to see me. Though I was still but a captain my reputation in battle had been well publicized in my hometown and I enjoyed a notoriety that opened every door with nothing more than the presentation of my card.

I asked my lawyer friend if he would mind safeguarding my will, a request to which he gladly assented, not knowing that I owned nothing but a uniform and a horse. As was usually the case in such meetings the lawyer asked me to sit down and discuss the war news. We talked for perhaps five minutes before I was able to work in a lighthearted aside to the effect that the life of a junior officer isn't very close to that of a Governor's Club member.

He laughed and now that the gate was open I pushed my advantage, making a series of meaningless inquiries about the club. I thought he would never ask the question but he finally did.

"Why, have you never been?"

"No, I haven't."

"Well you must go," he said unconditionally. "I'll take you myself and make introductions. When are you free?"

"I have some time tomorrow afternoon."

He glanced down at a schedule on his desk and asked, "Would four o'clock be all right?"

"Four-thirty would be more convenient," I said.

We met at the appointed hour on the next afternoon and I was escorted to the Governor's Club by my friend the barrister. The place was warm and comfortable, furnished in the typical, quiet elegance of similar clubs that populate the Midwest. Such places are normally too quiet and too constricted for me, but I was on a mission that afternoon and as such was happy to be established in the stuffy environment.

I was introduced to a dozen of the town's leading citizens, and after refreshments were in hand, I stood against the hearth, warming my backside and holding court. I sensed from the start that despite the wide reporting of my exploits, my low rank made me less an object of reverence than of curiosity. But as soon as I began to answer their questions about my adventures I could see a change in the inert expressions of the business and professional men who surrounded me. I felt fully relaxed in the same odd way I am before battle—the greater the pressure the more relaxed I become—and whatever natural charm I possessed seemed to be working at peak efficiency on that afternoon.

The first question I remember well. An old gentleman, sunken in a wing chair, asked whether my reputation for recklessness was truly founded. I remember that the room was still and I let it remain so a few seconds more before answering.

"When the two sides in a war of this proportion are utterly un-movable one of the few ways victories are won is through daring. If I see a weakness in my enemy's line I throw myself against it without hesitation. If surrounded, I fight my way free without hesitation. If it is a matter of kill or be killed I kill without hesitation. This is the only conduct for battle I know and without it I doubt I would be standing before you now. My conduct has been described with many adjectives. If one of them is 'reckless' it bothers me not at all. Recklessness is a word most often associated with disaster, but as you can see I am alive as any of you."

The old gentleman in the wing chair was clearly not the mirthful type, but as I spoke, I saw his eyes come more and more to life until at last they had begun to sparkle. His applause was followed with enthusiasm by the others.

I held forth in the manner of a storyteller for another half hour, careful to talk in short enough spurts to afford myself a glance now and then at a tall clock standing in a far corner of the room.

The members had crowded closer as time passed and I was describing what it had been like to serve at General McClellan's side during the battle of Antietam when I looked up to see the long, sallow face of Judge Bacon watching from behind the last rank of listeners.

I had no sooner finished my description when the judge's somber voice asked: "Are you a McClellan man?"

"I will always be a McClellan man," I answered.

This reply silenced the room again. The nation was divided on the question of General McClellan's record. It was assumed he would win the war by now and he had not.

"To serve with him," I continued, addressing the entire audience, "was an honor that can be attested to by thousands. If the dead could be brought to life they too would raise their hands in support of him. No commander could be more solicitous of his men, nor could he be more intelligent or determined. When General McClellan was relieved of command I can say with authority that our army was in disbelief. Our father had been removed from the head of the table. Disappointment ran so deep that I believe for a day or two the future of our army was in doubt. I felt the pain of his removal as much or more than any man but my personal distress was soon supplanted by my sense of duty. Judge Bacon's question, 'Are you a McClellan man?', while fair enough in itself is not to the point. I have served under a number of distinguished commanders and will continue under future ones so long as they have faith in me . . . for I am a *Union* man, and in the end that is the only thing that truly matters."

Again applause broke out in the room and though his enthusiasm still seemed guarded, I saw that Judge Bacon also made noise with his hands on my behalf.

It was natural now that I should meet Judge Bacon and I did so on leaving. He took my small hand in his large one and pumped it gently, his watery eyes boring into mine. The words "This is the father of the bride" burst into my thoughts and for some odd reason I felt like laughing. I suppose it was because I knew something the father of the bride did not . . . only death could deter me from eventually marrying his daughter.

The judge spoke a few words in praise of my impromptu lecture and then asked: "When will you be returning east?"

"In less than a week," I said.

"Well, I wish you luck, young man. You can be sure we will all have our eyes on you."

With that the interview concluded. Excepting a very few negativists I have always gotten on well with people, regardless of their political or social stripe, and Judge Bacon was no exception. In the few years that remained of his life we were to have a more cordial relationship than I might have suspected.

Our meeting at the Governor's Club lasted only a few seconds and we did not speak of Libbie. Still, I considered it a most glorious event. The judge had done everything possible to keep me from seeing his daughter, not the least of which was keeping me from meeting himself. But I had triumphed nonetheless and would leave Michigan with renewed confidence. I had baited and trapped Judge Bacon and the victory was made all the sweeter in that I had done this without his knowledge.

When the hours in the saddle grow long the country is monotonous and time creeps, I often lapse into what might be described as a state apart. I seem to lose conscious awareness of my surroundings, a phenomenon that frees me to journey along many pleasant roads of contemplation. Rocking to the natural rhythm of a horse induces me to muse upon what is probably my favorite subject . . . the mechanics and mysteries of destiny. The cause of my life—my union with Libbie—could have been altered had the judge deviated from his routine that afternoon. It could have been altered by anyone in attendance at the Governor's Club meeting. The very words from my mouth could have made a difference had they not been spoken just so. Destiny is insoluble but one can feel destiny without knowing it and in my life, whose course I believe has been fated from the moment of birth, destiny has never been more pronounced than it was with Elizabeth Bacon. In her case destiny seemed to function as my personal, silent partner.

This conviction was enhanced a few days later as I boarded a train back to the war. All of the cars were crowded with civilians and soldiers and on finding my seat I watched the throngs moving up and down the aisle and wondered if we would start on time. As I watched I saw Libbie's head appear among a mass of others in a doorway at the far end of the coach. She caught sight of me and pushed forward as I rose to meet her. Her expression seemed strange but I remember also that it was fully alive.

"I just wanted to see your face," she said in a rush. "And I want you to have this."

She pressed a locket into my palm and stepped back as if shyness had suddenly overtaken her. For a moment we looked into each other's eyes and I had the impulse to kiss her again.

"I shall be very disappointed if you do not carry it with you," she said rather strictly.

Then she turned, hurried back down the aisle and was gone.

I opened the locket. There was an ambrotype inside. It was a recent picture, perfectly capturing her usual expression, that of a serious, determined girl whose half smile hints at the playfulness that is so strong a part of her nature. It was the picture of the person with whom I was to spend my life.

I carried her image throughout the war. I slept with it and fought with it. It has been with me through every day of these last twelve years. It is with me now, lying open on my little desk as the camp sleeps, an everlasting reminder of the love I have for the girl I married.

MAY 27-JUNE 1,

1876

The Missouri River country, particularly the badlands we are traversing now, is always unpredictable, but it does appear that summer has come early to these northern plains. The heat today was suffocating and the country is badly broken, a condition that necessitates the constant construction of bridges over which our hundred wagons can pass.

Inevitably, getting the wagons across coulees, ravines, and streams is a laborious and frustrating task but I am still well satisfied with our progress. What we may lack in miles marched we are now making up in improved coordination of the column. I can feel a burgeoning intensity amongst the seven hundred souls marching at my back. I must explain my orders less and less and their execution is carried out with a dispatch one would expect of a veteran regiment such as ours.

Talk and expectations of Indians had died to nothing, for though we are now deep in enemy territory we have not seen a single, dusky foe. Nor will we for some time. There are signs in the country we presently occupy but the travois scratchings and fire rings I have seen are years old.

The entrance to my tent is facing west and as I look out I see the sun has dropped beneath the horizon, leaving a wide orange band to fire the day's last light. That is where they are now, perhaps a thousand enemy fighters who I am sure have taken note, as I have done, of the day's passing. The drama in these skies is irresistible to all. Freedom too is irresistible and I know many of them will fight when we corner them.

There is sufficient wood here and the water is passable and the men seem in good spirits. We went into camp early again today and I should say that a short march of ten or twelve miles never fails to lighten a soldier's heart. The fleshpots of Bismarck are worlds away as is the whiskey peddler's bar and I can sense that the regiment's focus is falling squarely on the campaign at hand.

Were it not for Libbie and my love of theater and its sister arts I could spend the whole of my life tenting in the field. The freedoms here cannot be duplicated anywhere else. Life in the open infuses the soul in many ways that the human species, despite the gains of civilization, still yearns for.

There are times when I have tried to extricate myself from the grasp of this unique freedom. I have tried sincerely to ingratiate myself with the captains of industry, but while my efforts often produced blossoms there has never been fruit. Often I have wondered why, but cannot conjure an acceptable answer other than that

I was meant for this life of soldiering . . . that my creation was meant to serve this purpose alone.

For reasons I am still attempting to comprehend and accept, I doubt I will rise much higher in the army. But I refuse to think of it for it spoils the joy I feel at being with the Seventh again. Perhaps I will achieve distinction as a writer, but failing that, I know I shall remain what I have always wanted to be: a horseman riding to battle.

Somewhere outside they are singing "Motherless Child." The beautiful words and melody are floating through my tent like something borne in on the breeze. The soft sounds of their voices in twilight belie their toughness in battle. We have a number of recruits, boys who have only fired a few rounds at painted targets and who are riding many miles on horseback for the first time. At anything more than a walk they pitch and reel in the saddle like sacks of corn and are constant objects of derisive entertainment for the older troops. When we meet the enemy a few will lose their nerve and cry. Most will lose their nerve but fight anyway. Some will die and rot away on the plains.

Those who survive the crying and the fighting will do so with the help of the veterans. Little is as dear to a commander as a veteran. Men who do their duty without wavering are of the greatest value and the power of this regiment is heavily vested in numerous ranks of tried-and-true veterans.

My feelings for them are often mixed. In the main they are men whose lack of education or initiative or money or family drove them into the army as a last resort. Their lives are largely colorless, woven from the bland monotony of life on post, where they live more as menial laborers than soldiers. They put their backs to make-work much of the day, grousing and complaining incessantly, eager to spend a month's paltry wages on one night of debauchery. There are times when I regard them as dregs of the race. I cannot argue with the commonly held notion that those unfit for society enlist in the army.

But any disregard I may harbor toward the common soldier is made pale by the curious, precious respect I reserve only for those who answer the trumpet's call. While I fault these men for a thousand failings I must also salute them. To see them covered in the grime of battle, to see them after a fight, sitting on their knees, unable to move, to see them in each other's arms crying out their grief for a lost comrade, to see them marching resolutely toward an enemy who ravenously desires their destruction, to see their faces warm at the smallest favor, to see them fight as if possessed. To see these things is to see what the public cannot, for a large part of the reason they are not well matched with society is because they are doing the work society cannot stomach. They are doing society's killing and whether they are regarded as fools or heroes in society's eyes is determined by how well they kill.

I do not know any of them well enough to love them as individuals but I truly love them as a body. Occasionally, one becomes as family. My striker, John Burkman, has seen to my wants, those of Libbie's and the dogs and horses for nine years. He is an uncle to us all.

The others I treat as soldiers and there can be no doubt that I am frequently an object of their wrath for I demand more than they can willingly give. They blame me daily for fifty miles of pain in their backsides and for mouldy bacon and wormy hardtack. They blame me for the banishment of the alcohol they crave.

But I have never asked anything from them that I was not willing to endure myself. I have ridden as long and hard. I haven eaten the same foul rations and drunk the same undrinkable water and when the enemy stands to make a fight I have never failed to go first. The men know that, above all, I would never put them in death's path without putting myself there too. And they know that I have never been defeated in the field. They will follow me into any fight and for that I love them all.

The men with me now are content to serve and eager to fight and I feel especially proud for it has not always been that way. This command was built from the ashes of the Great War and in the beginning, the ash left a bitter taste in the mouths of everyone, not the least myself.

General Sheridan sent me to Louisiana shortly after the close of the Civil War, and even after a dozen years of mutual support and affection between us, I find myself reluctant to forgive him for doing so. Perhaps he did not know what I would be facing at Alexandria but he is far cleverer than I and it is hard to believe that he could not have guessed what would happen. If he did, he never provided me with a clue.

Louisiana is a place I rarely speak of unless involved in a discussion of the eccentric pleasures of New Orleans. I do not speak of my military life there because the darkness of that time is so great that I would gladly erase the memory if it were in my power.

My assignment was to form a cavalry division with which to police the state of Texas, a region whose population had difficulties accepting the war's result. I was thrilled nonetheless to be traveling to Alexandria on a special train, one entire car of which had been reserved for me, my family, and staff.

My confidence at that time was running higher than could be imagined. I was still just a boy but a boy who had presented the country with a long unbroken string of victories. We were all basking in the aftermath of war, the crowning glory of which had been a mammoth review of troops on the streets of Washington, D.C.

It seemed that the whole nation had turned out to honor its army. I was mobbed as the parade began to form and on gaining the saddle an aging veteran actually took my hand and kissed it, an act that moved and embarrassed me simultaneously.

The veteran Michiganders, many of them marching in scraps of shoe leather and uniform remnants, glowed through their rags with a tangible pride as we marched down Pennsylvania Avenue. The brigade's colors snapped overhead in a bracing spring breeze while thousands upon thousands hugged the sides of the street.

My Wolverines were widely renowned and the cheers raised in

our honor as we passed were tumultuous. All of the horses were rather unnerved by the screams of so many thousands, and the horse I had selected for the review was driven absolutely crazy by the noise—it took all of my strength to keep him under control.

Not far from the reviewing stand a group of schoolgirls, laden with flowers, rushed from the crowd and surrounded me in the street, thrusting bouquets into my hands and strewing petals at the feet of the hot-blooded Don Juan. One of the girls attempted to slip a wreath over my steed's neck. Don Juan ducked his head to one side and the girl tried to improvise by tossing the wreath. It struck him on the neck and in the next instant I found myself rising into the air as Don Juan stood on his hind legs, staggered a step or two, and bolted forward as I tried to hang on.

He streaked down the avenue with the bit between his teeth, and pull as I might I could not slow him. We sped past the president and other high government officials at a full gallop and I remember seeing sparks fly from his hooves as they clattered over the pavement. The crowd, thinking I was making a demonstration, roared as I passed, and for want of any other response, I made the best of it and doffed my flop hat in the president's direction as we flew by.

After another hundred yards I succeeded at last in bringing Don Juan to a stop. There was nothing to do but trot back the way we had come, which of course took us past the reviewing stand again, this time against the parade's tide. Again, for want of a better manoeuver, I sheepishly lifted my hat.

When I finally rejoined the Michigan Brigade I was greeted with smug smiles and suppressed laughter. Unable to contain himself, one of the men called out, "Kinda eager aren'cha General?"—a remark that released a round of guffaws from the ranks.

This was followed rapidly by "Who ya chargin' General?" and "Somebody tell that officer the war's over."

At this the whole brigade was carried into convulsions. My face must have turned a very deep shade of red but the laughter was so infectious that I could not help but join it. The memory of that spectacle, the memory of being in it, sends a surge of excitement through me still.

To have peace after a long and ugly war is a feeling of immeasurable joy. To me, there is no more happy condition on earth. It was in that festive spirit that our special train pulled out for Louisiana not long after the triumphant and remarkable review of troops in the streets of the capital.

Inside our special sleeping car all was merry mayhem. Among our party was my younger brother Tom; whenever he and I found ourselves together and at leisure there were likely to be very few serious moments.

When Tom is up to something he wears a phantom grin and has difficulty looking me straight in the eye. Such was his demeanor as we sat down the first evening out. I immediately suspected that there was mischief afoot. I watched the table carefully as I ate but detected nothing unusual except that Libbie was absent. I asked Tom if he knew where she might be.

With pursed lips he arched his eyebrows and shrugged his shoulders, dubious actions that increased my suspicions. I had no idea that an evil scheme had already been set in motion, not until my fork struck something solid in the mashed potatoes. Parting the spuds, I discovered a squirming cockroach that had undergone a premature burial.

Seized by sudden, overwhelming spasms of laughter, Tom fell from his seat and was attempting to crawl to safety when I started after him. I had not gone two steps before I was on the floor too, a result of my bootlaces being tied together. As I struggled to free my feet, Libbie emerged from under the table and rushed after Tom. As I sat on the floor in ignominy fumbling at the knot in my laces our friends at the table laughed and clapped in delight at my misfortune. Someone remarked that it was the first time they had seen "a general unhorsed."

When my feet had been liberated I thought of going after the two perpetrators but decided instead to remain where I was, there to let my mind sift through various options for revenge.

Before a plan had time to take shape Libbie reappeared, standing in the far doorway of the car with a cautious and hesitant expression. She was waiting to see if I was still hot for retaliation.

I remained seated at the dinner table and I suppose the sight of me, so calm and cool, gave her the courage to come forward. This she accomplished to the accompaniment of a stream of explanations.

My fellow diners chuckled as she described the affair of the wriggling cockroach and knotted laces as being wholly my brother's creation. She had not known of the interloper in my potatoes and had allowed herself to be employed as Tom's accomplice only because he had threatened to make her the target of some dark deed should she refuse to help him.

I forgave her on condition that she swear not to divulge my future plans for Tom. She swore she would not.

Tom did not reappear that evening and I suspected correctly that he had taken refuge in the smoking car, a public place in which he knew I would not dare to challenge him.

His absence, however, gave me free access to his sleeping quarters, and here, at the foot of his bed between the sheets, I placed the rib cage of the chicken we had consumed at dinner. I knew that on his return, Tom would be on guard and that my retaliation would lose its potency through lack of surprise. Surely, Tom would see the bump under his covers and discover the chicken.

Knowing Tom's habit of falling asleep on his stomach, hands tucked on either side of the pillow, I retrieved a selection of inedible chicken parts from our cook and placed a portion of these underneath Tom's pillow, carefully centering them so they would remain undiscovered until just before sleep.

We ate dessert and concluded the evening with a few rounds of cards. When it was time to retire there was still no sign of Tom. This suited my plan perfectly, and as Libbie and I lay talking in bed, I would from time to time be overpowered by laughter at the thought of my brother slipping into his bed.

We waited until at long last doors were heard opening and closing at the far end of the coach. No longer able to contain myself, I began to giggle, a hand over my mouth. Libbie was giggling too, and with our stomachs rolling we held each other as we waited out the seconds.

From out of the darkness came Tom's high voice, purposely flat in an attempt to deny me satisfaction.

"That's very funny, Autie."

Libbie and I giggled on, making no reply as he continued, his words partially drowned out by the sounds of his bed being rearranged.

"But you know what? It bothers me hardly at all, Autie . . . hardly at all."

He said nothing else, but like children in a closet anticipating what was yet to come, we could not stop laughing. Curiously, nothing happened and I began to think I had been too subtle with the chicken innards when his voice came again, floating out of the blackness in a long, mournful wail.

"Oh, my God!"

In moments he was standing before the drawn curtains of our compartment, demanding that I come out or he would come in and get me.

Libbie told him quite properly and firmly that he could not enter. In my mind I could see Tom quivering with rage as he stood in the darkness of the aisle. I laughed uncontrollably and as I did I heard him say: "I'll get you for this, Autie . . . I will. I promise you."

Then he was gone.

Libbie and I lay back with tears in our eyes and let laughter carry us into the arms of sleep that night. Nothing could have been more satisfying.

The duration of our trip was conspicuous for its war of pranks, which reached their climax when I dropped a live and ill-tempered 'possum onto the bed in which my brother Tom was slumbering.

Inside, we were having the gayest of times but outside was a different matter. We were steadily pushing into the enemy's former territory, which was more different than we could image. Outside the train there were no light hearts.

Our stops in the East were exciting. News of our impending appearance always seemed to precede our arrival in this town or that with the result that our car was inevitably surrounded by crowds of supportive citizens. They would call for me to come out and I believe I answered every summons.

To receive the unanimous adulation of strange masses always provides an uncommon thrill. On these occasions I have always tried to conduct myself in an authoritative, amiable manner. I say "tried" because I was only twenty-five at the time and to be the beneficiary of public demonstrations, particularly in out-of-the-way hamlets, made my chest swell and my mind run.

To be treated as a conquering hero necessitated that I act the part, and though I enjoyed my role immensely and actively dreamed how far such adulation might take me, at the time I felt I was only playing a part the public had thrust upon me. I cannot say I suffered but I felt uneasy, realizing that in accepting public plaudits I was somehow changing the character of my life.

I had detected a change in the perception of others from the time I had won my star. With every triumph that came, these perceptions altered my existence, but I was not fully aware of how deep the alterations were until taking the train to Louisiana.

Perhaps I had failed to perceive the very subtle nature of these shifts in perception, perhaps I had not wanted to accept them, but by the time of my postwar assignment they were succinct. Even my friends and family seemed to walk more softly in my presence. My opinions were deferred to with greater, quicker ease than ever before. My counsel was praised beyond that of others. Thankfully,

Libbie remained down to earth but there were times when I saw that she, too, was looking at me not as husband or lover but as an object of celebrated mystery.

My father, with whom I had always maintained the most facile relations, fell into the habit of addressing me as "General." At first I laughed, reminding him of our father-and-son relation, but he persisted with such obvious good nature that I finally gave it up and would simply reply, "Yes, Father."

What I have just described should not be construed as any type of complaint. I love the attention and respect that comes with elevated status and I have to say that all of my life I have wanted to sit atop the common heap. But a position of such height and all that comes with it can be anticipated by no one. The experience of it comes as a surprise.

I remember that each time we pulled out of a station I would linger on the platform and invariably someone in the crowd would shout out, "Three cheers for General Custer." I would watch as the people grew smaller and boys broke away, calling my name as they ran after the train. The fading cheers impelled me to reach up and tip my hat, usually sweeping it off my head and holding it aloft. How they would cheer then!

And yet, what could I make of it? In reality I was nothing more than an actor who had become skilled at seducing his audience. I had entered a new and lonely dimension that could be fully shared with nobody and, as I soon found out, was constantly subject to change.

My first important instruction as to the shifting attitudes of the public mind occurred when we stopped after traveling all night at a midsized town of southern Tennessee.

Our party alighted from the train and in order to stretch our legs and eat a breakfast untainted by the odor of a train we proceeded to the first café we could find. A restaurant was quickly discovered and we trooped inside. Our high-spirited group pushed several tables together and commandeered most of the chairs. As we settled at the table, a woman appeared bearing plates and utensils. In the midst of distributing these items the woman suddenly stopped. At once I perceived what had made her cease such a normal activity.

It was the image of Eliza, who was sitting at the far end of the table.

Eliza had escaped her master during the early stages of the Great War and had been blown by fate to the door of a young captain of cavalry who was myself. She appeared at my tent one night and appointed herself my cook.

At first I had laughed at the idea; a tiny, tough Negro woman of indeterminate age appearing out of the night and ordering me to accept her into my life. I had no experience with people of color and matters of race had never held much interest for me. Even the issue of slavery, which was not a concept I embraced, was a topic I rarely considered. My service in the Civil War was motivated entirely by an oath to defend our Union.

At the time of Eliza's arrival, however, my eating habits had for months consisted of stuffing my mouth with handfuls of food whenever food was available. I knew the addition of a cook would make my soldier's life more efficient in every way.

Taking Eliza in that night proved to be one of Armstrong Custer's smartest moves ever. She followed me down every road of war for the duration of that lengthy conflict. She made her home in any place I could find for us. She lived in the mud and rain and heat and cold. She packed my belongings on a moment's notice, marched with me for days and weeks at a time, cooked delicious meals, and made me laugh when I most needed to.

Although she fully acknowledged our separate roles and stations, Eliza never shrank from expressing her true opinion, nor did she shrink from ordering me about when I invaded her sovereign territory. She stayed in perfect step with my rapid advancement, sensitive to the increasing needs for discretion and dignity without losing one iota of her forceful personality.

Twice during the war Eliza had been captured by the enemy but had escaped each time and found her way back to us, traveling alone through many dangerous zones to do so.

When Libbie joined me at last they took to each other almost like sisters and overnight the three of us became an inseparable and largely indomitable force.

Abruptly, and with our breakfast ware half distributed, the woman retreated from our table and I watched curiously as she disappeared into the rear of the restaurant. A moment later she reemerged with a man whom I guessed was the proprietor. They exchanged a few words, the woman nodding toward our table as she talked. The proprietor listened with folded arms and an obstinate expression.

Wanting to know what had halted the breakfast process I rose and made my way to where they were standing.

I said, "Good morning" and started a hand forward but the proprietor's arms remained folded.

"I can serve you but I can't serve that nigger," he said sourly.

I looked back at the table and saw Eliza. She was sitting still as a stone, staring at her lap.

"You have to get that nigger out of here," he commanded.

The blood was rushing to my head and because I have a tendency to stutter when excited I waited to reply as long as I could so as to make each word absolutely clear.

"She will not leave, sir . . . and she *will* be served. If not, I can guarantee you your establishment will be no more."

After enjoying our breakfast we returned to the train and found the usual crowd of bystanders waiting there. But unlike before this group greeted us somberly, disdaining the cheers and applause to which we had grown accustomed. They said not a word as we passed through them on our way to the car but they stared at us with the cold gazes normally reserved for the perusal of biological specimens. I offered "Good morning"s to several of them but received only silence in return.

Libbie and I were the last to gain the platform; assuming the crowd had come to see me, I paused and, turning, faced the people standing below.

Thrown from somewhere in back of the onlookers, a raw egg struck me on the shoulder. I heard Libbie utter a small shriek. In the next instant someone shouted out, "Blue butcher!" Other voices rose, calling out foul names. I stood before them in shock, making no answer. Then I turned my back on the insults and walked into the car to join my family and friends. Being hated by strangers carries many features similar to being loved by strangers, but the emotional impact is as different as fire and ice.

We made no more appearances for the remainder of our journey and were relieved to arrive at the Alexandria station well after dark. Alertly, we made our way to the post accompanied by a large, well-armed escort.

∾

I have let Alf the Mouse out for his nightly sojourn around the tent but he seems content this evening to maintain a perch on my shoulders. I can feel his tiny, clawed feet from time to time as he crosses from one shoulder to another. Usually he takes a walk across the floor and investigates the darkened corners of my abode before venturing out for a midnight dinner. Then he returns and I feel him again, climbing up the back of my arm.

Like all mice I have known—and I have known a few—Alf is meticulous concerning cleanliness; without fail he pauses on my shoulder to wash his face and hands. Satisfied with his bath, he strolls furtively down the length of one arm and returns to the spare inkwell on this little desk, which is his home. It is furnished with long, sweet grass, the strands of which I have arranged as his nest. Apparently my taste in bedding agrees with him for it is clear that Alf loves his house.

I am always amused by his bedtime routine. The inkwell stands perhaps two inches off the surface of the desk and as Alf approaches he rises on his hind legs. He then grasps the lip of the inkwell with his small hands and pulls his body up. This requires some effort as Alf is rather fat of bottom but I don't believe anything would keep him from his cup-shaped bed.

He is vigilant about the order of his nest and spends some time sniffing its borders and nosing bits of stray grass into more acceptable positions. Gradually, he runs out of things to do and calms down, sinking low on his stomach. Not long after I will glance over at the inkwell and see Alf's round, wet eyes resting at a sleepy half-staff.

John Burkman takes charge of him in the morning and has found a place somewhere in a wagon for Alf to ride along, secure in his inkwell. After mess John returns him to my tent, where he spends the night. Our relationship is but two days old, yet our ease at companionship has the feel of a much longer stint together.

John originally found him cowering at the side of the trail, probably shocked into senselessness by the close passing of a horse or wagon. John then brought him to me as he does all orphans of the march.

"John," I exclaimed, "what do you propose I do with a mouse?"

"Well, I didn't want him to get run over, General, and you have such a way with creatures that I expect him bein' in your company for a few days might make him feel himself again. If you want, I can put him out of his misery."

We have had the same exchange, nearly the exact words, on so many occasions that I sometimes feel we are two entertainers performing a familiar comedic sketch.

I tell John that it will not be necessary to end the foundling's life, at which point we begin an examination of the new addition and set out the terms for its care. It was just this way with Alf.

That he would rather warm himself on my shoulder tonight than eat his dinner is ample testimony that my meteorological prediction was, as usual, wrong. Summer must wait a few more days for it is raining again, a soft, driving rain that is blowing across our camp here in the badlands of the Little Missouri River.

This means, of course, that tomorrow the trail will be a bog of sticky, clinging clay. My only consolation is that we are on the great, high, western plains, an ocean of windswept country that will always be preferable to the stifling swamp that is the Deep South.

If weather had been the sum of my difficulties in Louisiana I would have been fond of the time spent there, but a series of complicated and grave social conditions poisoned my tenure, which I might compare to being dropped into a dark, slippery-sided well from which there was no escape. Each day consisted entirely of disagreeable and frustrating challenges. And each challenge required decisions made in the spirit of one condemned who must choose death by hanging or stoning.

The local populace was at once frightened and defensive, a combination that forced me and my command to operate in an atmosphere of vicious, unpredictable antagonism. Trouble always came to the surface when soldiers mingled with citizens and in a short time I had no choice but to place the entire town off limits.

By then, however, animosities had gone too far and the barely repressed hatred between citizen and soldier constantly resulted in acts of lawlessness. Men in uniform were forever sneaking in to steal extra rations and anything else of value that opportunity placed in their path. This trespassing and plundering ignited the already resentful townspeople.

Because I represented the Union in all its manifestations, particularly that of justice, I severely punished those of my command who were caught outside the post. The punishment was quick and harsh, but without it I cannot imagine what travesties might have transpired. As it was there were horrors enough.

Our division was made up of veteran regiments of volunteers from the Midwest. They were hardened, worthy soldiers caught in a web of untimely circumstance. Each felt he was serving against his will. After four years of warfare, virtually all my command wanted their enlistments canceled. All wanted to return home, to rejoin their families and resume their livings.

I sympathized with their desires but could not grant their wishes. I was then functioning as the Union government and my mission was to restore full order to the Union. These men had taken oaths of allegiance and had a duty to serve just as I did and there was only one way to make them toe the line; to mete out punishment that was swift and sure. Had I given an inch I am certain there would have been an insurrection.

It came to pass that I found myself policing a population who loathed us with a division who loathed me.

Filled with spite, the men carried out their duties lethargically, questioned their sergeants and their officers to distraction, and continually groused amongst themselves. They behaved like surly convicts instead of soldiers. My officers applied ever harsher discipline and tensions rose with the passing of every day.

I had thumbed my nose at discipline in the years at West Point. Placing a boy of youth and spirit in an environment of order and academics could hardly have produced another result. So long as I played the soldier I was a devotee of play but the Great War was play with mortal consequences and it forever changed my attitude toward discipline.

It came quickly clear to me that our army was useless without it. The commands in which discipline was highly observed were often able to achieve victory and survival whereas those without discipline were defeated before the first shot of battle.

During the war our volunteers fought in a cause they were willing to die for, but to my regiments in Louisiana the war had been won and the cause was finished and it was only through the strictest discipline that our force could be maintained at all.

Those who preyed on citizens were given twenty-five lashes and had their heads shaved. Those who committed lesser offenses were required to carry a log of at least twenty-five pounds as they performed their duties over the course of a day. I issued orders that anyone found guilty of desertion or mutiny would be shot. These measures I took reluctantly, knowing that while they might preserve order they were also sure to increase hostility. And they did.

There was little peace in our household at this time. Each day was permeated with torturous levels of anxiety. I had a picture made during a short trip to New Orleans that shows everything. My expression looks blasted as if the impossibility of existence has turned my features to stone. It is an accurate depiction in every way.

The troops became more and more bold at insubordination. Word of assassination plots against me were reported almost daily, and the outrages against townspeople continued unabated. When it came to my attention that an entire regiment had openly refused an officer's lawful order and another regiment had appeared before its colonel in makeshift costumes I knew that the time had come for a reckoning. The specter of catastrophe didn't affect me because catastrophe had already become a part of the day's routine. I decided to end the conflict between the men and their commanders with direct action.

The tension came to head when a young private who was a persistent malcontent made a public announcement of his intentions to desert, then did so on the spot. One of my officers ordered man after man of the regiment to detain the deserter but all refused to comply. The runaway was captured by other troops but in the meantime a leading sergeant of the offending regiment got up a petition to replace his own commander, a document that was eagerly signed by all.

The sergeant, whose name was Lancaster, had a highly valorous record and was immensely popular among the rank and file. He had also instigated an act of mutiny and I had him arrested. He and the deserter were found guilty at court-martial and sentenced to death by firing squad. I directed that the sentence be carried out within forty-eight hours.

Each one of those hours seemed interminable. I was besieged with numerous deputations pleading for the lives of the condemned, especially that of Sergeant Lancaster. A small group of my own officers questioned the sentence, advancing the opinion that they might be unable to control their men were he executed.

The pleas on behalf of Lancaster had the desired effect and I changed my mind, but as commander I could not allow myself to appear swayed by public opinion.

My conclusions were confirmed when I visited the guardhouse on the eve of the execution. The young malcontent showed no remorse for his action but Sergeant Lancaster was a different matter. I found him as he had been described: youthful, vigorous, brave, and highly intelligent. His ardor for insurrection had cooled and I knew from the beginning of our interview that I had condemned a superior man.

He rose to meet me and accepted the offer of my hand without hesitation. He answered my questions without emotion and throughout the interview met my eyes with his own, which were steady and bore a striking shade of gray.

I asked whether he had contemplated his actions and the sergeant replied that he had spent his confinement thinking of nothing else. I wondered whether he had reached any conclusions and asked what they might be.

"They're mixed," he replied, "and I suspect they always will be. I know that such defiance of authority is intolerable but I guess standing firm for my men became more important."

As he continued the sergeant looked at me pointedly.

"I have served under many diverse commanders," he said, "but the discipline this command has imposed is not discipline, sir, it is simply torture."

"Indeed," I replied, "I believe you are correct, but you understand I have been given no choice."

"Is it so difficult to choose for justice?" he asked.

"Not in the least," I said. "But this conflict does not concern justice, it concerns who shall command, you or I. Any man who conducts himself as a faithful soldier has my respect. Those who do not jeopardize everyone's lives and will be swept aside by any means necessary. I do not demand this. It is demanded by military life and I am a servant of military life."

Sergeant Lancaster nodded his head in the affirmative and as I stood, he came to attention, offering a salute, which I returned.

"Will I see you in the morning, General?"

"You shall," I answered.

The convict seemed crestfallen and I asked if he would rather I not attend.

"No, sir. But I have heard from many quarters that there are men who are ready to sacrifice their lives in order to take yours."

"I have heard the same, Sergeant. I shall see you early."

"Yes, sir," he said.

My night was sleepless and so was Libbie's. We have endured much but this was a time when the tension in our home was at an hysterical pitch. Libbie senses trouble unlike any person I have known and in addition to finding the punishment of death too severe she was deeply concerned about my personal safety. The assassination rumors had found a way to her ears and on the night before the executions she was consumed with fear. She articulated these fears through the whole of dinner and insisted on pursuing the subject as we retired.

The general turmoil was heightened by regular appearances from the officer of the day, whom I had instructed to report to me personally through the night. We also received brief visits from other key officers who requested clarification of the orders I had issued for the following morning. I should say that the atmosphere was one of barely controlled chaos.

When faced with such moments my instinct has always been to fight through. I consider a fighting spirit my personal talisman, and under severe pressure I have always summoned it. This affair was no exception.

I wanted every man to have a first-hand knowledge of disobedience's price and gave orders for the entire garrison to turn out at dawn and form ranks around the parade ground. I also gave orders that my personal review of the troops would be conducted without escort, armed or otherwise. This edict created consternation on the part of my most faithful officers, but after volumes of thought I decided it was best that the troops see their commander as he is, as a man alone.

Libbie could not sleep and in the early-morning hours, tired and desperate, she begged me to forgo the action that was shortly to take place. I said, "I cannot," and with a fitful sob she threw herself facedown on the bed. There was nothing I could do to reassure her, and as it was nearly dawn, I dressed quickly and left the room.

Even Eliza, who was up and preparing breakfast, gave me a grumpy look as I walked into the kitchen.

"You might as well give me your opinion," I said. "Everyone else has."

"I ain't got a 'pinion," she replied, stoking the cook stove. "Alls I no is, yo' got yosef a worl' a nerve. But Ginral we both know that. You jus' do what you gonna do. I sho' ain' goin' stop ya."

The breaking day was already hot and sticky when I and my mount arrived at the parade ground. Nearly four thousand men had been assembled as ordered and were flanking all four sides of the field. Standing under guard in the center were the condemned, open graves at their sides.

In silence I began my review of the regiments, moving at a slow, calculated walk. My eyes roamed over the eyes of thousands of others and nowhere could I find a neutral expression. Making that promenade was the loneliest thing I have ever done, but strangely, I was not in the least afraid. It was the same here as it had been in battle. My life was at stake and the mysterious, automatic mechanism that forces me to risk all had assumed control.

A spring wagon carrying coffins rolled into the yard, momentarily diverting all attention. I kept to the business at hand and was nearing the end of my inspection when a soldier called out, "Goddamn murderer." He uttered this not at my back but to my face. I pulled up my horse and looked down at him. He was perhaps eighteen and

I remember he had very large ears. His teeth were clenched and his eyes were moist with emotion.

In the most even tones possible I said, "I will shoot you too, if that's what you want."

The boy's face began to vibrate. It turned utterly red as I sat in the saddle waiting for his answer.

With a coughing sob, his head fell and a trembling hand rose to cover his eyes.

I had just passed the last rank of men when a steady drumming announced the arrival of the firing squad, a group of eight soldiers marching onto the parade ground with an armed escort of their own. A rumor had surfaced at the last moment that the firing squad intended to execute me.

I quickly joined the squad at the scene of the execution, there to command it personally.

The coffins were placed next to the waiting graves, the orders of execution were read aloud, and it was enquired of the prisoners whether they desired blindfolds. Sergeant Lancaster refused. The deserter accepted and a strip of cloth was tied around his head.

A final drum roll commenced as the riflemen formed a line in front of the condemned. I called out, "Ready," and the squad brought their weapons up. At the command "Aim" the troops obediently sighted down their weapons. Responding to a prearranged wave of my hand the officer in charge of the firing squad stepped forward and pulled Sergeant Lancaster to one side, out of harm's way.

I called out, "Fire," and eight rifles boomed. The young deserter's knees buckled and he slumped sideways, falling head first into the grave, his legs left angling out of the hole.

As the rifle smoke dispersed I ordered the stunned Lancaster released to return to his regiment, at the same time directing the regimental commanders to dismiss their troops. The men made no trouble as they broke ranks, returning to their places of duty in abject quiet.

Libbie was waiting on the porch of our home as I rode up. She was perfectly still save for twin rivers of tears that I could see streaming down each cheek. She put her arms around me as I mounted the steps and held me.

It was one of the few times I can remember expressing a need for rest. Libbie led me up the stairs and pulled off my boots as I sat on the bed. Then she helped me off with my clothes and gently pushed me down. She spread a sheet over my frame, kissed me on the forehead, and slipped out of the room, closing the door softly behind her.

When I awoke the long shadows of afternoon were falling across the bed. I looked out the window and noticed that the breeze was up. Then I lay back down and slept again, all the way to morning.

The execution on the parade ground in Louisiana proved to be a catalyst for change in the entire division. It was as if a large bubble of pressure had been popped and in the days that followed military life resumed its normal routine.

Barely three weeks later we marched into Texas with the purpose of dampening the imperialist schemes of Mexico under the emperor Maximilian and subduing Secessionist groups still roaming the country.

The march was long and incessantly hot, but being on the move had a deeply calming effect on the ragged spirits of all, including my own.

To ride again at the head of my own column, straddling a fine, strong horse, every mile greeting the eye with something heretofore unseen, to listen to every beat of an army's heart while moving constantly forward nourishes my spirit like nothing else. And that feeling has lost none of its intensity through time. It is the same today as it was then. I am most happy when free of constraint, when intoxicated with the taste and smell of new adventures.

Libbie rode in an ambulance that was converted each night into our bedroom. She adhered carefully to the schedule of the march and through all the rigors of such a trek she refused to complain.

Nor did she upbraid her husband concerning his frequent, pro-tracted, and necessary absences.

It was my restless habit, after the column had gone into camp, to take the dogs and ride into the twilight, ostensibly to hunt but mostly to clear my mind. Sometimes I would return to camp well after dark but even then she had no words of chastisement for me. Though we disagreed about many things in life and were not above having hot words for each other from time to time, Libbie routinely placed her own needs in the background when I was in the field, sacrifices for which I will always be grateful.

When at last I returned, I would lift her into our bedroom and together we performed the ungainly ritual of undressing for sleep in a wagon-sized room. I would start a smudge for the mosquitos and Libbie would wriggle under a sheet. There she would quickly whisper a prayer I could never quite make out.

I would then dive through the blanket of smoke the smudge had created and take possession of my portion of the sheet. Lying on our backs we would enjoy a silent time, together in body, alone in our thoughts. At some spontaneous moment which always seemed well timed Libbie would rise up and blow out the candle. Then her bare feet would come searching for mine and we would fall asleep with toes entwined.

One night as she moved toward the candle I broke this routine. Sometime before I had taken vows for Christ Our Savior, but if the truth be known I only did it for her—destiny is a god on whom prayer is wasted and I had always tried to politely distance myself from religion, wherever and whenever it might be afoot.

But Libbie's nightly prayer intrigued me. I could not understand her constant cheerfulness. Perhaps the prayer was its source and, if so, I was curious to know its power.

"May I ask you a question?" I said.

Libbie turned and smiled at me like an eager schoolgirl. "Of course," she exclaimed.

"You have not complained," I said, "not once."

Her smile widened and she said, "Isn't that nice!"

"Yes, of course," I laughed, "but you are alone in a strange country with four thousand men, riding in a bumpy wagon, enduring extreme heat, while I attend to this or that, and you never complain, Libbie . . . and it makes me wonder whether your nightly prayer isn't a cry for help."

Smiling tenderly she listened to my long question, looking into my eyes for several seconds after it was finished. Then she blew out the candle and lay down.

"Come here . . . give me your head," she commanded gently.

I squirmed closer. Taking my head in her hands she pressed it against her chest and stroked my hair. I could hear the little bellows of her lungs and the light, steady thump of her heart.

"My prayer doesn't ask for anything. It's a prayer of thanks. I thank God that I have my Autie and that he is safe. Everything is easy so long as I have my Autie."

Our marriage has often been vulnerable to stresses from outside events but inside it has been blessed, almost always, with the same stillness found at the center of a storm. To have each other, secure in the knowledge that death alone can part us, is a joy we have never lost. Hearing her recite her prayer that night in Texas has sustained me through many tribulations and those happy words "I have my Autie" are alive in me now.

The destination that summer was the town of Hempstead, Texas, and by the time we reached it, lapses in discipline had again become a problem. There was even grumbling about my practice of letting the dogs ride with Libbie in the ambulance when they became weary or footsore while the men were compelled to march. I ignored these complaints.

Rations were a bone of contention as always, but I could produce no better, and as I was determined to treat the defeated populace with complete respect, these complaints I took as a signal to institute greater security in order to prevent foraging in the homes and gardens and chicken pens of civilians.

These measures proved successful on the march but were impossible to maintain when we reached Hempstead. The men were crazed with the desire for fruit and parties of them quickly began to make unauthorized visits to the town which was nearby. I punished those who were apprehended with lashings and head shavings, and murmurings of mutiny surfaced a second time.

I wrote to General Sheridan and he surprised me by coming in person to review the situation. The general gave me his full support, which was passed on to the rank and file, and from the time he departed I heard no more talk of sedition.

France was already withdrawing from Mexico and suspected outlaw units of Confederate resistance had not materialized. Our mission was reduced to policing the local inhabitants, a duty I find distasteful and degrading for all.

Essentially there was little to do but follow the daily routine, and though Libbie and I participated in the life of the region by socializing with various prominent citizens, we soon became lonely for family.

Tom had not traveled into Texas but I was able to effect his transfer and appointed him my aide. The division was also in need of an official civilian forager and I thought of my father. Though advanced in years and inexperienced in military ways he had always been a shrewd bargainer and I had him installed in the exalted position of division forager.

These additions were not only a reflection of a wife and husband's need for familiar company. The troubles in Alexandria pointed out to me in bold terms the need for a circle of dependable advisers who could protect me from threats coming at any hour from any quarter. Brother Tom and father Emmanuel were the first members of what was to become a large group of trusted allies who have provided me with many extra eyes and ears and brains through the years and it is for my family that I reserve my deepest love.

Tom is with me now, as is young, sweet brother Boston, my only nephew and namesake, Autie Reed, and my capable brother-in-law

Jimmie Calhoun. Family always comes with disadvantages but in my clan the credits far exceed the debits.

In Texas it was only father and Tom but our time together was passed in the Custer tradition. In fact, there hardly was one day in which our noses were not alert to the aroma of some sinister plan that could be sprung at any time.

My father is composed in equal parts of the strange, the powerful, and the comical. His blacksmithing and judgment of horses is peerless but his true passion is politics, an arena in which he has never achieved a high status. I don't believe that, despite a lifetime of public espousal of his political views, my father has ever influenced a solitary vote in support of his convictions. I do know of many whom he drove to the other side.

This I attribute to his comical bent, for my father Emmanuel has rarely evinced a desire to take life too seriously. He led our household to be sure and was, in most instances, obeyed by myself and my siblings. But we, like most of those outside our family, found it impossible to take him seriously. My father did not, why should we? There was constant clowning in our home and my father served enthusiastically as the ringleader.

For the first several months after his and Tom's arrival in Texas, elaborate jokes were held in abeyance and we subsisted on jibes and jabs. Tom was busy disseminating my orders and familiarizing himself with personnel while Father set about to charm and cajole various goods out of the town at unreasonable rather than outrageous prices. The busy newcomers had little time for pranks and just as they were becoming adapted to Hempstead the division was ordered to the town of Austin, Texas.

There we took up residence in a two-story stone building that was bestowed on us for use as a headquarters by the governor of the state. It had previously been an institution in Austin called the Blind Asylum, from which the inmates had been evacuated to an unknown locale. How it served them I do not know, but it served me, my staff, and my family well.

The Asylum was located in a portion of the town that was pleasant but quite private and we were delighted with the space its many rooms afforded us. For many townspeople the idea of our occupying an asylum of the blind was the raw material for numerous jokes. For those of us who lived there home was affectionately referred to as "the Asylum," and as a defense against the boredom that haunted our days, idle minds applied themselves to the construction of devilish pranks that, it was hoped, would thoroughly confound and humiliate the victims.

A classic example of these elaborate hijinx was a hoax perpetrated by Tom and me on my father, which is still referred to by those who recall the event as "the affair of the dead alligator."

It began on a lazy Sunday morning in September as we sat on the porch of the Asylum, drinking coffee and sharing the newspaper. No one wanted my father to have the paper first because he took forever in the reading of it. He read the fine print on the advertisements as if they were outlandish gossip or fresh war dispatches.

Tom currently had possession of the paper and, knowing that my father was next, made no haste to finish. This irritated the old man and he squirmed about in his chair with anticipation. As Tom finally folded the periodical, Emmanuel leaned forward and stuck out his hand. Pretending to be unaware of my father's eagerness, Tom faked a sudden second thought and reopened the paper. This was more that the old man could take.

"Give me that paper, Tom," he snapped.

"I'm not done with it, Father."

"Yes you are . . . you're drawin' out your time 'cause you know I been waitin' for it."

"Well," started Tom languidly, "if you want it that bad—"

"I want my paper."

"Yes, Father."

Tom feigned a final, lingering interest in some piece of meaningless text as my father waited, a prominent vein on his temple beginning to swell.

"Tom . . ."

"All right, Father."

At last he closed the paper once more and then, to his antagonist's consternation, he deliberately began to open the paper once more.

My father, whom the years had begun to slow, lurched forward in his chair, snatched the paper out of Tom's hand, and fell back in his chair, perfectly satisfied now that he had his prize.

As the old man read I noticed that Tom was glancing at him now and again, then returning his gaze in thought to the vacant country in front of the porch. After a few minutes of this he caught my eye, nodded toward my father, and winked at me. This covert signal informed me that some fun was now to be attempted. I rose from my own seat and casually stepped nearer the action as Tom turned toward my father.

"It's odd there wasn't anything in there about the alligator."

My father, who has always been entranced by oddities of nature, immediately lowered the paper and looked at Tom with suspicion.

"What alligator?"

"Fella told me a big alligator got killed."

"How big?"

Tom narrowed his eyes, struggling to recall.

"I can't remember exactly what that fella said but I guess it was pretty big. He called it a monster."

The paper now fell into my father's lap as he leaned forward, bowing his head in thought. Now he looked at me.

"Do you know anything about this, General?"

Tom had baited the line and the bait had been swallowed. It was now up to me to set the hook.

"I was told it devoured a child. A gang of citizens were able to kill it. I believe they cut it open in order to remove the corpse."

My father was now on his feet, one hand pulling on the long carpet of beard beneath his chin.

"I'd like to see that alligator," he said, half to himself, "They didn't chop it up or burn it?"

"I don't know," Tom replied. "I only know that it was killed at a place called Jensen's Fill."

The old man reached for his hat.

"Where's that?"

Tom was the picture of sincerity.

"I think it's north of town quite a ways . . . I don't know exactly. Are you goin' out there?"

"I want to have a look at that alligator," he said resolutely. "Do you know where this Jensen's Fill is, General?"

"I know of it," I said, "but I've never been there. Are you sure you want to go, Father? It's going to be a long ride in this heat."

"What would you have me do?" he said brushing past me, "sit around here all day and wait for one of you boys to hide my teeth?"

Without another word he walked down the stairs and into the blazing sun.

"Father?" I called.

The old man turned around.

"I wouldn't make mention of the alligator if I were you . . . people are touchy about it because of the child."

My father waved a hand as if he understood, turned, and made a beeline for the stables.

Tom and I stumbled into the Asylum so that our laughter could explode out of earshot. We stood at a window, hugging each other gleefully as we watched him ride off for Jensen's Fill, the outline of man and horse shimmering in waves of heat.

When Libbie found out what had happened she severely questioned the wisdom of sending an old man out on such a day in search of a nonexistent alligator.

Tom and I threw off her concerns, but as morning passed into afternoon and afternoon to evening we both began to wonder if we had not gone too far. We were sitting in the parlor, growing more nervous by the minute, when at last a footfall was heard on the step outside.

Tom leaped to the window and pushed aside the sash. "It's him," he said, starting to laugh, "and he looks pretty well done."

My brother resumed his seat and we all waited in silence as the front door opened and closed. In a moment my father appeared in the parlor doorway. His arms hung limply at his sides as he glared at us from a scorched and weary face.

"There's nothin' at Jensen's Fill exceptin' a putrefied mule."

Tom and I burst out laughing at the same time.

"There weren't no alligator," he announced grimly, a remark which sent Tom and me rolling to the carpet in hysterics.

As we laughed we could see Father. He was still standing in the doorway, seemingly too tired to move a muscle. The sight was so pitiful that we laughed even harder.

"I'm gonna fix you boys," he said solemnly, but the threat was wasted on us. We had crossed the threshold that separates a casual joke from the laughter of pain and were too immersed in our happy seizures to make a reply.

Thoroughly defeated, our father's heavy steps carried him out of sight and into his room. Long after he was gone Tom and I lay on the floor trying to catch our breath.

Our remaining months in Texas were infested with similar high spirits. Father exacted revenge on both his sons many times with varying degrees of success, and though there was a close call or two no one of us experienced serious injury as a result of the ongoing pranks. Libbie occasionally wearied of our games but never lost her good humor completely. Actually, I believe it would be fair to say that she was more often active as a participant than as an observer.

Professionally, it was a rather colorless period. Our mission, failing engagement with any enemy, quickly reduced us to functioning as a force of police. The army was being dismantled and I knew that my division of volunteers would eventually realize their dream of being mustered out.

I too would be mustered out, losing the rank of brevet major general of volunteers, which I then held. I assumed I would continue in the army but the unforseen is always a part of service life, and Libbie and I had many conversations about what might happen to us, trying in vain to prepare for a future we could not divine.

Having never been anything but a soldier made the world of business a mysterious place in which I was never quite comfortable. Though I flirted heavily in years to come with the society of profit and loss, like a lover who cannot give up I always dropped whatever I might be doing and returned to uniform at the army's call. The barest whisper of boots and saddles induced me to come on the run.

In military life alone have I been able to build a kingdom of my own. Only in this world have I been able to live as a knight of war and of love. I cannot imagine anything greater.

❧

The day's end has been one of misery for the horses. We experienced a tremendous hailstorm shortly after going into camp and the force of the stones has drawn blood on many of the horses' backs. Burkman and I were able to get Vic and Dandy under the fly of my tent, and though it took some effort to keep them there, fortunately neither was injured. They are calm now, for the hail has turned to snow. Snow on the first day of June. It is clear that I would never have gained greatness as a predictor of weather.

The dogs are inside tonight, curled here and there. One of them is cowering under the bed. He devoured Alf this afternoon and I greatly miss my midnight companion. I will forgive Bluecher in time but at the moment I cannot stand the sight of him. Of course it is not his fault. He has always received praise for his kills and cannot tell the difference between a deer and a mouse. I wish that he could.

JUNE 2-5,

1876

In September of 1867 Libbie, Eliza, I, and several others in our entourage boarded the train in Saint Louis for our trip to the western end of the line. In the space of a few months I had been reduced to the rank of captain in the regular army, lost the two general's stars I had won as a leader of volunteers, been promoted to lieutenant colonel in the regular army, had my brevet's stars restored through the influence of General Sheridan, and been given command of the nation's newest cavalry regiment, designated the seventh, whose mission was to protect the frontiers of America. I was actually to be second-in-command. But my superior would be headquartered in Saint Louis, and as agreed beforehand, I would lead operations in the field.

To build a thousand strangers into a smooth fighting regiment was a challenging task, and through the first phases of our train trip west, my head was abuzz with anticipation of how this would be done. These anticipations were minor, however, when compared with what was preeminent in everyone's mind, for we were entering a strange new domain known only through the descriptions of those few who had entered it before us.

No word picture could have prepared us for the spectacle spreading everywhere we looked as we neared our destination. The trees and hills of Missouri gradually disappeared before vanishing altogether as we burst upon the vastness of the great southern plains of Kansas. It was as though we had suddenly entered a trackless sea of grass and sky and clouds and as we penetrated deeper and deeper into the endless landscape it closed behind us, sealing off the rest of the world.

I was fascinated by the existence of such a place, by the mere wonder of its flatness, the height of its grasses, the length of its horizon. But my heart pumped with excitement when I thought of who inhabited this region and who, until recently, had ruled over it almost unopposed.

I had never seen Indians before, excepting those who had already endured years of subjugation. The Indians of the plains are of a completely different cast. They do not lounge on street corners or tend small farms. They are not of the hoe and rake. These people carry the lance and shield, prideful of their status as warriors and their freedom to roam as they please. They are as different from us as the plains they live on are different from our cities in the East and they rigorously practice the art of war.

As the wild, unbroken plains enveloped us these realities became more acute. This alien land was home to a race of warriors who were certain to defend their territory, and I resolved to learn as much about them as quickly as I could.

Were it a simple matter of fighting I felt confident that the new regiment would, when fully assembled, be equal in strength and tenacity to any foe. But it was not to be that simple a matter. While our government had engaged in what I considered unduly harsh measures in respect to the vanquished South, it had, virtually at the same moment, initiated a strict peace policy in regard to the wild warriors of the southern plains. This peace policy was undertaken just as the great southern railroad was nearing the heart of the aboriginal hunting grounds, as settlement continued to flow into western spaces for the purposes of farming, and as mineral wealth was being uncovered and exploited in the territory of Colorado.

I failed to grasp how a displacement or suppression of hostile native inhabitants could exist side by side with peaceful policies administered by high civilian officials who were then following the mandate of the President, the same President who was our Commander-in-Chief.

That confusion and waste would ensue because of so many varied interests and policies seemed likely, but I knew it would be a mistake to consume myself with forces that neither I nor anyone else could sway. A perceptible wave of growth and expansion was rushing across the land with a power that many still believe to be divinely inspired.

The Seventh Cavalry was charged with preparing the path of progress, duty bound to sweep all obstacles from the road of Manifest Destiny. The difficulty of our task only added to the excitement of what I perceived to be sacred service . . . to serve the will of the people.

As mile upon mile of lonely prairie passed behind us we became more and more still, and I do not believe anyone entertained much thought beyond this new world in which we found ourselves.

The terminus of the Union Pacific, a raucous settlement of rail gangs, was reached at last, the animals were unloaded safely, and we clambered into ambulances, which struck out into the prairie night. Spirits were high as we jolted over the final miles of our long journey and we became positively joyful when the lights of the post twinkling in the blackness ahead were sighted at last. Nothing is as comforting for a soldier and his family as reaching the warm glow of home, especially when they beckon for the first time. Libbie hugged me and asked question after question about our new home and life, which of course I could not answer.

We made a brief inspection of our quarters, had our baggage piled inside, did the best we could to settle our menagerie in their new surroundings, and fell into yet another of the thousand different beds we have shared.

The day's excitement had invigorated us, however, and, unable to sleep, we placed chairs next to our bedroom window and looked out at the dark shapes of the fort as we talked in whispers about the new beginning that was upon us.

Libbie does not enjoy campaign talk, particularly if the campaign is forthcoming. She told me from the time of our marriage that she didn't mind hearing about engagements after they had happened. It takes all her stores of resolve to wait out the result of my efforts in the field and Libbie has never felt she can waste her fortitude on speculation of what is to come. When I am gone she fights constantly to suppress thoughts of my death. Why should she be subjected to these thoughts while we are together? I have always thought her demand a fair one.

Preparation and the talk that comes with it cannot be avoided but I have striven to spare her as much as I am able. Libbie has never shied from reminding me, sometimes with an irritating persistence, that while my role may exceed hers in social importance, the pressures on both of us are in many ways equal.

Especially equal are the gymnastics of mind we must perform during prolonged separation. In many respects her part is the more difficult, for while I am immersed in the trials of the campaign she must busy herself through the interminable waiting hours. And even the most frenzied or satisfying activity cannot blunt the anxiety of being apart.

I attempted to broach the delicate subject of separation that night as we chattered back and forth in front of the open window. A great expedition, the size and depth of which Libbie knew little, was being seriously contemplated by the supreme army powers. The campaign would likely begin with spring and would probably last through summer. It was being designed as a show of massive force, sufficient to cow the Indians rather than combat them. The hope was that the mere sight of the army's might would awe the hostiles into a fast and lasting peace or at the least the beginning of a permanent confinement, thus allowing the wheels of commerce and settlement to roll over the prairie unimpeded.

Perhaps it was my wife's enthusiasm for the positive aspects of life or it may have been a conscious effort on her part to sidestep an unpleasant subject. Whatever the reason, I was unable to instigate a serious discussion of the realities of army life that I knew would soon engulf us.

On that night, at the mention of a campaign Libbie would associate it with a pleasant memory of our married past and in her usual happy way insisted on recounting any number of our considerable triumphs. For two years we had never been effectively separated for more than two weeks. This was achieved, despite the presence of the Great War, not so much as a result of fortuitous timing but rather because of our mutual, unshakable commitment to being together.

The most conscious resolution of our courtship and marriage had come in the form of a sacred vow that we would depart from the traditions of separation in most unions. Our commitment was not simply to be married but to be together for all time as neither of us believed that the dictates of work and protocol need drive couples apart. To us the point of marriage is lost when couples pass long periods without each other and from the first we declared that togetherness would be the cornerstone of our holy bond. It was a beautiful ideal and a marvelous defense against the world of insecurity rotating around us.

Threats of any kind to our marriage neither of us could abide and if I had succeeded in raising the issue that night, no amount of talk could have led us to accept separation. Looking back, I cannot see that avoiding the topic made any difference in the final outcome.

It was our fate to see our worst fears come true, and though we have suffered mightily we are still together after twelve years of struggle, wanting each other close as much as ever. I have learned to manage my anxiety and so has Libbie. We are veterans.

But that night at the window we were very young and afraid. What would become of us out here?

The more we talked, however, the more our excitement took over. Talk constantly drifted back to the new post and how cozy our new quarters would be when finally put together. We dreamed about the newly invented Seventh Cavalry and how grand the regiment would be. We have always been great admirers of music and that night we also talked about the possibilities of a regimental band. For Libbie, music is a link with heaven, particularly when times are hard; and I happily share that view; I have always believed music to be essential on the march and the battlefield and have used it to further these ends whenever possible.

It was the Michigan Brigade's band that first alerted me to the tremendous power of a heartfelt tune in battle. Among many other songs our band frequently played "Yankee Doodle Dandy" and whenever the band struck it up I noticed that it enlivened our men to the point of causing them to stop whatever mundane task might be at hand. Though I would never have picked it personally as a tune of glory I could not deny the power it had over the men. Many would gather around the band to sing along or tap their feet. Horseplay around camp increased whenever it was heard and I soon informed the bandmaster that I wanted to hear it on a regular basis. The more the band played it, the more it meant to the brigade and before long it became inconceivable that we would go into battle without it.

I led many charges with that eerily jaunty tune at my back and by the end of the war it had become a weapon against the enemy. Those who had not heard it feared it and those who had heard our ditty associated it through experience with defeat and death.

Libbie and I agreed that it would be best not to resurrect "Yankee Doodle" but instead find a new tune the Seventh Cavalry could make its own. For some time we idly searched through our repertoire of favorite songs but could not find one that was just right.

At last we fell into a long silence, which Libbie gently broke when she began to hum "Yankee Doodle" in the absent fashion of a memory. Then she lifted her eyes to mine and began to sing the words in the same somber way the band had played when marching into battle. Soon I was singing along.

It was a remarkable moment for I remember as we sang together in the still of night it occurred to me that we were able to recount much of our wartime experience in a single song, that the careless tune known by every American schoolboy held our memories like a magnet.

As we sang I also experienced a curious phenomenon that Libbie has produced in me many times. Watching her mouth form the words of the song, seeing the shine in her eyes, looking at the skin move up and down on her beautiful throat; these visions and uncounted others sometimes move me to distant places even though I am sitting next to her. At these times I am no longer the familiar husband or lover but the secret admirer I have always been. As such I watched, overcome with a desire that had to be expressed in a kiss.

I kissed her that night before we finished our duet and she responded in kind. We would certainly have kept on kissing had Libbie not suddenly drawn back, squinting into the darkness outside our window.

"What's that?" she whispered.

Peering down, I saw immediately that something was moving across the parade ground. They were animals, animals I had not seen before, six or seven of them. They were moving easily, their heads down, browsing here and there as if out for a midnight stroll. The size of them, so large and monstrous, startled me.

Several sentries suddenly appeared on the fringes of the parade ground. I suppose they did not want to wake the post because they started toward the animals but did not fire their carbines. The buffalo raised their heads almost as one and the next I knew they had run off with a speed that rendered them invisible in the blink of an eye.

While it was thrilling to see the beasts we had so often heard of, it was sobering, too, more evidence of the new and wild region that we were now inhabiting as uninvited guests.

The weight of a long journey and of so many new sights and sounds suddenly fell on both of us and before we knew it we were in bed and asleep.

For the next few days Libbie saw to the organizing of our latest home while I began the tedious but satisfying work of building the new regiment: overseeing the influx of men and material and making the multitude of decisions, large and small, that were required of me. This work had barely begun when I was called back to Washington for administrative reasons that, while important in themselves, separated me from my wife and my regiment at a critical juncture. Without enthusiasm I boarded a train for the long trip east, not knowing that this separation was only the first in a long series that would, with other as yet unforeseen circumstances, make the next eighteen months the most disappointing of my career.

My duties in the bureaucratic halls of the capital seemed to drag on forever and I did not return to Fort Riley until just before Christmas of 1867.

My arrival coincided with news of the Fetterman Massacre, an event that sent waves of horror through the nation and especially the army. On the northern plains a series of forts had been built to protect an emigrant road passing through the Sioux hunting grounds, the same hunting grounds upon which we are now marching these many years later.

The Sioux were opposed to the road and the forts from their inception and, being a large and intensely warlike tribe, had opened relentless hostilities which by their hit-and-run nature had effectively placed the troops of each garrison in a state of siege. After being pestered for most of the previous summer the troops were eager to strike back, and when a woodcutting party was attacked in full view of one of the forts the eagerness for retaliation, so long held in check, was at last released with disastrous result.

Captain Fetterman, who I understand was a competent but inexperienced officer with an impetuous nature, raced out of the fort with eighty men seeking to relieve the party of woodcutters. He assumed this mission with explicit instructions from his commander to drive off the attackers but not to follow them past a specific point, which would take the troops beyond view of the fort.

Sadly, Captain Fetterman failed to follow these instructions and was decoyed into a natural basin where the enemy waited for him in huge numbers. Surprised and overwhelmed, Fetterman's command quickly exhausted their ammunition and tried vainly to escape the trap, an attempt that proved impossible. They were wiped out to a man.

That the Indian is an able fighter has been a point of common knowledge since colonial times, but that he could destroy eighty-one well-trained, well-armed, and well-mounted cavalry of the United States Army in this modern day and age was unthinkable, despite mistakes made on the part of Captain Fetterman.

The Fetterman massacre dominated talk and thought for months afterward, a topic to which I was no more immune than anyone else though I gave it much more thought than talk. Because I myself was inexperienced in fighting the painted warriors of the plains I pondered the Fetterman affair in depth and came to the conclusion that there were two lessons of paramount worth to absorb.

The fact that eighty-one men were decoyed to their deaths demonstrated that the Indian was capable of a high degree of sophistication in warfare. And it was clear that Fetterman's force had, in the effort to flee, turned its back on the enemy, an action that never fails to inspire the Indian warrior.

Regarding the latter, I was especially moved by the curious fate of a bugler in the Fetterman debacle. The relief party that reached the battlefield first discovered that one body, and only one, had been covered respectfully with a buffalo robe. It was that of the bugler, and on closer inspection it was discovered that the horn he yet clutched in his dead hand was disfigured by numerous dents and bends. Lacking anything else, he had used his instrument as a weapon and must have fought with great valor to have been acknowledged in such a way by his enemy.

It is clear to me that the Indian reserves his greatest respect for power and courage, none at all for faint hearts. Fearlessness is the aspect of character he admires most and is the only way to fight him.

Repercussions from the massacre were felt up and down the chain of command and altered plans for the coming expeditionary campaign against the southern tribes. Instead of taking the field in late spring, when the Indian and his ponies are at peak condition, it was decided that we would be in the field no later than the end of March with a force a third larger than had been originally planned.

During my sojourn in Washington, higher authorities decided to move up the mammoth campaign, an action that made the work now confronting me even more difficult, and on my return to Fort Riley I threw myself into the task of building a fighting regiment from the many disparate parts I had inherited.

The close of the Great War and demobilization had effectively dismantled the army, and though much effort was given to maintaining a semblance of continuity, it would not be too much to say that confusion reigned supreme. Many thousands of officers were left to compete for a few hundred commissions and competition was carried on without the benefit of order. Politicians and high commanders were lobbied around the clock, the applicants utilizing a limitless array of pleadings and subterfuges to gain commissions. A large number of appointments were made on the basis of political consideration or favors owed or the luck of the draw. The officers' corps this process produced constituted the most diverse hodge-podge of temperament and quality of character imaginable.

It was a game that everyone had to play, and though my commission was more secure than most, I was forced to engage in the same capricious lobbying in order to procure the individuals I needed with which to form the nucleus of a regiment.

Had I not entered the fray I would have been left to play a hand dealt from the inscrutable brokers of power in Washington. I was moderately successful, being able to push through commissions for several solid officers who had served under me previously. Included among them was an old Monroe friend and Civil War comrade George Yates and, most important, brother Tom.

The remainder of my officers came in surprise packages. Some had navigated their way through the enlisted ranks, some were academy graduates, and some had distinguished themselves as ex-patriate soldiers of fortune in foreign wars. The mildest adjective I can apply to this blend would be "exotic." Some, like Tom and George, were loyal from the beginning and are serving with me now. Others, for reasons ranging from petty jealously to pure malice, created difficulties from the start. Ironically, some of these men are also with me now, nine years later.

Owing to these vast differences in background, the officers' ranks squabbled constantly that winter. Making matters even more infirm was the fact that the same officers suffered a uniform lack of experience in the business of pursuing and fighting Indians. It fell to me to assemble a pirate crew that had had no time at sea, a job not unlike having to fashion a fine and seamless quilt from remnants found on the sewing-room floor.

Enlisted ranks were beset with many of the same difficulties and worse.

The farmers and lawyers and doctors and merchants who had served so bravely in the Great War had all been mustered out, leaving in their wake a profound vacuum that was to be filled by those who desired a dangerous career of extreme physical hardship, served at lonely outposts, featuring substandard pay and substandard rations. Good men did come forward, some of whom are still with the regiment, but a far more significant number of those who filled the void were luckless immigrants, fugitives from the law, illiterate drifters who had known only failure in life, and chronic deserters.

The defects and drawbacks of these troops were visible to all, including Libbie, who was deeply affected. Through concern for me she frequently despaired at the prospect of a disciplined, proud, and motivated strike force being manufactured out of such uncertain material. I assured her with what I had always known to be the truth: that a fighting regiment could not be such until it had run the gauntlet of battle. Combat alone had the power to weld disparate units into a polished whole. This was not a very effective argument, for it brought images of combat to Libbie's mind and no amount of reassurance would suffice once she began to contemplate my mortality.

What I did not tell Libbie was that squabbling officers and derelict troopers were factors that could make little difference in my outlook. In the end, there was only the mission with which I had been charged: to meet the warriors of the plains and convince them by force, if necessary, to submit to our authority. That recruits were green, that my officers had no experience fighting Indians, and that I myself had never been on the plains before were matters of fact that had to be ignored when faced with the paramount duty of carrying out America's wishes, emanating from the government itself, a body of men legally elected by the people of the United States. So long as I have been in uniform I have dedicated myself to serving the people's will whether I agreed with it or not. It was this conviction which inspired my efforts as I absorbed the myriad, never-ending detail required to mount a campaign of the size we undertook that summer.

Neither I nor anyone else foresaw the thousand plagues that would be visited upon the army in the months to come. Looking back, I am not certain that foreknowledge would have made a significant difference in my own case. I was still very young, not yet twenty-eight, and it seemed eons since I had led men in battle. I had been forced to sit on my laurels for too long while the usual demons of jealousy and spite harassed me from all sides. I would have gone into the field that spring and summer with a command of walking dead if need be. As it turned out that is precisely the command that our campaign concluded with, the thousand plagues having at last overwhelmed the army and its most stalwart supporters, including myself.

But even had I known what was to transpire I would have been powerless to change it. Fate was—as always—my driver and I did my best to serve what was to be a thoroughly disheartening destiny.

Desertion was a monster I could not vanquish, a constant and insufferable demon that tore the heart from my regiment. No punishment, no matter its severity or humiliating effect, could staunch the flow of those taking the Grand Bounce. Before we had marched a step, fully ten percent of the recruits had run off, and even in the wilderness men continued to melt away, at one juncture in front of my eyes. By the time our initial campaign was over, my frustration had given way to fury.

The brother of desertion is whiskey. I punished its lovers and banished its presence wherever and whenever I found it, but I could not dissuade men from embracing its poisonous charms. Despite knowing my aversion to the use of strong drink, especially in the field, a sadly significant number of officers continued to serve their alcoholic masters each and every day. The army's strength and vitality has always been compromised by whiskey and I suppose it always will be.

Major Reno is one of those who is still with me who has never been able to give up the mistress who lives in his cask. Lamentably, it is his right to keep her and in vain I continue to set the example of abstinence, though it has never been followed by Reno or scores of other officers who are lifetime members in the fraternity of drink.

In a wider sense, food is the deepest cause of a regiment's distress, particularly among the enlisted ranks, and while a soldier can rarely expect a fancy meal, I often sympathize with the men who are subjected over and over to deprivation at mealtime. The corrupt and neglectful excesses of the commissary department are today as they were then—abominable. I was forced to commit an inordinately high and time-consuming amount of energy in attempting to intercept and inspect the shipments of rations that flowed into Fort Riley.

Our shipments of meat, which consisted exclusively of bacon and salt pork, the former being commonly referred to with the colorful and mysterious sobriquet "Cincinnati chicken," were often packed with rocks.

Bread came to us from eastern warehouses as surpluses from the Great War that had waited years to be consumed and were now glazed with mold. In addition, these breads had hardened to a consistency that rendered them inedible except by frying after they had been soaked in water.

Bean-sized pebbles were constantly being separated from actual coffee beans and on one occasion an entire shipment of coffee was discovered to be composed of stones.

Hardly a day passed when I was not composing a letter of complaint to functionaries and luminaries alike. Though I was promised many times that "deficiencies would be promptly corrected," no such thing in my experience has ever happened with the tiniest modicum of regularity. I believe I have waged more war in my career against various departments of supply than I have against the armed foe.

This worthless warfare against those who supposedly support us in the field continues unabated. Through years of battle I have learned the ways of my enemy well and have become wiser to the workings of avarice. Some time ago I reached the conclusion that greed in all its manifestations, numerous as the stars, cannot be defeated, for it is a permanent condition of human life. It can be opposed. Occasionally, it can be checked. But it cannot be defeated.

The difficulties I faced in forming the Seventh Cavalry were routine challenges of military life, but when added to the newness of the unit, the alien country and the alien enemy it contained, the schizophrenic nature of government policy and the calamitous, unpredictable weather, the effect was overwhelming. In hindsight, it is a simple matter to see that the great Hancock Expedition was doomed long before it began. I would have taken the field regardless, for I was as eager as everyone else to put training into action, and it is always a commander's duty to carry out his orders with what he possesses rather than what he wishes he had.

It was raining the morning we departed Fort Riley, but I don't believe any condition short of a cyclone could have wetted the high spirits of our column, for it was a magnificent assembly, the most magnificent I had seen since the Great War.

The band was excellent and the tune we had selected as our theme, the stirring "Garry Owen," cut the drizzle like sunshine as we marched out onto the plains, fourteen hundred strong.

I rode at the head of six companies of cavalry, followed by a battery of artillery and seven companies of infantry. A huge train of supply wagons gradually fell in behind us, stretching out for more than a mile.

No sight can compare with the grandeur of an army starting into the field. Every uniform is clean, every button polished. Every horse glistens. Flags wave unsoiled. Orders are sharp, responses quick. Every heart dreams of brave deeds yet to be done, victories yet to be won.

What the expedition lacked in experience was forgotten. Each member's mind was linked in the knowledge that we constituted the full power of the United States, so great a power that no army of aboriginal fighters, despite their reputation, would have the suicidal courage necessary to oppose us—that no one did was the great irony of that first, ambitious, and naïve campaign.

Marching west we reached Fort Harker without incident and, as the weather was clearing, pushed on for our primary destination, a small outpost built on the Pawnee Fork of the Arkansas named Fort Larned.

It was previously believed that most of the southern Cheyenne nation was wintering on the Pawnee Fork, and already runners had been sent there with the news that we wished to meet their leaders on reaching Fort Larned. Once all were assembled, General Hancock planned to inform them of our government's expectations for the future.

Aside from the originality of the country, there were few diversions on the march and I filled the cavalry's time with regular drill, of which they were sorely in need. Many of the recruits were unfamiliar with horses, much less mounted manoeuvers, and I often shook my head at their clumsiness.

But the excitement of being on the march and the prospect of meeting an enemy spurred even the greenest troop to apply himself, and soon the Seventh was looking like a regiment—it thrills me still to remember our horsemen far out on the column's flank, drilling at a gallop in wind and sun on the vast prairie stage.

If one could overlook the oddities of the troops themselves, there was one bizarre addition to the expedition. We had with us a Cheyenne boy, a child of many strange fates. He had been born on the plains and raised for several years as a wild Indian. At about age six he had survived the despicable affair known as the Sand Creek Massacre, which had occurred in late 1864 and had damaged relations with the Cheyenne immeasurably.

A large village of Cheyenne had been attacked by an irregular force of Colorado militia under the command of a self-appointed former preacher who felt it was his duty to enact God's vengeance on the hostile Indian. His men had murdered large numbers of women and children and had tarried at the scene for most of a day, drinking heavily, mutilating the bodies of the dead, and collecting trophies which in addition to scalps included the private parts of slain women.

The boy in question had been spirited from the field by a morally upright officer and was discovered years later employed against his will in an Eastern circus.

His discovery in the circus coincided with the planning of the current expedition and a brainstorm had occurred in the Department of the Interior, the result of which had delivered him into the hands of an army on the move.

Part of the impetus for the expedition was provided by the ever-increasing raids of the southern plains tribes. They were attacking rail crews and occasionally carrying off women and children.

The abductions were especially painful to relatives and accounted for the Cheyenne boy's presence with us. It was thought that his repatriation would be a strong signal of the expedition's peaceful intentions. It was also hoped that the gesture of returning the Indian boy would pressure the savages to give up at least some of their white captives.

Personally, I felt it a hollow effort and my heart went out to the boy who had been jerked from one world to another and now back again. He did not know his age; I guessed it to be eight or nine. He spoke English more fluently than many of our soldiers and swore like a mule driver, a trait he had apparently acquired while traveling with the circus. Though I never knew why, everyone called him Milton. He disapproved of the moniker but, unable to produce one of his own, the name stuck.

He dashed about camp in a boy's suit, the front pocket of which was usually home to a rather large jackknife, an instrument he wielded with amazing dexterity. He railed against his predicament, ceaselessly voicing his opposition to "going with the damn Indians," but of course Milton's protest went unheeded. The government had thought him useful and so he would be.

Despite his clothing and speech Milton was clearly a member of the Indian race, though this fact was not admitted by him. He became more sullen and withdrawn as we neared Fort Larned, supplanting his bravado with a quiet fear that could only be expected of a little boy.

Up until the final minutes of his time in our custody I struggled with the notion of speaking to General Hancock on Milton's behalf. But I could not bring myself to do so. I had no better idea of what to do with the half and half boy than anyone else. He was to be returned to his people. That was all.

Though it had existed for some years, Fort Larned was nothing more than a small collection of rough buildings in the wilderness. The camp made by the expedition, which was within hailing distance, dwarfed it completely.

The first day was taken up with establishing a base and readying ourselves for the delegation of Indian leaders whose arrival was expected the following day.

The next morning it snowed so hard as to make everyone feel that we had somehow been transported back to January and fixed close to one of the earth's poles. It snowed through the whole of the day, a huge, wet snow driven by winds in which a person could not walk upright. At midafternoon word was received that the Cheyenne delegation would be delayed, a development that came as an anticlimax.

Their failure to appear provided my first vital lesson concerning life on the plains. Nothing can be predicted, for this is a region that exercises its powerful will without warning and when that happens the visitor's most assured plans are crushed so completely as to make them laughable. The great plains, as the Indians know, calls its own tune; to survive there the absolute power of the place must be acknowledged. One must work with what the country yields and not the other way around.

The temperature dropped fifty degrees, and as darkness descended and the snowfall slackened, the camp plunged into a killing freeze. To create more warmth, two-man tents were filled with as many men as were able to fit. A detail of a hundred men walked our lines of horses all night in order to keep them moving and alive.

I brought my own horses up and to give them some shelter from the drifting snow placed them under the fly of my tent. There they availed themselves of what little heat was coming from inside. The dogs lay tightly curled in a mass on my bed. When not checking on the horses I sat next to the stove, watching my breath turn to ice in front of my face.

No one slept. The entire camp shivered through the night in disbelief that this could be happening in April.

By morning there was equal disbelief at the clearness of the skies, the brightness of the sun, and the rapidity with which eight inches of snow disappeared into the ground.

The Indians appeared on a rise late that afternoon. We were dismayed to count only fourteen silhouettes: twelve warriors and two chiefs. We had expected a hundred warriors and at least twenty chiefs but as the dark figures on horseback rode out of the sun we made ready to receive them in honorable fashion.

It had been decided beforehand that to make the strongest impact, General Hancock would not speak until after the meeting had begun. But the small size of the arriving delegation made the special attention to appearances seem almost a charade. After a series of hasty discussions, during which no one came up with a better idea, it was agreed that we would go forward as originally planned.

With Captain Yates on one side and the expedition interpreter on the other I rode forward to meet our wild visitors. As the ground closed between us I was able to make out details of their features, but even before I could see them clearly the depths of our differences were apparent.

A quality surrounded them, something about the way they carried themselves, that made the realization stand out in my mind for the first time that I was on the threshold of holding conversation with men who still belonged largely to the Stone Age.

Their ponies lunged and pranced like the half-wild creatures they were but the men atop them controlled each animal with amazing ease. This was done through the power of a single hand as the other was invariably occupied in grasping a lance or rifle or war ax or some other weapon.

One of the chiefs carried a small bow, the other a stout lance of at least ten feet. On their backs rode small, round shields. They came forward with what I can only describe as a unique quality of presence and it was obvious to me before they had spoken a word that these men, the two chiefs in particular, were plains royalty. They were not acquainted with any form of deference, save what they accorded their peers. To us they showed none.

We halted a few yards apart, and while their bodyguards looked on, jockeying their uneasy ponies back and forth, I absorbed the vision of the two chiefs sitting before me.

The older of the two, whose name was Bad Bull, was powerfully built and possessed a face seemingly hewn from stone. The other, who was addressed as Left Hand, was much different in appearance, almost feminine by comparison. His face was as polished and smooth as rubbed wood. His lips were thin, his eyes were small, and whereas Bad Bull's hair was woven into twin braids the ends of which lay far down on his chest, Left Hand's long, raven tresses, anointed with oil, flew down the sides of his face, traveling all the way to his waist.

The sound of the Indians was something else to be noted for the snorting and stomping of the skittish ponies was merely background to the jingle and jangle of the horsemen themselves. Weapons clanged against weapons as did the many items of jewelry worn by each warrior. Every man seemed to have a bracelet wrapped around his wrist. Some wore medals around their necks. Some had clusters of tin cones sewn on the outside legs of their breeches or knots of tiny bells sewn high on the flaps of their moccasins. Even the feathers that had been inserted in varying amounts on every long-haired head produced a whirring as gusts of air from the prairie breeze passed through them.

The noise emanating from this body of men was as light and cheerful as the sound of wind chimes on a summer afternoon.

The pleasant lullaby stood in stark contrast to the men themselves, who were obviously seasoned fighters. Even Left Hand, the most delicate of them, had the aura of a man who had never known defeat. Lying close along the top of his head was what seemed to be most of a large hawk whose feathered skull and yellow beak rested in the middle of Left Hand's forehead, producing the impression that man and bird were one.

Our visitors from the well of time gave vague answers to the question of why so few of their number had come to the Fort Larned conference. I suspected at once that the memory of Sand Creek and the size of our present force made them frightened and distrustful, an assumption that was reinforced throughout subsequent events.

They asked to be fed and were escorted to a large tent which had been prepared for this purpose. The delegation said nothing as we rode through camp, but it was clear from their wide-eyed expressions that the enormity of our force impressed them greatly. Their curiosity about the food we provided was exceeded only by their appetites. They ate with the rapidity and gusto of the starved.

While they devoured their dinners I waited with General Hancock and others of the staff in the headquarters tent. We waited long into nightfall while our visitors satisfied their stomachs and performed their drawn-out preparations for the council.

At last they came, appearing out of the darkness in single file. I and my fellow officers were in full dress for the meeting; although the warriors said nothing, their gazes were frequently absorbed with our raiment, particularly the plumed and helmeted heads of the artillery officers.

This gazing at one another took place as we all engaged in the lengthy ritual of smoking the long-stemmed pipe that Bad Bull produced. This was passed from one member of the gathering to another in several revolutions, during which not a word was spoken.

When these preliminaries were at last ended, General Hancock announced his intention to speak. At this he rose and began in what I thought were clear and businesslike terms to present our government's position. He noted his disappointment at the scarcity of chiefs, taking care to express his satisfaction with those who were sitting before him. He announced the existence of Milton and of the government's desire to return him to his people. At the same time he told the assembled group that he had heard they were holding white people captive and expected they too would be returned.

He told the chiefs that he not only intended to visit their camps but that the soldiers of the government would remain among them to keep the peace. Mincing no words, he said that he had heard the Cheyenne were thinking of getting up a war against the white man. If that were true and the Indian people wanted to fight he said he was ready and willing to oblige them. He said quite plainly that our soldiers expected to be killed and those that were would quickly be replaced.

Indicating the surrounding officers, he announced that our war chiefs had fought in battles much larger and more numerous than their Indian counterparts. Singling out me as an example he said that Indians that did not lie about their innocence would be treated as brothers, but that those who deceived us would be treated as enemies and their punishment would be severe. General Hancock again pointed at me and indicated that I, like my brother officers, would be ready to fight if peace could not be attained.

General Hancock then talked specifically of the railroad and telegraph and stage lines and how important it was that the molestation of these entities be stopped immediately. If they did not stop there would be war and the Indian would be sure to lose.

He told them to stick to their treaties and all would be fine. He then assured those present that if white men molested Indians they would be punished, a remark that caused a considerable stir in our visitors, apparently because punishment of those who make war on an enemy, regardless of reason, is practically unknown in their society.

General Hancock concluded with the well-intentioned but unfortunate statement that we were better at redressing wrongs committed against them than they were themselves, a comment that was taken as a deep insult, a reaction that caused General Hancock to cut short his speech.

The pipe was lit once more and passed around the fire. I had been watching the Indians as General Hancock spoke, for it was impossible to keep my eyes from them. The fire in front and the night behind made their appearance all the more amazing. The men sitting wrapped in blankets, their heads covered with feathers, had painted their arms and faces after dinner and as they watched us through narrow, unblinking eyes there were moments when I thought I must be dreaming.

Bad Bull got to his feet to make a reply. He stood staring down at us as he gathered a rich, red blanket about his shoulders. His speech was given entirely without emotion, which in retrospect, I believe, made his words even stronger.

He said that his people were presently at peace and had no wish but to be left alone. He said that young white men should not shoot at Indians for sport because it only led to bad blood between our races. He said the railroad was bad for the country because it frightened the animals but promised he would leave it alone in the name of peace. He mentioned the presents of food and weapons and clothing which the government had long ago promised. The Indians, he said, had given up hope of ever seeing these presents.

He expressed the opinion that the government said one thing, then did another and wondered respectfully if the government was not feeble-minded—a statement so true that we who were representatives of the government could not contain our laughter.

Bad Bull concluded by saying that he was willing to be friends with the white men but that if we came to his village tomorrow he would have nothing more to discuss than he did now. In other words, he considered our proposed visit a waste of time.

It was I thought a brilliant display of diplomacy and Bad Bull quickly parried any reply or objection to what he had said by asking to see the Cheyenne boy.

Milton was ushered in and placed before Bad Bull and Left Hand and it was obvious that they found him an object of intense curiosity. Left Hand reached out to touch Milton's shoulder and as the boy jumped back, out flashed his jackknife. This produced instant and unbridled laughter among the Indians, laughter of which I had not thought them capable.

I was close to the boy and explained to him that they were only curious and meant him no harm. At my prodding he reluctantly stepped forward again, allowing a closer examination, first of his shoulders, then his head, and finally his mouth.

Bad Bull consulted with his companions briefly and told us that no one recognized the boy but that they would make an attempt to locate his relatives once they had returned to their village.

The Indians rose as one and terminated the council by leaving, taking Milton with them.

I saw them once more as they departed at first light. Milton was riding behind one of the warriors. I called his name but he did not hear, or chose not to—but he seemed at ease as the little party rode slowly into the enormous maw of the prairie. He did not look back and his jackknife hung open in his hand, as if ready for a great adventure.

The delegation had been reminded before departing that we would be marching this day to the vicinity of their village, an announcement to which they made no clear reply. Eager to follow them, our military city on the plains broke camp quickly and forty-five minutes later the column was following their trail.

We hoped to travel more than twenty miles that first day, but the air was numbingly cold and together with the strong wind that was blowing over the prairie left the column no choice but to go into camp early. The wind was still raging on the next day and, along with the massive nature of the expedition, precluded our starting the morning's trek until eleven A.M.

I could not help but compare the slowness of our movements to the leanness and mobility of the Indians I had seen leaving the council. It did not take much thought to reach the conclusion that our sluggish column could never expect to catch or corner such fleet and well-conditioned nomads. It seemed ludicrous but I held my tongue.

As it turned out, my opinion was of little value, for we did not locate the Cheyenne—they located us. Experience has taught me in the years since that except under the most favorable circumstances, soldiers of the United States Army have no chance of surprising or catching wild Indians. Unless one is very fast and very crafty one is left to chase mirages.

We contacted the Cheyenne that day only because they wished it. The time and place and terms of the contact were decided solely by them. We had barely begun the march when mounted silhouettes, looking as though they were rising out of the earth, began to appear. At first sight they resembled isolated clusters but in no time the gaps in their ranks filled and in short order a solid wall of several hundred warriors occupied the horizon, effectively blocking our line of march.

Nonetheless, we moved resolutely forward and soon I could see our opposition in detail. It was the first and to this day most spectacular display of savage cavalry I have ever witnessed. Hundreds upon hundreds of fighting men, sitting bareback on their painted, half-wild ponies. Every warrior was bristling with arms both ancient and new: bright-colored shields and streaming lances, bows and arrows and battle axes, six-shot pistols and repeating rifles, most of these obtained as peace offerings from our own government. Never have I seen a force better outfitted for fighting.

They came up as one and I could only marvel at the discipline and control, which I had somehow not expected. But despite the monolithic order their cavalry demonstrated so convincingly, a powerful spring breeze produced a contrastingly festive effect as they approached.

The manes and tails of their ponies waved in the gale like flags as did the feathers and numerous other accoutrements of the Indians themselves. Among them were dozens of chiefs wearing full bonnets of eagle feathers, the trains of which trailed over their ponies' haunches and flew in the wind with lives of their own as their owners galloped back and forth, instructing their fighting men.

We were in the process of hurrying our wagons up when the Indians halted, an action that created a flurry of new business on our part. The infantry was quickly brought to the front and deployed, our artillery was wheeled into line and aimed at the enemy, the cavalry swung into position on the right of the cannon and I gave the order to draw sabers.

Then there was silence . . . save for the snorting of the impatient enemy ponies, a sound that to my ears seemed as incessant as waves lapping the shore.

At the far end of the Indian line, where most of their chiefs had congregated, a white flag suddenly appeared and started toward us. Two interpreters were dispatched to meet them and after a few minutes' talk, a conference between both sides' leaders had been arranged.

In ten minutes' time General Hancock, I, and several other officers rode out to meet a corresponding delegation from the Indian ranks.

As we drew up they did the same, and one man moved out of their group to meet us, an extraordinary presence whose name we soon learned was Roman Nose. He was at least six feet tall and extremely muscular. An officer's jacket, complete with epaulets, covered his torso. His face was framed in a wild configuration of feathers, part of an enormous headdress the end of which lay on the ground bouncing in the breeze. His face was long, his nose prominent, his full lips pressed together as if glued, his eyes black and bottomless. His escort, who looked on only a few steps behind, clutched their weapons as if they would use them at any moment. My own hand was tight on the pistol grip at my side.

With an expression that remained totally inscrutable, Roman Nose immediately enquired as to what business we had with the Cheyenne and when told, replied that while he did not mind having white people in his country he did not want us coming near his village because the women and children were scared and would run away at our approach.

General Hancock reiterated the basic points of our mission and assured Roman Nose of our peaceful intentions. Then he said quite coldly, "But if you desire war, we shall give you that."

As this was being translated a small smile spread on Roman Nose's mouth. It spread until it had exposed two lines of sturdy, incredibly white teeth.

"If I desired war," he replied, "I wouldn't come so close to your guns."

All during our conference segments of the Indian force had begun to disperse, creating the impression that they were sinking back into the earth bit by bit until at last the entire enemy contingent seemed to have vanished.

I suppose I must have realized then that everything would be against us. Not only the Indians, who had so clearly demonstrated that it was they who were in control, but the empty land we stood on, the chill air we were breathing, the harsh wind buffeting our faces so relentlessly. All these things and every other element of the environment seemed to be having their way with us.

Citing the windy conditions, General Hancock suggested the discussion be continued on reaching the village. To this there was no reply. Roman Nose's pony, as though commanded by sleight of hand, suddenly backed several steps, rose into the air, whirled on his back feet, and streaked away, the other chiefs following behind.

The speed of them was marvelous, made more so by the ease with which it had been achieved. They flew to the horizon, hung for a moment as if suspended, and were gone, leaving the field entirely empty save for the presence of Bad Bull, who now seemed totally alone in the world. He rode with us for several miles, constantly reciting his concerns about our coming to the village.

I shake my head in wonder now. It was all a ruse. Bad Bull's heartfelt pleas were nothing more than a preconceived delaying tactic, one facet of the overall Indian strategy, a strategy that had been applied to us from the first with great effectiveness.

When the Indian fears for his life or those of his loved ones he will adopt any protective measure necessary, duplicity being the one most commonly used.

The last leg of the march was brisk, for anticipation over something heretofore unseen and mysterious was high. Our excitement came to fruition in late afternoon, when the conical tops of the Indian lodges came into sight. The village was a large one, rising with a certain majesty from the prairie floor on which it had been erected. It was an intriguing sight, like that of a forbidden city appearing out of the fog of eternity.

⤮

Perhaps I have in my scratchings summoned past ghosts, particularly as pertains to the wind, for I have just returned from a nocturnal adventure involving my tent. While writing this the breeze suddenly rose, level after level of succeeding insensitivity, with the result that my tent was ripped from its moorings.

At the same moment I was blown off my seat and when I regained my senses, I found myself tossing about in several yards of liberated canvas. Fortunately, John Burkman came quickly to my aid and extricated me from the tangle of my former quarters. Together, we were able to salvage the errant canvas and luckily were also able to retrieve those personal belongings that had been blown into the wilderness.

All of this was done in total darkness on a moonless, starless night. The main camp has suffered much more turmoil than I have been subjected to.

It is still unseasonably cold, the country is so hard that it must be conquered mile by mile, and the phenomenon that struck us tonight—perhaps it was a cyclone—has thoroughly disrupted the camp. Thankfully, I am told the wrath of Mother Nature did not bring fire or serious injury with it. I have managed to find the inkwell intact and have now reseated myself, have relit the candle, and am resuming my narrative in hope that it will not be interrupted again.

The wind is still up, however, and, as the walls of my tent shudder with intermittent gusts, it is easy for me to return to memories of those first breezy days of the Hancock Expedition.

My experience is so much greater now, but in some ways the feeling of adventure and excitement in a strange land is the same as it has always been. It was certainly like this nine years ago on the Pawnee Fork of the Arkansas.

We went into camp at a respectful distance from the huge village of roughly three hundred buffalo-hide houses. Bad Bull was sent ahead with his few associates to make arrangements for another council.

We waited in the shadow of the Cheyenne city for something to happen, but all was quiet until twilight, when Bad Bull returned with the news that many women and children had fled.

General Hancock was disappointed and chagrined. In a near rage he ordered Bad Bull to retrieve those who had fled and report back as soon as they had returned to their homes.

He was still angry at a staff meeting shortly before tattoo and, looking pointedly at me, ordered all of us to retire at once for we might need our full strength to face whatever was to develop at dawn.

Faithfully I followed this order, only to find myself being awakened at one-thirty in the morning with instructions to report immediately to General Hancock. Scouts had informed him that the Indians were now fleeing en masse. I was ordered to mount the Seventh and encircle the village to prevent any further flight.

In a matter of minutes hundreds of troops ringed the village. No soldier was closer than twenty or thirty yards from the nearest lodge as we did not want to further agitate the remaining occupants.

But as I sat waiting in the darkness at the north end of the Indian town I felt a palpably eerie stillness that, despite the flickers of light from inside some of the tipis, convinced me that we had surrounded a city of ghosts. I soon received a message ordering me to enter the village and ascertain what was or was not there. I ventured inside with an escort of half a dozen mounted men and for fifteen minutes we rode up and down the deserted avenues of the tidy, well-ordered settlement.

The only sounds were those we ourselves made, the steady fall of our horses' hooves and the occasional banging of a sword or canteen. The Indian town seemed suspended in time and I was seized with images of the people themselves, picturing the life of the place from a peculiar position of invisibility. It was a rare and unsettling experience to be in such a place, an experience I have had neither before or since and one I do not wish to repeat.

No human emerged from the Indian houses and when the initial swing through the village was complete I gave orders for the troops surrounding it to commence a close inspection of all three hundred lodges.

I dismounted at one of the tipis from which light was glowing, stooped down, pushed aside the buffalo skin flap serving as a door, and looked inside. I was amazed to see how swiftly and silently the home had been abandoned. Couches and beds were intact and all manner of personal items lay about the floor or hung from the rafters. A bow and quiver with a full complement of arrows lay among these miscellaneous items, and a cooking pot, still bubbling with some Indian delicacy, was suspended over the yet burning embers of a central fire.

The other lodges were in the same general condition; after searching for more than an hour, we discovered only two exceedingly pitiful souls still inhabiting the town.

One was an elderly man found reclining alone in a destitute

lodge. He was suffering from some malady that had so weakened him that the old fellow had to be carried when moved.

The other person discovered was a girl whose age I estimated to be eight years. The poor little thing had been raped nearly to death. Whether she was white or Indian could not be determined and her mind was so shattered that she was unable to speak but a few words. We did the best we could for her and the old man but I was told that both died.

General Hancock was so enraged on discovering that the thousands of residents had slipped away that his first thought was to burn the village, but I and several other officers advised against this. It seemed obvious that the village had been deserted not out of defiance but out of fear. After much discussion, General Hancock, though not fully convinced, decided to await further developments before putting the village to the torch.

In the meantime I was directed to take eight troops of cavalry and at first light pursue the Indians, an order that meant the remainder of the night was a sleepless one as my command prepared for a lightning march.

While the troops made ready I held a series of councils with my scouts, Indian and white. Considering that we would be unencumbered by wagons and artillery and considering the size of our quarry, as many as three thousand panicked savages, I felt confident we could catch them, even in view of our late start.

But my excitement was dulled by skeptical responses from the scouts, who to a man doubted that we would run them down. I listened to these opinions but was unshakable in my belief. Surely eight troops of cavalry, moving without impediment, would overtake so many refugees.

We left as soon as we could see, moving onto the prairie at a quick trot. Almost immediately a large trail was discovered, and as I was encouraged in my belief that our Delawares and the white frontiersmen were wrong, we maintained our brisk pace.

But after thirty minutes of hard riding I was dismayed to find that the main trail had suddenly split into two, taking different directions.

This proved to be the first of many halts that morning and at every stop my frustration grew. How many times the Cheyenne trail split I cannot remember, but I know that the whole column waited while each new path was investigated, then discussed at length, before one was followed. The deviations became greater and greater as we marched. At last they all but turned to dust and in the end we could not find a single footprint of the three thousand. That they would rendezvous at some future place was certain but we could not possibly know where that might be.

There was no choice but to break off the search and head straight for the Smoky Hill Road, which now lay only a few miles to the north. The road was the main thoroughfare of the region, populated by an occasional isolated farm and a string of stage stations.

It was on this road, at an outpost called Fossil Creek, that we found the Indians had preceded us. The station had been burned, all of its livestock stolen, and the three men employed there brutally killed. In fact, they no longer resembled men.

Their bodies were remnants of bitter war. Blackened from burning, they lay scattered and headless in the depot's yard. Several limbs had been hacked from their torsos and these too had been strewn about. Each stomach had been opened, allowing masses of intestines to bloom. Their heads, arrows still jutting from the eye holes, had been flung far onto the prairie.

These depredations had been committed with a ferocity surpassing the normal heat of battle. The work had been done with a kind of ritual glee. Soldiers were detailed to gather up the body parts and while this task was being completed I watched and imagined that the station had been attacked and its keepers murdered by a mob of psychotic children.

This scene had a chilling effect on me and my men. We later discovered that for miles in either directions the results were the same. The Indians had rolled through like a fiery tide destroying all in their path.

I immediately dispatched two reliable riders to inform the expedition of what we had found. The remainder of the afternoon was spent getting bodies under ground and scouting for signs of the Indians.

It was not until the early hours of the following morning that anything of note transpired. It was then that I found myself staring in disbelief at General Hancock's reply to my message of the day before. He had construed the attacks on the stations as open acts of war and had burned the huge Cheyenne village.

At that moment I was merely puzzled by the general's action, but with the passage of time I have come to view it as an act of monumental stupidity. That the Indians must be subdued and removed from the course of national destiny was inevitable. But the burning of the Cheyenne town effectively guaranteed that the removal would not be peaceful. Ironically, it later came to my attention that the depredations on the Smoky Hill had been committed by the Sioux and that the Cheyenne had played no role in the attacks.

I was ordered to march east to Fort Hays, there to receive forage and rations while we waited orders for what would surely be an active summer of campaigning.

We covered one hundred and fifty miles in four and one half days, arriving at Fort Hays with exhausted mounts and no food.

To say that Fort Hays at that time in its history was a ragged post offering little comfort to soldiers coming in from the field would be a positive description of its attributes. The post's condition was, however, to be expected, and thus forgiven.

What I could not forgive was that the promised rations and forage were nonexistent. There were no shoes for our worn-out horses, nor was there anything for them to eat, nor were there any replacement animals.

The post was already rationing its meager supplies of foodstuffs and there was not a single vegetable in residence. Water was marginal and had to be carried from a brackish stream.

These deplorable conditions drove the command's already flagging morale even further down, the testament of which could be read in the face of every man.

Exercising as much emotional control as possible, I sent a message to General Hancock by rider and to the division quartermaster by stage. They were as messages in a bottle, for the replies, when they finally arrived, only made more vague promises of rectification. Effectively, support of the Seventh Cavalry was ignored for almost a month while General Hancock turned his attention to further discussions with other plains tribes and the division quartermaster dilly-dallied.

There was nothing to do but watch the prairie's grass grow taller, a sight made wrenching by the knowledge that with every day's growth Indian ponies became fatter and stronger. Had we been able to move quickly I believe that summer's campaign may have had a different conclusion. As it was we were as stuck as a ship run aground.

The weather during this month of interminable waiting and privation was maddening. It rained and hailed and sleeted and snowed. The wind blew as if it would never stop. Training was sporadic and my frustrations bubbled and boiled as I watched each opportunity to shape the regiment and maintain its readiness wither away.

Gold had been discovered in Colorado, and this development, when linked with lack of rations, inclemency of weather, and grinding boredom proved too great a temptation for many of the soldiers. In the six weeks we languished at Fort Hays, ninety men took the Grand Bounce. Only a handful were run down and brought back to face court-martial.

Those who remained on post were, under the conditions, easy prey for itinerant whiskey peddlers. The paymaster arrived midway through our stay and I could not have been more displeased for I knew that most of the men would squander their paltry earnings on the bottle. Sadly, this was true of many of my officers as well.

As I expected, those who did not desert took the first opportunity to drink themselves into stupors. Emerging from my quarters on a bright, beautiful, and heretofore rare day at the end of May I beheld the noxious sight of an inebriated trooper lying facedown in the dirt outside my door. I didn't know how much he had drunk but he was unconscious at my feet and if I had let emotion be my guide I would have assembled the post and shot him in front of everyone . . . with my own revolver.

Instead I accompanied his removal to the guardhouse, where I directed that a lidless coffin be placed over him and nailed to the floor. I left orders that on waking, this man was to be ignored no matter how loud or unruly he might become.

In about an hour he apparently woke for I noticed that a crowd of snickering soldiers had gathered around the guardhouse. In a short time the captive became dissatisfied with his unique form of confinement and began to yell quite loudly for assistance. His pleas fell on deaf ears and before too much longer he began to cry for water. At length he became hysterical, his moans and wailing echoing over the post all afternoon. These morbid cries frayed the nerves of everyone, but to my ears they were sweet music, clearly indicating to all the penalty for intoxication.

He was still crying at sundown when the officer of the guard, along with several others, came calling and asked respectfully that I have the coffin removed as some men had heard enough to push them to a breaking point. They also expressed the fear that the drunkard himself might lose his mind or even die.

I acceded to this request with the stipulation that once released from his premature burial the trooper be confined to the guardhouse for three more days and that he dine solely on bread and water.

Whiskey continued to flow in and out of the post but it did so with discretion. The drunkard did not die, nor lose his mind, but remained in the army. He is now a first sergeant on this campaign against the Sioux. In the years since I have never asked about his current drinking habits and he has volunteered no information on the subject, but I have never seen him raise a bottle since.

Due to the activity of marauding bands of vengeful Indians the mails ran only occasionally and I received few letters from Libbie. Through the trials of outfitting the Hancock Expedition, the chaos of dealing with the Cheyenne, and our desultory stay at Fort Hays I began to pine for my wife with an intensity I had not experienced before.

The bottle was not for me, I despised it, but excepting the pleasant distraction of hunting, holding the regiment together was a debilitating struggle. There was little to cushion my life. The only vice open to me were games of chance, particularly cards, but even this amusement gave me empty pleasure under the circumstances.

Though she was hundreds of miles away Libbie became my only relief from the hellishness of that spring. My letters became ever more bold in descriptions of my longing for her and I cringe at what I can remember of the piteous sound of my own words on paper. I even found myself daydreaming scandalous liaisons between ourselves while in routine conversation with officers of my command.

These desperate delusions were but poor substitutes for the real article. They were charades I had concocted as a hedge against the terrible uncertainty I faced in being without her. The yawning hole of her absence was far greater than I had imagined and I was made fully and forever aware of what I had suspected since our marriage: that my wife was preeminent in my life, far outdistancing the importance of my own career. Without Libbie, all satisfactions were somehow hollow at the core.

Adding to my personal misery were her intermittent replies to my letters, for while they contained all the normal news presented in her lighthearted and indomitable spirit, I could feel a restless anxiety running below the surface of her lines.

We were still very young at that time and I suppose some of our mutual fear could be traced to the natural insecurities of a youthful, deeply attached couple living in the bright light of public scrutiny. But the predominant cause of our worry at enforced separation had more to do with the depth of our feeling. The feelings were as real as anything on earth and we could not stand to think of losing them.

My spirits seemed trapped in a steadily descending whirlpool from which I was powerless to effect escape. I was constantly doubling my effort to surmount the minor frustrations of each day and I actively began to wonder whether the downward spiral of my mental state might have madness as its final destination.

Then one morning, about two weeks before our departure, a small train of ambulances and wagons, accompanied by what was barely large enough to be called an escort, appeared out of the east. Customarily I would have jumped on a horse and sped forward to hear the news or inspect the supplies that had reached us, but my enthusiasm was at such a low ebb that I found myself on foot, walking listlessly with the rest of the garrison toward the little line of vehicles. While still some distance away a voice called out from one of the ambulances. It was only a single word but it is still impossible to fully describe the impact it had on me. My steps froze as I heard a familiar woman's voice cry, "Autie!"

I stood as if poleaxed, watching her slim form clamber out of the ambulance and come running, both hands clutching the front of her dress, lifting it high to give her strong, skinny legs freedom to move.

She struck me so hard that I staggered. As she climbed high into my arms, locking her own around my neck, my hat flew off my head and skipped away on the breeze. But I barely noticed for I still could not speak and stood oddly mute as I held my wife. We clung to one another mightily, and as we did I felt all my burdens lift and fly into a wide, limitless, and suddenly happy sky.

When I was at last able to form a question her reply was simple and sincere. "I just had to see you," she said, her wet eyes shining. Then she kissed me on that barren plain in full view of the entire command.

Through resourcefulness and sheer pluck she had traveled more than a hundred miles through hostile territory to be with the one she could not be without. For her to come so far, at such great risk, and to unabashedly press her lips to mine so publicly might appear overwrought to some. But such demonstrations of supreme devotion have been hallmarks of our life together and we could no more temper our love than live apart.

The affectionate machinations of our love have prompted skepticism and even ridicule on the part of some, and I truly believe that envy and jealousy lie at the root of these perceptions, just as they do when it comes to my celebrity as a military figure. Those who have lampooned our marriage merely reflect the poverty of their own romantic lives and we have never felt wounded by their arrows. From the moment we fell in love we resolved not to be guided in any way by gossips or naysayers. That we have not is another hallmark of our marriage, worn by both of us as a badge of honor.

Remarkably, Libbie had brought along Eliza and together with the dogs and horses she made my large tent at Fort Hays a very happy place the last week of May 1867. Eliza ordered me about as always, the dogs were constantly underfoot, and the horses provided us with many wonderful outings. We retired early, lying in my rough bed through the hours of darkness, telling silly stories about the people we knew, talking in whispers of what our future might be, and making hushed love in the early hours of morning while the camp slept all around us.

Her presence imbued me with extra strength to face the coming campaign. Such an infusion is an enduring and common example of the difference she has made at every critical point of my life. I drank as deeply as I could from the reservoir of her in the vain hope that it would see me through what might be months of separation.

When we parted on the first of June I felt that if all else failed I would survive the ordeal ahead by virtue of my unfailing desire to see her again—if my will to live is made of steel Libbie must be its forge.

But even the tonic of Libbie's visit could not smother the trepidation I felt when we finally took the field a few days later. For weeks, General Hancock had been imploring me to begin the campaign, a request I repeatedly and respectfully declined owing to the condition of horses and men and the lack of supplies. We were unable to move until the first week of June.

Desertions had further depleted the command, but we marched out of Fort Hays with what was left: three hundred and fifty men and a train of twenty wagons. Not the least of my burdens was the mission itself, for it seemed to be at cross purposes. The burning of the Cheyenne village had raised the roof in Congress and the White House. And there was jurisdictional friction between the War Department and the Department of Interior, which caused almost ceaseless conflict.

My orders were to clear a huge area, from the Smoky Hill Road to the Platte River, of all hostile parties. This Herculean task was to be accomplished in a peaceful manner! How this was to be done no one gave a clue. How we were to be supplied no one knew precisely. How the remaining troops would behave on the march and how they would fight, should they need to, was an open question.

All that I knew was that one more dreary day of inactivity at Fort Hays would have been unbearable and I led my command onto the prairie with the single-minded thought that I had a duty to perform. That my command was not at full strength and that my duty was unclear was beside the point. We were going, no matter what.

I should not give the impression that I was embarking on a hopeless errand, for I did not think so at the time. Whatever my misgivings may have been, my blood was up and running.

Ahead of us lay a march of two hundred and fifty miles over what many in the East characterized as "the Great American Desert." Since its acquisition, this region had been derided as worthless, tract upon tract of uninhabited land unbroken by fence or plow or track, as empty and monotonous as a great sea.

Although its value to America has been realized in succeeding years I cherished it for precisely the same reasons it was for so long judged useless. The country was as wild and open as the day it was made, still subject to the irrefutable laws of nature. Its unpredictability, its emptiness, and its never-ending potential for danger stirred my soul.

To penetrate such a country, to travel its grasslands and escarpments, to cross its rivers, to rest in the shade of its stately trees, to sleep beneath its black and starry skies rouses my imagination even at this moment. As a voyager of untamed territory I am freed from the shackles of my own or any time. Then as now I am liberated, no longer a captive of an age but an ancient Argonaut, plumbing the depths and scaling the heights of the unknown, absorbing all that is new in this wide, wide world.

The longer our column traversed the unknown the better I felt, and although the specter of desertion and dissipation weighed on me I knew that there were many stout warriors at my side on whom I could relay. Yates and Moylan and Hamilton . . . Keough and Cooke and Elliot . . . and brother Tom, the best right hand a soldier could possess. For all our pranks and horseplay it is my brother on whom I depend. His loyalty is unswerving and his fighting ability, which was worth two Medals of Honor in the Great War, has always been above reproach.

There were those who, while not practicing disobedience and being good career soldiers in themselves, took no great pains to conceal their dislike of me personally. The reasons for this animosity seemed to reside more in opposition to style rather than substance. Fortunately, they were in the minority and as the column wound its way north I felt optimistic that our small force with its large challenges would be successful.

But this confidence began to erode after only a few days on the march. On the third evening out I was at table with several other officers when a single shot sounded somewhere outside. We all dropped our utensils and hurried out to see what had happened.

Men were already gathering around the tent of Major Cooper, a capable officer who had absented himself from our mess frequently because of depression over a sick wife he had left pregnant in the East.

Complicating his misery was the fact that I had never conversed with him without smelling the sour, sickly odor of alcohol on his breath. Alcohol had sunk its claws into Major Cooper's back many years before, and though a bullet had now carried him out of the mortal world, it was alcohol that had pulled the trigger, placing a perfect shot deep into his brain.

He was on his knees, his head cocked weirdly against the ground in a dark, spreading pool of blood. He had not died as a soldier but as a wretch. Still, protocol dictated that we carry his corpse along with us as we marched, an inglorious and unwelcome burden to say the least.

Sadly, the major's fast decomposing body did nothing to dissuade the enlisted men nor certain of the officers from their affection for drink. The major's body functioned as nothing more than an annoying ball and chain attached to the rear of the column, a persistent reminder of deeper frustrations . . . the primary one having to do with the whereabouts of the enemy.

After very little time on the trail my heart began to sink for we could find nothing of the hostiles we were supposed to chastise. Neither the Delawares nor our experienced white scouts could find anything of the Indians. On moonlit nights I rode out with them, searching the prairie through hour after silent hour, but though I learned much about tracking and the colorful character of the frontiersman, we found nothing of military interest on the rolling, silvery grasslands.

※

I have been interrupted again in my solitary nighttime pursuit, this time not by violent weather or random rifle fire but by a single eyeball starring through a crack in my canvas door.

Startled by what I at first thought was a ghostly apparition, the flap opened a little before I could react and the granitelike countenance of Bloody Knife was revealed. What brought him to my quarters at such an early hour was a mystery I did not pursue, but apparently he was attracted by the candle flickering in my tent, the only light in camp. With a wave of my hand I asked him to come forward. He took a step or two and stood just inside the entrance, fascinated at the sight of these pages and what might have induced me to sit so long into the morning at my little desk.

Through signs and the few words we knew of each other's language it was soon clear that my energy was at the source of Bloody Knife's curiosity. I had covered fifty miles the previous day, many of them in his company. It was now a little after three A.M. and my stalwart chief of scouts wanted to know whether I would be sleeping through the coming day instead of riding.

I assured him we would be on the march as usual, and after a few minutes he was able to make me understand that he was unsure as to how I would be able to march all day without sleep.

With gestures, pantomime, and a few intelligible words I was able to tell him that I did not need to sleep when following the enemy, that the scent of the enemy kept me awake.

At this Bloody Knife was deeply impressed. His eyes widened. He nodded his head, and then the seemingly eternal solemnity of his expression was replaced by a good-natured and knowing smile.

He tapped at his chest and proudly muttered the same phrase several times in rapid succession. Though I did not know the words the meaning was quite clear.

He too went without sleep when the smell of the enemy was in his nose.

JUNE 6-7,

1876

The column made more than twenty miles today, and I rode more than forty. I have taken to riding Vic because Dandy is beginning to show his age and is greatly deserving of comfort at the end of a long and successful career. He has carried me over seemingly impassable crags and innumerable swift running rivers without error. And most important, in the face of the enemy he has never flinched.

Were it up to Dandy we would continue on, but I too can feel the extra effort he must give to do his simple duty. The legs are not as sure, the heart a little less strong. A little more goes out of him after a difficult day.

Vic is the ablest of substitutes, but for all his power he lacks a certain sixth sense that Dandy has always possessed, a quality that I cannot expect to be replaced. I have ridden hundreds of the finest horses but never one like Dandy, and I will do all that I can to see that his life is extended to a serene end.

I wish I had been able to do the same with all of my four-footed colleagues, but I know even as I write what a hollow hope that is. Though my sentiments are true I know that realizing them is but a boy's dream. Death and destruction have been the working environment, and though I have striven to preserve life whenever I could and even to celebrate it, the imperative has always been to steel myself against the upturned face of death I have known through every phase of my military existence. I believe that only by accepting death's final judgment have I been able to endure.

This result was never tested more strenuously than on the plains of Kansas in that summer of 1867, the summer of the Hancock Expedition. Death was dealt out over those months not in the glory of hard-fought battle and victories won but in the piteous manner reserved for the unprepared, the uninformed, and the impotent. That summer I was a fool among fools.

The march to Fort McPherson on the Platte River continued uneventful until we were only two days away from completing the first long leg of our bitter scout.

It was at that time that we first contacted a roving band of warriors. They were not Cheyenne but Sioux, a group of several hundred led by a man called Pawnee Killer. We sat in council for two hours on the banks of the muddy Platte and all was cordial. I expressed our desire to have him and his people confine their activities to regions north of the Platte. To this Pawnee Killer agreed and, professing nothing but peaceful intentions, we parted most amicably.

While greatly satisfied with the bargain struck, I felt a lingering doubt, which centered almost entirely on the man with whom I had spoken. His easy smile was agreeable enough on the surface but there was a distinct and elusive aspect of his demeanor that left an unsettling aftertaste.

On the face of it all seemed well, but I had never encountered such a supreme example of the inscrutability so commonly associated with members of his race. His eyes were especially salient, for they always remained as slits, as if guarding access to the true convictions of his soul.

My uneasy feelings were exacerbated on reaching Fort McPherson the next afternoon. General Sherman happened to be in temporary residence, having forsaken his administrative duties in Washington to come west for a first-hand look at the costly workings of the Hancock Expedition.

I briefed him on the uneventful march and was bold enough to express my displeasure with the Commissary Department. The general listened to my report without comment, and didn't show much interest.

Sherman is a commander who prizes results above all else—my outlook is much the same—and I happily informed him of my recent parley with the Sioux. I was taken aback when the general interrupted me. He did not openly chastise me but made it clear that my meeting with Pawnee Killer had been superfluous at best. He said that if I had been wise I would have ensured that Pawnee Killer kept his word by taking hostages. I agreed with my commander's evaluation but still expressed confidence that Pawnee Killer would uphold his end of the agreement, a confidence based more on hope than result.

I saw the general frequently over the next few days and he stressed many times the importance of moving the Indians out of the country so that the progress of national expansion could proceed unabated. He directed me to scout the headwaters of the Republican River far to the south and return to Fort Sedgwick in the north for resupply before about facing to march another three hundred miles south to Fort Wallace. These orders were to be changed at my discretion, particularly if in hot pursuit of the enemy, in which circumstance the general urged me to spare neither man nor horse.

To my mind these directives countermanded the letter and spirit of the expedition, whose policies had been formulated by no less a personage than the President of the United States.

I had taken the field on a mission of peace, but now the commanding general of the army instructed me to pursue war. It would not have mattered whether the policy was peace or extermination: as a soldier I would have dutifully followed either course. But Sherman's orders muddied the waters, and taking the field again, I was stricken with the queasy feeling that I was now occupying the disagreeable space of purgatory.

I had no choice but to make a choice and I decided to sustain the expedition's original intent. While maintaining a readiness to fight, I would extend the hand of peace to all those we encountered.

In theory this could be easily done. In practice, however, it was another matter. My force was steadily declining. Thirty-two men had run off while we rested at Fort McPherson, and talk of desertion continued openly as we marched south to the headwaters of the Republican, a position roughly equidistant between the Platte River to the north and Fort Wallace on the Smoky Hill Road to the south.

The rations we had received at McPherson were abominable. All of us were eating hard bread out of boxes marked 1860, virtually every piece coated with mold. And these were the best of our rations.

Summer was reaching its height, the tempestuous weather of late spring having been supplanted by scorching temperatures that turned the treeless plains into an endless griddle of heat. The dogs that trailed along with the column began to die like mayflies, and by the time we reached the Republican both men and horses were beginning to break down.

The water of that silty stream was barely drinkable and had to be strained repeatedly before a single bitter drop could be drunk.

Any vestige of adventure had now been replaced with the grind of ordeal, and as we wandered down the river I began to visualize Libbie as the cool, clean antidote for my predicament. I rationed my thoughts of her, hoarded them as a traveler hoards the last swallow of water while crossing a waterless waste.

I had asked Sherman if she might be allowed to come to McPherson and he had assented. But as we took up the march I realized we would be scouting south, in the direction of Fort Wallace, and suggested in a letter written before leaving McPherson that if she could reach Wallace instead we might be more easily reunited—I wish it could have been so.

Morale continued to sink as we stumbled down the Republican in search of Indians. The heat was torture for man and beast, the water failed to improve, game was frustratingly scarce, and the object of our mission, the Sioux and Cheyenne, were practically invisible.

Only once did we scare up our foe, surprising about a hundred mounted Cheyenne at a ford around midday. They fled like a covey of flushed birds and though we gave chase it was hopeless. While our heavy horses strained over every yard of ground, the Indians seemed to fly across the prairie on far superior mounts, many of whom were sublime animals stolen from the stage lines.

By this time, after almost a month in the field, even the most dull-witted of soldiers knew implicitly that we would not overtake the quarry if we chased him a thousand years.

I dreamed of Libbie day and night, and when unable to concentrate on my living dream found myself snapping at anyone in the command who came near.

When not dreaming, I was trying to divine a way out of our impossible situation. I could not halt the scout without orders and I dared not move to Fort Sedgwick for supplies as requested. The country was even more difficult in that direction and as Sedgwick was situated next to a major emigrant road, I feared that so many men might desert that I would be left without a command. Nor could

I stay where I was, to remain becalmed in an empty, searing, nearly waterless land.

I was at last forced to concede that our mission could not possibly succeed. I decided on a radical plan I hoped would save the column and give me some prospect of seeing my wife again. It was the sole chance for salvation I could conceive.

Instead of marching our whole force to Sedgwick I sent Major Elliot and a dozen picked men to see if any new orders had been received there.

At the same time I sent the ever-reliable Lieutenant Robbins and two squadrons south to Fort Wallace with orders to procure whatever supplies existed there and bring them back via wagon train.

I myself would continue to scout the Republican as ordered, intercepting the Platte as it curved south into our path. There were stage stations along that stretch of the river, and while they might pose a temptation for further desertion, it would be far less temptation than that of a major center like Fort Sedgwick.

We made our way west, combing the breaks of the Republican slowly so that Major Elliot and his small attachment might more easily find us on their return, which was expected to be rapid.

We could see no sign of Indians but they apparently had us in sight. Barely twenty-four hours had passed before a combined force of Sioux and Cheyenne tried to stampede and capture our horses shortly before dawn on the day after Major Elliot had departed for Sedgwick. This attempt was thwarted by the alertness of the sentries, one of whom was killed.

Leery of being decoyed into an ambush and unwilling to risk a fight in the open against superior numbers of enemy cavalry, I did not give chase. I held the command in camp, close by the river.

This lack of action was correctly deduced by the Indians as an indication of weakness, and while the horses were brought into camp and a defensive perimeter established, the enemy happily lingered in the neighborhood.

They appeared on hills and rises in a perfect circle around our camp, popping up at irregular intervals like targets in a shooting gallery. They dashed back and forth, careful to remain beyond rifle range, performing feats of horsemanship that stretched the boundaries of believability.

When they tired of these games and demonstrations they contented themselves with shouting taunts and obscenities, in remarkably good English, that called into question our manhood, the legitimacy of our births, and the sexual habits of our mothers.

At one point a group of half a dozen warriors dismounted, discarded their aboriginal underwear, turned their backs, bent at the waist, and in unison presented the command with a sun-splashed view of their bare buttocks. At this display many of the men angrily started forward but the officers succeeded in restraining them.

About midday these activities ceased, but the Indians continued to lurk in sight of us. Obviously they were discussing their next move, and I decided to take advantage of this lull in the "action" by sending a delegation consisting of myself, my adjutant, and a handful of scouts under a flag of truce several hundred yards into the field.

We were soon met by a corresponding delegation from the ranks of our tormentors, and after a brief discussion it was decided to hold a council, the primary condition of which was that the participants would be unarmed.

A tent was quickly erected not far from our camp and the council, which included five chiefs, me, two interpreters, Captains Keough and Yates, and two orderlies, swung into action.

Our group reached the site first, and as our savage counterparts rode into view I was chagrined to see Pawnee Killer among them.

Despite the broiling sun of early afternoon each man was wrapped in heavy blankets, the purpose of which was clear as soon as they had dismounted and started forward. The chiefs were so weighted down with concealed weapons that they could barely walk. Of course we had concealed many of our own, so I should say that the council began on even terms.

The Indians entered the tent and we all stood about awkwardly for a few moments. With so much steel hidden beneath blankets and coats, neither party was anxious to attempt the manoeuver of sitting. There was nothing to do but make a clean breast of it. Through the interpreter I suggested that we all make ourselves comfortable, taking care in the process to see that no firearm was accidentally discharged.

The directness of my statement momentarily shocked the Indians, but in no time they were seating themselves with casual ease. As they did this a fantastic array of weapons was produced, which they then laid at their sides.

We did the same, and as the inevitable pipe was lit, each side openly studied the others' armaments. Pawnee Killer asked to handle my long-barreled pistol, a request I granted after I had removed the bullets. As I watched him test its heft in his palm it seemed clear to me that these free roamers had come to council with one self-serving purpose in mind; they wanted to learn at close quarters all that they could of our force's strengths and weaknesses.

After several revolutions of the pipe Pawnee Killer asked the purpose of our existence in country he characterized as belonging to himself and his cohorts.

I replied that our mission had always been and yet remained a mission of peace and that we were here to foster good relations. But I reminded them all that we were good fighters too and would fight if that was what they desired. Before he could reply to this I asked Pawnee Killer why he was so far south of the Platte when he had agreed only days before to remain north of the river. Then I asked him why he had attempted to steal our horses.

He pointed out that he and his people were following the buffalo and were only exercising their right to hunt meat for their families. Not knowing who we were, they had decided to appropriate our horses as punishment for trespassing, and that was only a slap on the wrist. The punishment could have been much stronger.

Not wanting to open an argument over the details of intent I let

Pawnee Killer's lame excuses pass. Instead, I informed him that from this moment on he would have to hunt north of the Platte and to make certain that he would do so we would now follow him to wherever he and his friends might be camped.

He did not agree but he made no fuss either. He and the other members of the delegation grunted at one another and got to their feet. Everyone shook hands and the council broke up.

By the time my men had saddled and mounted, however, the Sioux and Cheyenne force was far out on the plains. They stayed together until they had led us in a zigzag of several miles. Then, abruptly, the large party broke up into smaller and smaller groups that traveled faster and faster before disappearing altogether.

I was furious at having been deceived again. While the troops made coffee, I, the officers, and our scouts held an inconclusive meeting. There was nothing to do but go back the way we had come, empty-handed once more.

After a long, hot, and dispiriting ride we reached camp in late afternoon only to find that the duplicitous Pawnee Killer had doubled back and thoroughly vandalized our temporary home.

Tent canvas was blowing across the prairie in every direction, utensils had been flung to the four winds, and those items which the Indians found attractive, including a regimental flag, had been stolen. I found the few personal items I carried with me submerged in the Republican River. Not until well after dark was some semblance of camp restored. But there was no rebuilding our pride. It lay scattered on the plains, the lost remnants of another futile chase. Without suffering a single casualty we had been whipped by a mocking enemy. I could not bear to face my men and retired to what remained of my quarters feeling myself to be the utterly reduced victim of an unceasing barrage of humiliating pranks.

My frustration smoldered all night and burned through the next day as we waited gloomily for the return of Major Elliot.

He and his detachment arrived unmolested the next afternoon but with vexing news. His dangerous ride had gone for naught. No new orders had been received, and I would not have stayed in that camp had it been situated on a mountain of gold.

We marched immediately for the Platte River, and after two days, the highlights of which consisted of the unpleasant duty of shooting ruined horses and dogs, we struck a place called Riverside Station.

It was nothing more than a stage depot but possessed enough stores to provide the men with fresh water and some bits of salt pork. And there were enough horses on hand to replace a few of those who had been lost. Most important, there was also a telegraph line, and I was able to wire the commandant at Sedgwick.

His reply told me that Major Elliot had missed new instructions by no more than a few hours. General Sherman himself had directed that we break off the scout and march back to Fort Wallace, there to await further orders from General Hancock.

Having missed Major Elliot, the commandant had sent a young lieutenant named Lyman Kidder—a name I shall never forget—into the field with an escort of eleven men and a Sioux scout in an effort to make me aware of Sherman's new instructions. This boy, only recently arrived from the East, was presently adrift somewhere in hostile territory.

As if there were not enough problems already, during the night we passed at Riverside Station a foul conspiracy was hatched and thirty-four more men, succumbing to the lure of civilian opportunity, took the Grand Bounce. The guards I had posted to prevent such a thing happening had apparently been in league with the deserters.

We started back up the Republican the next morning, hoping to rendezvous with Lieutenant Kidder and his party coming down from the north or the wagon train coming up from Fort Wallace. Each mile of that day's march was passed while the crushing cadence of defeat echoed in my brain. The regiment I had labored so long to build into a premier fighting force was in tatters.

The Hancock Expedition, which I was now spearheading, was a shambles, defeated in equal parts by hazy government policy and a clever, cavalier enemy.

I had lost control of my men and for the only time in my life my addled mind entertained its own thoughts of desertion. Images of Libbie were all that kept me on course as we backtracked over mile upon agonizing mile.

At the noon meal, thirteen men, made brazen I suppose by the aura of defeat that lay upon what was left of the column, decided to desert in full view of the command.

Taking seven of our best horses, they doffed their caps in merry adieu to their comrades and simply marched off. They were still in sight when brought to my attention and as I watched them disappear over a bump in the distant landscape all the frustrations and burdens of the campaign exploded inside me.

These thirteen men were not only thumbing their noses at the oath of service, they were ridiculing me as well. If I did not stop them now, if I did not punish them on the spot, I could not have given another order that would be carried out by anyone.

I sorely wanted to pursue them myself but that would be nearly as unseemly as letting them go. I quickly called for Tom and the ever loyal Lieutenant Cooke and ordered them to take however many men they desired and chase down the deserters. Major Elliot asked that he be allowed to join them and I granted him permission.

Raising my voice to reach the ears of as many of my command as possible I ordered the pursuing party to shoot the deserters when they were apprehended.

Once Tom and the others had disappeared the camp fell still as death. No one spoke. Few moved. After what seemed an extraordinarily long time riders were spotted. They were part of the detachment I had ordered out and, after reporting that there were wounded on the prairie, requested a wagon with which to bring them in. I ordered that a vehicle be sent out and, after another dreary wait of perhaps half an hour, it reappeared on the horizon with Tom and Lieutenant Cooke and Major Elliot riding in front.

The seven mounted deserters had escaped. Three of the remaining six had been shot. While engaged in conversation with the returning officers I noticed that our surgeon, Dr. Coates, was making his way to the wagon that held the wounded. I immediately ordered him, again in earshot of most of the command, to stop and render no aid whatsoever to the wounded men. I then gave instructions for the march to resume and within twenty minutes the column was again on the trail.

The thirteen had been part of a larger conspiracy that had planned to desert that evening. The conspirators were under the impression that we would remain in the camp where we had stopped for lunch until the next morning, affording ample time to make preparations for a night flight. But the impatience of the thirteen had spoiled the larger, more rotten scheme.

When we had covered several miles I summoned the surgeon and told him to give what aid he deemed necessary to the wounded men. I told him to do this discreetly as I wanted the troops to have a lasting impression of what fate awaited them should any others contemplate desertion. None did.

Keeping the command intact was but one of a plethora of worries that now clotted my thoughts.

The whereabouts of Lieutenant Kidder and his tiny detachment were on everyone's mind. That a young man with no experience, despite the presence of a Sioux scout, could make his way through miles of territory being patrolled by large bands of mature warriors was the cause of much speculation. Some of the men amused themselves by wagering on his fate.

The wire I had received from Sedgwick also informed me of renewed raiding on the Smokey Hill Road. Posts all along the line were being attacked repeatedly while we were flailing about in a vacuum a hundred miles to the north of the action. As Fort Wallace was one of the posts being harassed I was deeply concerned over the wagon train coming up to meet us. There were only fifty men to protect it and if Libbie had received my letters she might be with them. I detached a squadron to ride ahead at a forced march until they made contact with the train.

But there was even worse news. The dreaded death's head of cholera had appeared in the East and was making its way along the Smoky Hill Road. This scourge, against which there was no defense, carried away almost everyone it touched and in camp that night as I tossed and turned in fitful sleep I dreamed a horrible dream.

Lying on her side, Libbie lay in a bed at some unknown place, curled almost double in the terrible pain of cramping, her awful screams circulating through the room like an ill, unrelenting wind.

Her eyes were open wide and her bedding was soaked in perspiration and vomit and urine and feces.

As I stood before her, unable to help, her screams would gradually subside. Then, just as it seemed peace had finally descended, my girl's eyes would pop open and her tortured cries would begin anew.

I watched uselessly as the cholera cruelly teased the life out of her. In the end she had wasted down to a moaning, breathing skeleton, heaving and wailing on the filthy bed.

I awoke on the floor of my tent, a blanket spread over my lap as first light was breaking. The one thought I had in my head was that I must bring this command out of the field without a moment's delay.

Many of the horses were but a few days from death; at the next night's camp, after digging for hours, there was only enough water to keep the men alive. After a march of thirty terrifyingly hot miles none of the horses had anything to drink.

I posted officers as night guards to prevent further desertion but I doubt if any men were still thinking seriously of leaving. I believe everyone now knew that we were marching for our lives and survival depended on sticking together.

The horses finally drank at noon of the next day when we struck the trail leading south to Fort Wallace. The water was so alkaline that everyone had to hold their noses as they drank. The poor horses were not capable of doing that but they drank anyway.

One of our guides, Will Comstock, who had been indispensable throughout the journey, was certain that the trail to Wallace would tell something about the fate of Lieutenant Kidder and his party . . . if they had survived to come this far. After only a few miles we came upon the first clue when the tracks of ten shod horses were discovered. They had been moving at a walk which meant they were not being pursued and our hopes were momentarily lifted.

A short distance ahead we found a white horse lying dead and stripped in the middle of the trail. On closer inspection it was ascertained that the animal had been shot and that it carried a U.S. brand. There were no pony tracks around the carcass and it was speculated that the horse may have played itself out and been destroyed to deny the enemy use of it.

We hurried on and two miles later another dead horse appeared in the road. The ground around this animal told a different, less hopeful story. The shod horses of Lieutenant Kidder's group had begun to gallop and they were being followed by hundreds of unshod tracks. The country had turned level and open, perfect terrain for hunting hostiles to encircle and destroy their prey.

It was I who first saw a column of gliding vultures spiraling into the air no more than a quarter mile ahead. We galloped on, and almost immediately the unmistakable stench of rotting flesh filled our nostrils. Shortly after that we saw the bodies.

They were grouped close together in a small declivity on the hot, lonely prairie. To call what lay on the ground bodies is a generous characterization. The vultures and wolves had picked through most of the flesh and scattered limbs and appendages all about the grass. Some of the corpses had been set afire, indicating that a number of the young men with Lieutenant Kidder had been tortured. Our efforts at identification were stymied by the condition of each soldier's skull. Chopped to pieces by battle axes, they were utterly unrecognizable.

Twenty-five or thirty arrows protruded from each former human. The scout Comstock identified them as being of Sioux origin. This was further confirmed on finding the body of the Sioux guide. His name was Red Bead and he was the only member of the party who still retained a face. His scalp had been sheared off and dropped at his side, a practice that Comstock regarded as unique to the Sioux when dealing with those of their own whom they perceived to have gone bad.

When the column came up a burial detail was formed and we waited in that ghastly spot while the trenches were dug, the bones gathered, and the corpses interred.

As I sat atop my mare, Fanchon, forcing myself to watch this sad ritual, I could not help but think again of the enemy's fury. And again, I likened their zeal in combat to that of monstrous, unholy children.

We marked the spot with a small pile of stones and departed with new urgency. I had directed each member of the command to gaze upon the carnage of Kidder's massacre and am positive that each soldier stepped with renewed purpose as we left that cadaverous place behind us.

That night we had to dig for water again and after tattoo I performed the unpleasant task of composing a letter to young Kidder's family. I told them that he had died bravely, in the line of duty, and urged them to gain solace from the fact that he had fallen in service to his country. I did not touch on the gore I had seen. Nor did I share with them that he had died as a result of a foolish errand that he should never have been ordered to run.

I thought of Lieutenant Kidder long after I had written the letter, that boy who was only two years younger than myself, sacrificed so needlessly to a mature and bloodthirsty enemy.

Tonight it is nine years later and the fate of Lyman Kidder remains with me still. It could just as easily have been I, smashed to nothingness and left to decompose slowly into the uncaring ground.

Viewing the spectacle of those slaughtered men hardened me. I could never again give quarter to Pawnee Killer and those of his ilk. From that moment I have thought only of destroying the enemy when ordered to do so. I have always excepted women and children as that is a line I cannot cross, but any Indian male who has since raised arms against me or my men I have striven to dispatch as swiftly and ruthlessly as possible, for I know what he would do to me if given the opportunity.

∽✦∽

I cannot think of Kansas without thinking of this summer's campaign of 1876. If we can catch and corner the free roamers, the result will likely be far different than it was those many years ago on the Republican River.

I expect that if only we can place our hands on the enemy's throat the outcome is much more likely to be as it was on the Washita. The Seventh Cavalry is now a seasoned regiment and wholesale desertion is no longer the nightmare it once was. In fact, from all I can tell the men are eager for action, though some are growing skeptical of seeing any this summer. And why shouldn't they? Our sojourn on these northern plains has thus far been more like an extended tramp than an ordeal of war.

We endured another violent hailstorm this afternoon, but thankfully it struck us before camp had been set up. Although it was fierce enough to kill two antelope who were watching our arrival, everyone here was fortunate to gain cover under the trees and only a few of the horses were injured slightly.

We are nearing the Yellowstone River and a rendezvous with Colonel Gibbon's column and the steamboat *Far West*. Spirits are high all around for that same boat will be carrying fresh provisions and several bags of soldier's treasure: mail from home. Knowing Libbie, I expect she will have found a way to be on board. At the least there will be letters from her. I am eager to see her, to feel her cheek against mine, but we have both learned from experience that if she does not appear it could be for the better.

It was a nonappearance that saved her life that summer of 1867 in Kansas. The train coming up from Fort Wallace was met the day after we buried Lyman Kidder and I learned to my horror that in preceding days it had been under severe attack by a force of Sioux and Cheyenne. The fifty-man escort had managed to keep the savages at bay for most of an afternoon but had exhausted their ammunition and would undoubtedly have been overwhelmed were it not for the timely arrival of the squadron I had sent ahead to meet them.

Long before I had given instructions to all of my officers that if they came under attack while my wife was with them they must kill her immediately, death being more agreeable than having her carried off.

Indian fighters are ever keen for taking white women and the fate that befalls a grown woman who finds herself in their hands is unspeakable. A grown woman who is not instantly killed in the most gruesome way will invariably be beaten and pressed into servitude. If she actively resists or is unable to perform her duties she becomes a target of carnal contempt, after which she is discarded.

I have managed to effect the release of several white women from the hands of Indians, but simply gaining their freedom—no mean triumph in itself—has never been fully satisfactory to the captive or her family. What is returned alive is, in the main, wreckage. No woman I know of who has experienced abduction and captivity returns as the same person. The damage cannot be repaired. The very souls of the captives have been torn in pieces and rearranged by their experience. They are consigned to carry the scars of their ordeal for the remainder of their lives.

I could not allow this to happen to my Libbie. I never told her of my orders to the officers but she knew full well that she was taking the same chances in the field as I. I believe she also knew that she was far too delicate and sweet of nature to survive such a catastrophe.

With held breath I asked Lieutenant Robbins whether Libbie had been with the train.

"No, General," Robbins replied, "there's been no word from her."

I felt as if an ominous cloud had suddenly passed off the face of the sun. But my relief was short-lived as I digested the rest of the lieutenant's report. The Smoky Hill Road was practically aflame. Every stage station had been repeatedly attacked in the last two weeks and Roman Nose himself had tried to take Fort Wallace the week before. Our troops had met him in hand-to-hand combat; although the post had survived the assault, our soldiers had been forced to withdraw from the field, having suffered seven killed, seven wounded, and half their horses destroyed or captured.

The rumors of cholera that had so long been uppermost in the minds of all were now confirmed. The disease had not yet reached full force, nor had it arrived at Fort Wallace, but it was making its appearance everywhere along the Smoky Hill Road.

I decided to press the march to Wallace. We pushed the horses and the men and the unwilling wagons over every obstacle in a supreme effort to reach our destination.

With barely enough energy left to put one foot in front of the other, the command at last collapsed in a makeshift camp a mile west of Fort Wallace on July 13th, 1867. We had marched through hostile territory for almost six weeks, scouting a distance of more than seven hundred miles.

I rode over to the fort and had its commander, Captain Keough, brief me on current conditions and events of the past weeks. Libbie was not there, nor was there a single letter from her, and I knew at once that my own correspondence had not gotten through.

The whereabouts of General Sherman and my immediate superior, Colonel Smith, were unknown. General Hancock was believed to be in the city of Denver but there were no instructions from him.

The telegraph wires were down and stage service had all but ceased, owing to attacks on the stations.

Cholera had not yet arrived but was expected at any time.

The post still possessed provisions but they were of an inferior quality and offered little in the way of nutriment. There were no foods on hand that could arrest scurvy.

And there was not one horse available with which to replenish our worn-out mounts.

I could not sit and wait for all these elements to become worse. I still had energy and the will for action. It was imperative that the post be resupplied and in order to do so communication had to be established with powers that could effect change. Instead of waiting for divine deliverance I decided to break out and called for the ablest men of each troop to make a forced march east. More than one hundred came forward and of those seventy-five were picked, along with the best of the remaining horses.

Libbie was as much in my mind as anything else and while I was willing to give my life for my country once, I would gladly have given it a hundred times to assure her well-being. I had to know whether she was safe.

We left at sunset on July 15th, intent on covering the one hundred and fifty miles east to Fort Hays as quickly as possible. The march would be continuous and the rigors we would be facing had been made clear to the volunteers. Traveling at night gave us no real advantage over opportunistic bands of the enemy for I knew from Captain Keough that the road was so thick with them that no travelers, especially a group of our size, could march a mile without being noticed. Approaching stage stations at night was in actuality a dangerous proposition, for the men guarding them had so often been besieged and so often tricked that they were disposed to open fire at anything or anyone moving about in the dark.

But we left at sunset despite these difficulties because it was essential to spare man and horse from the tremendous heat of day, the most formidable enemy of all.

By noon of the next day we had reached a point on the stage line called Downer's Station, which in addition to its normal keepers was being guarded by a troop of infantry.

Contrary to explicit instructions, some of our men had been straggling behind since dawn, and when I called for Fanchon I was angered to find that she was being led by a man who had fallen far behind down the road. At that juncture any delay was intolerable, but the horse I was presently riding could go no further. I had no choice but to send a detail back down the road to have the mare brought up.

After waiting more than half an hour, members of the detachment I had sent out raced into the station with the news that our stragglers had been attacked by a small band of hostiles. Instead of mounting a defense and driving the attackers off, the dawdlers had fled and two of their number had been killed.

Fortunately, Fanchon had survived the attack and I was well mounted once again. Every moment was precious and I had no intention of wasting more time chasing an enemy that had no doubt melted into the landscape moments after their strike. As to the dead, I instructed members of the infantry to collect the bodies and see to their burial.

We continued to press east and made Fort Hays the next morning at three A.M., after covering one hundred and fifty miles in fifty-five hours.

Here I learned that Colonel Smith was in residence at Fort Harker, another sixty miles to the east. Leaving the bulk of my escort to rest, Lieutenant Cooke, Tom, I, and two enlisted men remained in the saddle. The country was relatively free of danger, and after twelve hours of hard riding without incident we reached Fort Harker. The telegraph was up and I wired Fort Sedgwick with the tragic news concerning the Kidder party.

I then searched out the quarters of my superior, the amiable Colonel Smith, and roused him from his bed. I briefly outlined the events of our long scout and informed him of conditions at Fort Wallace. I also told him that Captain Hamilton would arrive in twenty-four hours with the remainder of my escort. They would begin outfitting the train that would carry needed supplies of medicine and food back to Fort Wallace. Finally, I asked him about Libbie and was told that she was safe at Fort Riley, ninety miles farther east.

Knowing it would take at least a day to organize the relief wagons and start them back to Wallace, I inquired of the colonel whether I might take leave during that time to see my wife. Fort Harker was then the terminus of the rail line and I had been told that a train to the east would be leaving within the hour.

"Don't you want to sleep?" the colonel asked.

"I would rather see my wife, sir."

The colonel smiled in a fatherly way and said, "Of course you would, my boy."

He insisted on walking me to the station, and I waited nervously as he dressed. The thought of missing that three A.M. train after the many trials of the last six weeks was unbearable, but the locomotive was still there when we arrived at the station and to my great joy it pulled out on time.

I cannot remember enduring a longer trip than the ninety miles to Fort Harker. When at last I saw the twinkle of its lights in the predawn my heart began to race.

I must have seemed a strange apparition as I dashed about the post covered with trail dust trying to find out where she was. It did not take long and soon I was walking through a strange door that opened into a strange house.

There was noise in the kitchen and I found Eliza there, stoking the cook stove. She grasped at her breast when she saw me. Her jaw seemed to drop to the floor but luckily for me she had a momentary loss of breath and made no sound that gave me away. Before she could say a word I was holding her fast, gently cupping her mouth with my hand.

"Where is my girl," I whispered.

Eliza's eyes tilted toward the ceiling.

I left her with the hushed admonition to admit no visitors and bounded noiselessly up the short stairway to the second-floor landing. I found the door to the bedroom slightly ajar and pushed my way inside. For a few moments I stood still in the near darkness and watched the phenomenon of dawn spread through the room like a lamp being turned slowly up. I could see her small form slumbering peacefully as she lay on one side.

I did not want her to wake and walked on tiptoe to a nearby chair. I laid my hat softly on the floor, stripped off my tunic, and sat as softly as I could. With great care I managed to pull off my long boots without making any noise. Then I wriggled out of my underwear, crept to the bedside, lifted the cover, and slid against the back of her nightgown.

She stirred then but before she could come fully awake I snaked an arm over her shoulder, held her close and whispered, "It's all right, Libbie, it's me."

Though she was startled, sleep was too heavy upon her to allow a scream or a shout. She rolled to face me and without opening her eyes murmured, "My God," over and over as her lips covered my face with kiss after loving kiss.

The frustrations of the last month and a half evaporated with the smell of her skin and the taste of her mouth and the touch of her fingers. Those first moments of reunion were the most wondrous two lovers could possibly have. Through the unshakable application of will and determination I had fetched back my life. It was here against me again in the shape of a single soul whose existence fed my own, the only entity who could make me feel healthy and whole by the mere fact of her being.

The hurried kisses produced many more, each longer and deeper than the last as both of us surrendered to the divine purity of touch. I do not know how long we made love that morning. I only know it was done with matchless freedom, unencumbered by speech or memory or longing for anything else on earth.

How much time passed as we lay listening to the sound of each other's breathing I do not remember either, but detail is of little value to my memory for it was the whole of that encounter, so romantic in its abandon that it cannot be recalled with distinction. That single encounter somehow provided a rare, supreme spark, the remembrance of which has done more to keep our marriage alive than any other event in its history. No occurrence, no matter how large or devastating, can ever erase that July morning in a second-floor room at Fort Riley, Kansas. Libbie has since referred to it as "our one perfect day," a description that could not be more apt.

Time came back to us eventually, but the recollection of its return is as hazy as all the rest. We began to talk but I could not keep my eyes open, and after three and a half days without sleep, I lost consciousness, most likely in midsentence.

I awoke sometime that same afternoon, brought to my senses by the aroma of food. I sat up to find Libbie on the edge of the bed with a large tray of eggs and potatoes, half a loaf of Eliza's hot bread, and a fresh pot of coffee.

With my back to the wall and the tray on my lap I devoured every delicious morsel as Libbie reclined at my side. We talked in a gay flood of chatter and when the last of the meal was installed in my stomach I surrendered again to sleep.

When I awoke again I was alone but fully refreshed. The shadows of late afternoon filled the room as I threw on a clean uniform and skipped downstairs, where I found my girl in the kitchen with Eliza.

Instead of a smile her face wore a troubled look as she handed me a recently arrived telegram. It was from Colonel Smith. He was ordering me to return to Fort Harker at once.

Unable to imagine what the cause of such urgency might be, we packed quickly and hastened straightaway to the station in order to make a prompt return. Our anxiety and apprehension was drawn out by various delays owing to disruptions along the rail line and we did not arrive at Fort Harker until late the next afternoon.

Greatly concerned, we made our way to the commandant's quarters, where we found the usually genial Colonel Smith, with whom we had always been on the best of terms, surrounded by officers whose faces were as wan and grim as his own. He greeted Libbie stiffly and suggested that she absent herself from our impending interview. I insisted that she stay.

The colonel placed himself in a chair behind his desk, fingered a few pages of official documentation, and lifted his gaze to me.

"It is my unpleasant duty to inform you, sir, that you are under arrest."

I was too stunned to speak. The colonel continued.

"You are charged with being absent without leave from your command."

"Who is preferring these charges?" I asked.

Colonel Smith sighed unhappily and cleared his throat. "I am," he said.

JUNE 8-10,

1876

I am restless with General Terry's grand design for this campaign. Laid out on paper the plan has much to recommend it. Gibbon's column pushes down from the north, we drive in from the east, and Crook marches up from the south. Together we pressure the free roamers to the west, there to encircle and entrap, leaving them only two options: fight or capitulate.

It is a sound strategy, but the sheer weight of it makes me dubious. We have been almost three weeks in the field, exploring ground that has seen not so much as a hunting party for months, engaging in nothing more than a sluggish, meandering walk in the wilderness.

The laying of our nets has a slowness akin to dripping sap. As we inch along, making scouts of every desolate valley in our path, the grass grows higher, making our enemy stronger by the day.

They will be at the height of whatever powers they can generate by the time we catch them. We should be streaking toward them but instead we are poking along, imitating the convolutions of a lazy stream in the far-flung hope that our three unwieldy columns will somehow converge at the proper moment, tightening the noose before the enemy realizes the rope is about his neck.

I am torn in two directions. As the plan is the only one we have, I am fully committed to doing my part to see that it is executed in a way that provides every possible chance for success.

At the same time, it seems idiotically slow, the pipe dream of some bureaucrat whose most vigorous activity consists of rubbing the seat of his pants against the bottom of his chair, thereby producing a glorious shine.

My discomfort is further aggravated by the sure knowledge that this monumental effort of the army is being influenced by the nearly invisible tendrils of a thousand political intrigues. Spawned at a distance of several thousand miles, they impact the life of this campaign as surely as an infectious disease invades an unknowing host.

Though I have experienced these dark and insidious influences on many occasions I must admit the deficiency of never being able to fully anticipate them.

These same influences that I feel about us now were the prime instigators of my downfall in Kansas. Then as now, I am sad to admit, I was naïve and uninformed and unaware of their presence—until they struck me with the force of a falling star. Perhaps it is simply not in my nature, but despite all effort, I have never been able to foresee a political snare before I have placed my foot inside it.

In the years since that summer of destiny in Kansas I have learned to defeat the Indian foe, but enemies in the halls of power have always remained one step ahead. I can only surmise that I have never learned the game because I have never held the cards that have been dealt to me from on high. But I have played them dutifully, perhaps too much so.

I am still haunted by what happened in Kansas because I feel as vulnerable at this moment as I was then, possibly even more so.

I have previously described the events that took place in Kansas, but always in a way that revealed little, while catering to the appetite of the popular reader. But now I am writing for myself and hope that through the process of putting it down, I can somehow wash out the ghost of the past.

I was told by Colonel Smith to get back on the next train and return to Fort Riley, there to remain under house arrest while the legal machinery that would manufacture my court-martial began its long, slow grind.

Libbie and I sat together on the train, at one moment unable to believe the bombshell that had landed in the center of our lives, at others fully outraged that it had landed at all. Whence the bomb had come and how serious its damage might be were questions we could not answer then. But we resolved from the beginning to assume a public face of confidence.

While we could not pretend that nothing had happened we were determined that our family and friends and especially strangers would not look upon us as suffering victims. We vowed to one another that, whatever we might face in the future, our heads would remain high.

Lack of information actually worked in our favor at the outset, and by the time we alighted from the train at Fort Riley we found ourselves in surprisingly good spirits.

For all those who might be cheering our misfortune we felt certain that there were just as many who would come to our defense. The charges might be dropped or squashed. It was up to Ulysses Grant, at that time general of the army, to order the court-martial, an action he might be disinclined to take. It was still early in the game, and we maintained our good spirits as we settled into the neat little house that had been the scene of "our one perfect day."

But as the long hours of high summer passed one into another, the news that arrived day after day on our doorstep gave little hope for bright prospects ahead.

The large picture of the circumstances that resulted in this calamity soon became clear. I realized with ever increasing certainty that I had unwittingly become entangled in a complex web from which it was unlikely I would be able to extricate myself.

In a short time I was able to learn that Colonel Smith had not brought charges against me wholly of his own volition. He had acted at the insistence of General Hancock. Why the commander of the expedition would be so eager to prefer charges on what amounted to a technicality was more readily understandable when I began to bring myself up to date on news of the nation.

The eastern papers had carried almost daily reports of a national debate that had commenced simultaneously with the start of the spring and summer campaign. Initially the debate was confined to bickering over the muddled peace policy toward the Indians, but as the expedition plodded on without success, the displeasure of each political side quickly produced a war of words that reached national proportion.

Some members of Congress inflamed the electorate with charges that the Hancock Expedition was fleecing taxpayers at the rate of one hundred and fifty thousand dollars a day. These claims helped to explain General Sherman's energetic point of view during our series of interviews at Fort McPherson in early June. He had encouraged me repeatedly to engage recalcitrant Indians with any force necessary. Though he made no mention of a national debate at that time, the general had in actuality delivered a political warning which I had failed to hear.

While my command had been concerned only with digging enough water to survive the march to Fort Wallace, national opinion was joining the camp of those who were loudly characterizing the Hancock Expedition as an abject failure. The reverberations of this outpouring reached all the way to the White House, further tarnishing President Johnson's administration on the eve of an election year.

As leader of the expedition, General Hancock made a conspicuous target for the ire of the parties fighting the issue of whether there was to be peace or no peace with the Indians. It was a desperately hot position for the general, and the temptation to deflect attention from himself to an even more conspicuous target proved irresistible. By focusing on one whose name was known in virtually every American household he could, at least momentarily, lower the flames licking at him from every side.

But there was barely time to absorb these revelations before another bomb exploded in our faces. Captain Robert West, long a member of my command and also a strong supporter of the anti-Custer clique, had preferred an additional set of charges. The new complaints concerned the pursuit, the shooting, and the alleged withholding of medical aid from the six deserters, one of whom subsequently died at Fort Wallace.

These new charges shocked everyone. Those in high command now feared a backlash resulting from the increasing public attention on the affair. Shooting deserters had long been tacitly acceptable policy. But because the policy was unwritten and because discretion was observed in all cases, I was powerless to oppose the charges except in military court.

I knew at once what had prompted them. Captain West's membership in the anti-Custer club was a fact that I had long acknowledged without rancor, having learned to accept animosity as a natural feature of military life. It is common knowledge that no commanding officer is universally loved by his troops and that he must accept the reality of detractors as one of the enduring difficulties associated with high responsibility. Captain West was a good soldier who carried out his orders quickly and efficiently, but lamentably he was also one of those whose career and character were deeply compromised by an inability to remove his lips from the mouth of a bottle.

He had been dangerously close to intoxication on several occasions during our march across Kansas and I was not disposed at that time to trust him with more than routine responsibilities. I had ordered him to Wallace to help organize and escort the supply train, but my misgivings based on his love of alcohol were such that I had placed Lieutenant Robbins in authority over Captain West. It was an action I took in consideration of what was best for the entire command, though I knew it would inflame his already considerable hostility toward me.

Whether this hostility had any bearing on his behavior at the time of our safe arrival at Fort Wallace I have no idea, but at that time Captain West became so completely drunk as to be unfit for any kind of duty and I had no choice but to place him under arrest, a development that did little to improve our relations.

A uniform characteristic of the anti-Custer clique has been the unfailing propensity of its members to hold grudges. In Captain West's case I believe he was made brazen by incessant drinking and in a fit of pique brought the serious charges against me. Ultimately they did not amount to much and were nothing but an irritating embarrassment to the military. Any long-lasting effect was suffered by me as it left certain segments of the public convinced that I was inordinately cruel.

All the while, communications poured in and out of our little home at Fort Riley. A constant parade of longtime friends appeared with declarations of support. Now and then a stranger came by to pay a respectful unsolicited call. Handwritten notes from military allies stationed at distant posts appraised me of support or the lack thereof amongst the officers' corps. A number of friends from the East came out that summer to provide moral support, sometimes for weeks on end. Overall, the dilemma kept us so busy that there was little time to dwell on its odious nature.

General Sheridan, who had risen to even greater prominence after the Great War, was in communication with me frequently, reasserting his backing and vowing to do whatever was in his power to exercise a positive influence on the proceedings. There remained between us, however, the unspoken understanding that despite his considerable power, the wheels of this peculiar form of justice might lie beyond his ken.

The editorial columns of the country's newspapers carried a wide range of views concerning the arrest and charges and we followed them closely. Some held the notion that the entire business was nothing but a petty prosecution and would be dismissed immediately, while others could not forgive my early and outspoken support for President Johnson. I was amazed and distressed at the often twisted reporting of the most elemental facts of my case, one paper going so far as to report that I had ordered men shot who I thought *intended* to desert.

I could not help but be burned by the vitriol that was hurled in my direction, and though I maintained a brave face throughout, attacks on my personal character and especially my merits as a soldier made me understandably blue.

Libbie never failed to lift my spirits at down times and constantly reminded me that after facing so many thousands of live rounds I could have little to fear from "paper bullets."

Waiting for General Grant was interminable, but our hopes were finally dashed on August 27th when he ordered the formation of a general court-martial to take place at Fort Leavenworth to begin on September 17th, 1867.

Fort Leavenworth served as district headquarters for General Hancock, and none of us could believe they would go through with the trial so long as he was there. We were right. Five days before the court was to convene, General Hancock was transferred out of the district, which effectively removed him from the hot seat and left me for all practical purposes alone.

General Sheridan was named to replace our late commander, a

development that was well received by almost everyone, though it was clear by this time that in the matter of my own difficulties his hands were tied.

The Indians had increased the scope and ferocity of their raiding since I had been relieved of command and it struck me as ironic that during this time the pendulum of government policy finally began to swing in a distinct direction—that of peace. It was doubly ironic in light of General Sheridan's appointment, for he was considered to be one of the army's most aggressive field commanders, a reputation very like my own.

A West Point classmate of mine, Captain Charles Parsons, had been designated to conduct my defense, and as he and I and Libbie prepared for trial it seemed to all of us that any evidence brought forward would be far less crucial to a final judgment than the composition of the court itself.

While I was technically guilty of leaving my command without authorization—according to Colonel Smith's testimony—such action was practically routine in the course of frontier duty. The underlying aspersion that I had done so solely to be reunited with my wife presented much graver problems, especially if the makeup of the court proved unfriendly.

We barely concerned ourselves with Captain West's charges. No one could imagine that the army would be prepared to discard a long-held policy for the sake of prosecuting me and none of us thought they would chance putting Captain West, who was now in the throes of delirium tremens, on the stand.

As the trial began and the composition of the court was revealed, our worst fears were confirmed. Of its ten members, half had served previously on General Hancock's staff. One of the remaining officers was attached to the Commissary Department and had been the recipient of complaints from me on many, many occasions. Even more disturbing was the fact that several of the officers selected to sit in judgment were subordinate to me in rank, a condition clearly contrary to military rules.

We objected most strenuously to this last discrepancy, but like our other objections it was quickly quashed and the trial went forward.

Though I felt from the outset that I would be convicted, the effort in making our defense consumed me to such a degree that I could not help but have my hopes raised. For more than three weeks I threw myself into the life of a defendant; keenly following the testimony of every witness, framing the questions posed to them and recording every nuance of the panel which sat in judgment. So deeply did I immerse myself in the proceedings that after a short time I felt I had lived my whole life behind the long, worn desk that sat upon a polished wooden floor of that barren room in an austere building on the grounds of Fort Leavenworth.

Occasionally I would glance out a window and lose myself momentarily in the turning of the season. Even the natural cycle of the earth seemed against me. The dismal campaign of summer had ended. With the coming of winter the hostiles would cease their raiding and the army would also cut back its operations. From a military point of view I had never felt so expendable.

There were few surprises as the days dragged on. The only events that slowed the ponderous wheels of justice were the sporadic absences of members of the court. Even the defendant contributed to the slowdown when a large boil developed and had to be lanced twice, causing a two-day delay while I recovered.

As the trial lumbered to a conclusion, I turned to the task of composing a final statement of defense, an effort made incredibly difficult by the persistent conviction that it was a hollow exercise. Each succeeding day of the trial had increased my belief that the court was preoccupied with making a political ruling rather than a judicial one and that no evidence, no matter how compelling, would dissuade them from this course.

My statement of defense, which Captain Parsons read so eloquently, was quite long. It is of no use now to reiterate it all—the testimony of the trial's each day is written down for anyone to see.

But I have carried the last words of my statement to this day for they adequately summarize my feelings and I believe the document itself serves as a far better reflection of my true heart than any memory I can record now.

After recounting in respectful and most thorough terms the absurdity of the charges against me I closed with the following.

"I have never been once absent from my command without leave as here charged. I have never wearied or in any way made use of my men for the advancement of my private wishes or interests—as here charged—or severely tasked any living creature as here charged, except under a sense of duty.

"I have never made use of any government conveyance, as here charged, except such as was universally conceded to be the right of an officer. I have never turned away from our enemy, as here charged, or failed to relieve an imperiled friend, as here charged, or left unburied or without having provided for the burial of a single fallen man under my command, as here charged. Or took upon myself the responsibility of a single summary action that did not seem to be demanded by the occasion, as here charged. Or finally, ever saw a man in any strait suffer when by my authority I could relieve him, as here charged.

"So if I felt guilty of all or one of the Charges or Specifications, it is an era of my life of which I am not conscious."

The verdict was guilty on all charges; the sentence: suspension of rank and pay for one year. The judgment was automatically forwarded to General Grant for review and a month later he issued a communiqué in which he not only concurred with the judgment but went on to express surprise at the leniency of the sentence, a comment that only added insult to the injury.

While the shock of what had taken place affected both of us deeply, Libbie and I resolved again to give no one the pleasure of relegating us to the status of pariahs. Though I was out of the army we decided to stay at Leavenworth for a time. If nothing else, we could demonstrate publicly that we were undefeated, at least until General Sheridan's arrival.

No reverse has ever affected me for very long and I cannot recall a single setback during my life on earth that has not fired me with an intense resolve to overcome. Being found guilty of charges that many in military and civilian sectors alike thought never should have been brought in the first place only stiffened my determination to rise again. My deepest secret heart burned with desire to meet and overcome what I perceived as a challenge rather than a defeat. If given the opportunity to return I knew I would do so with a powerful renewal of enthusiasm and fighting spirit.

That said, I should also admit that Libbie and I lived a double life for most of the next year. Outwardly we entertained military friends and a ceaseless number of guests from the East with our usual good humor. The lighthearted environment we created and maintained had the desired effect on those with whom we came in contact.

I was constantly reassured by officers, junior and senior, by journalists and ingenues and even passersby that my trial and its verdict were preposterous and that it would surely not be long before I was reinstated by a needful army.

Though such sentiments were never discouraged, I quickly wearied of the constant predictions of my glowing future and fought against the temptation to submerge myself in gloom.

The truth of the situation as I saw it was far more tenuous than most people thought. When there was peace in the house or when we were alone in bed I often drifted into a contemplative mood which I could hide from everyone but Libbie, who kept vigil over my dark moods and worked diligently to abort them.

While I knew her efforts were heartfelt, they irritated me more and more. She constantly asked to be apprised of my innermost thoughts, and the more she asked, the more suffocated I became. I wanted so badly to let my wounds heal, to open the gates of grief and let the resulting flood wash my sorrow away. If it had been up to me I would have traveled to some far corner of the globe, there to sit in silence until my wounds had closed. But the double life we had constructed and the fact of our marriage itself precluded such action.

I was now a general without a command, an inactive soldier with no means of supporting his family whose future, despite the assurances of friends and family, was veiled. I was a national hero who had suddenly been removed from the stage and spotlight, not by virtue of death in battle but by the stigma of wrongdoing. I was left to smile through clenched teeth with the hope that somehow my suspension would be lifted. On the surface I was the same old devil-may-care Autie but just beneath I was rudderless, bitter, and sad. My reputation and my rank, all that I truly owned, had been taken from my hands and locked away. On the outside I busied myself with presenting a positive outlook. On the inside, I loathed each minute of each day.

General Sheridan arrived to take command in December and his first act was one of amazing and chivalrous charity which has endeared him to me and my family ever since. He insisted that Libbie and I occupy his official residence at Fort Leavenworth, an act of kindness that boosted our morale immensely, for it was a supremely symbolic gesture, demonstrating to all that one of the highest-ranking generals of the army stood behind me and mine.

Privately General Sheridan told me that he desired my return to his command as soon as possible, going so far as to say that I was indispensable to him in the field and that he could never hope to make definitive plans without me, that doing so would be like carving meat with a spoon.

He advanced the view that my own troubles had come at an ironically fortuitous time. The clamor for peace had produced a presidential commission that had recently held a great council with the southern tribes of Cheyenne, Sioux, Arapaho, Kiowa, and Comanche at a place called Medicine Lodge in Oklahoma. This council, which took place shortly after my sentence had been handed down, produced a treaty that was hailed in the East as a significant step toward peace but was looked upon by those who had experienced the frontier as a complete sham.

The signatories did not include many of the leading chiefs. Hundreds of thousands of dollars in presents, annuities, and firearms had been lavished on the savages but in return the government received only the same vague promises to behave that I had witnessed firsthand during the previous summer.

Those of us with experience knew that despite the sincere avowal of peaceful intentions by the signatories, several facets of Indian behavior remained incontrovertible.

Any peace was destined to be made entirely of paper, for no single tribe had great influence over another. Even in the smallest bands, democracy was carried to what white civilization saw as ludicrous extremes. The old men, no matter their standing or sagacity, had utterly no control over younger members of their groups. And every Indian male whom I had ever encountered is trained from the moment of birth to become an instrument of war. General Sheridan knew, I knew, and every man on the plains, in uniform and out, knew that when the grass was up and the ponies were fat, great numbers of Indian men and boys would be on the warpath. Treaty or no treaty.

General Sheridan was certain that General Grant was going to run for president, that he had an even chance of winning, and that he would without doubt run on a platform of peace. That eventuality combined with the recently signed treaty at Medicine Lodge was sure to bind the hands of the military.

Neither I nor General Sheridan thought that peace could possibly last. But our private thinking was of no import. If the peace held, all sides would be satisfied. If it collapsed it would do so only over time. General Sheridan therefore had to content himself with keeping the troops in a stage of readiness and he advised me to take what advantage I could of my enforced absence. He subtly suggested that

I look around the wider world and see what it had to offer, cautioning me at the same time to temper my forays into civilian life.

When the time came, he would call and was counting on me to serve. I told him in the most forthright manner that nothing on earth could deter me from answering such a summons.

JUNE 11-15,

1876

I am camp-bound, a condition which in previous years my restless spirit would have rebelled against. In times gone by I would have been mad with frustration, but now, though I can still feel the power of that restless spirit pulling at its tether, I am old enough and wise enough to keep the hand I have been dealt close to my chest while I observe the antics of the other players.

General Terry has marched off to the northwest with a small escort, seeking the steamer *Far West* and Colonel Gibbon's Montana Column, now said to be bivouacked on the banks of the Yellowstone in the vicinity of the Tongue River.

There has been contact by messenger with Colonel Gibbon's column and enough information has seeped through to provide us with a few disturbing portents. Colonel Gibbon's column has been camped in the same general area for some time. It is apparent that he has forsaken several opportunities to strike the enemy, upholding instead the basic strategy of this expedition: that the mammoth proportions of the three columns, his, ours, and Crook's, will converge in some kind of ordered symmetry to enclose and crush the free roamers.

The odds of perfecting what is now on paper are at best minuscule, and my intuition, based on long experience, tells me that Gibbon has squandered any chance of dealing an early, decisive blow that would have the hostiles off balance as we came in for the kill.

General Terry has gone ahead to obtain a first-hand impression of Gibbon and his column but what kind of appraisal he is capable of making remains a mystery to me. I like Terry and I know I owe him a debt, for it was he, more than anyone else, who helped clear away my latest political difficulties. In fact, without his steadfast insistence I might not have been commanding the Seventh this summer.

But I think that he is a commander whose time these last few years has been spent too much behind a desk. Yesterday he came to me with the declaration that, instead of continuing our march westward, he had decided to make a long and thorough search of the Powder River Valley, a scout requiring many days of riding over country I am certain contains no Indians and will only waste more valuable time.

I believe I know why General Terry is cautious and I respect his situation. He can feel the eyes of Sheridan and Sherman and President Grant fixed on his backside. As a distinguished career officer he knows that one false step and he could find himself tumbling head first into the abyss, never to emerge again.

No matter how necessary it might be, I despise the reality of chains of command, the implacable system that fosters hesitancy and indecision, for I think on balance it forfeits more lives in combat than it saves.

Perhaps it amounts to nothing more than a clash of styles, but I fail to see what can be gained by searching every inch of ground for a foe who everyone knows has long since moved on.

I did not deign to change the mind of my commander, but when he expressed the desire that I lead this vacuous scout I respectfully declined, suggesting that Major Reno—who could make use of the experience, for he has practically none—lead it instead. General Terry assented and Reno is now gone, having taken half the Seventh Cavalry and Bloody Knife with him.

The question that bothers me more than all the others put together is, where can General Crook be? His column is marching up from the south along the Rosebud River but we have not heard a single word from him. Crook is known as an eccentric but at the same time is one of our most experienced and competent commanders, a man who under normal circumstances would not fail to keep his counterparts informed of his whereabouts.

For the moment I have been left alone to ponder these perplexing developments, but while I am becalmed I could not have ordered up a more pleasant spot in which to bide my time. The men who have remained with me have been allowed to deviate from the normal formalities of camp. Many have pitched their tents under sheltering branches of trees along the clear, cold stream called Mizpah Creek. Because we are holding here there is no scouting to be done. Sentry duty is light for there are no Indians of any kind in our locale. I will probably take a hunting party out this afternoon. I say "probably" because I too have succumbed to the sleepy, bucolic quality of life in this pleasant little camp.

The men who can write are busy composing letters. Others have settled down to card games, large and small, some of which are not likely to stop until we resume the march. Most of the band members are busy cleaning or reconditioning their instruments and impromptu bursts of melody are sailing overhead, as if the air itself were made of music. Most of the men have been at the stream toiling as laundresses and I have just ordered those who have not been to the stream to become better acquainted with the wondrously hygienic qualities of soap and water.

Because these June days have become very hot more of the men have taken to jumping in and out of the bracing creek at all hours. Just now someone has looped a length of hemp over a strong, low-hanging branch and a competition has ensued to determine who can swing most often over the water. Judging from the whoops and hollers, I would say many of them are landing a little short of the mark.

In this country, where water is plentiful, there are mountain trout and the camp skillets have been filled with tender filets of fish from the moment of our arrival.

I am situated alone, on a beautiful green bench of grass next to the creek. I cut a willow branch for a pole, had John Burkman procure a length of twine, a suitable hook, and some bits of meat and here I lie transformed.

No longer am I Autie, the fighting general who would normally be in the saddle, urging Dandy to the top of some summit just to take a look through the field glass. No, there is none of that. I am now Autie the contented angler, glancing every so often at my fishing apparatus in hopes of seeing movement at the tip of the pole.

Fishing, however, requires far more patience than resides in me. This is the first time I can remember trying it since the summer of 1868, a recollection that stimulates the recall of many poignant fragments of the past.

Libbie and I remained at Fort Leavenworth until the end of May 1868. How I managed to stay that long is a feat for which I cannot account. The winter had been pleasant in the extreme, a dizzying social season that did much to blunt the unhappy conclusion of the court-martial.

But the coming of spring and the attendant stirring it prompted in military ranks made me more and more uneasy. Despite many sacrifices to the altar of peace, word of new depredations perpetrated by wild Indians began to filter in at the first warming of the earth and increased as the prairie bloomed.

I knew that as a fighting general, Sheridan would not tolerate these outrages but would do everything in his power to punish those who were guilty and as spring reached its height, I noticed a certain look of intensity forming in his eyes, which materialized in an awakening of the troops. From that time on, each day saw more preparation for a summer campaign.

To be suspended was bad enough but to stand by was more than I could bear, for to be a passive observer of such events is the most frustrating role I could ever conceive of for myself. Put in the extreme, I would have to say that I would rather die in a battle than watch one take place.

Living in close proximity to purgatory was impossible and in early June Libbie and I found ourselves on the train east, rolling toward a long, bittersweet summer in our hometown of Monroe, Michigan.

It was to be our first summer of discontent as a couple. Libbie carried on in her irrepressibly cheerful manner but I could not keep up. It was as though I had been reduced to parts of myself and though I tried valiantly, I could not restore the whole. As day after monotonous day passed, I felt the parts gradually disintegrating.

There was but one way to redeem the life I loved and that was blocked by powers I could neither understand nor control. I had been relieved of the right to risk myself, the right to chance victory or defeat, and I simply could not envision life without it.

I never thought of suicide but I was deeply despondent, languishing in a kind of spiritual swamp from which all hope of escape seemed futile. Of course Libbie was aware of my slump and did all she could to lift me out of it. I loved her for her efforts despite their being largely unsuccessful.

We had contentious moments during that long summer, but the sum of many difficult times seemed to forge an even stronger bond between us.

Libbie honed the art of approach and at the end of summer had become an expert at determining when she should come close and when she should leave me alone.

For my part, I was taught that my problems and the self-absorption that accompanied them had limits.

No wife could love a husband more, nor could any wife be more devoted, and yet it was Libbie who, at a certain interval, informed me that she had grown tired of my dilemma and its effect on our lives. She suggested that I might take a first step in improving my outlook if I were to turn my thoughts to something other than myself. "*Anything* but yourself" is, I believe, how she put it.

While Libbie and I kept a tenuous hold on our relationship I did the best I could with the outside world. It was sweet to see so many old friends and family, but I quickly became aware that people had two basic reactions to my recent problems. One was to show solidarity in proclaiming dismay at the wrongs that I had suffered. This outrage was often spread thicker than I thought necessary. The other reaction was to sidestep the subject altogether.

Occasionally I would discourse at length with a friend or family member, laying everything out for dissection and speculation. But most often I was only made self-conscious and uncomfortable, by both those who were eager to make reference to my troubles and those who were not. In time I realized that the only antidote was to distance myself from events of the recent past. Without abandoning society I withdrew as much as possible.

This desire for detachment brought me often to the banks of the Raisin River, a lazy, pleasant stream close to town. I would leave early in the morning several days a week, taking the dogs along for company.

In addition to the requisite fishing gear I carried pen, paper, and ink with which to begin the task of writing my memoirs. While I proved to be a rather delinquent angler I made much effort and considerable progress in translating the thoughts in my head to a succession of words scratched on paper.

Being a neophyte in such pursuits I lacked confidence and wrote not so much with an eye for truth or beauty as with a desire to entertain the reader, a strategy that I hoped would impress the publisher and enhance, or a least keep alive, my standing in the public mind. In the years since, I have succeeded quite admirably, having published a score of articles and a book of memoirs relating to the events of my early years of service on the frontier.

But these efforts pale when compared to what I am recording now. For now, here on the banks of Mizpah Creek five hundred miles from anywhere, I am writing with no anticipation of reward. I am writing for no purpose other than to unburden myself of all that is swimming in my head. I am writing to be free.

Am I penning a confession? Am I offering a philosophy of life? Am I merely entertaining myself? In years past the why of it would have been paramount but now I find myself caring little about answers. I am more and more content to let all mysteries remained unsolved. Now as never before, the moment is supreme in every way. Now, as never before, it is clear to me that I control practically nothing. Like every other living thing I am but an actor, responding to this stimulus or that. Functioning in this most basic way, whether on a blank page filled with symbols of writing or on a battlefield surrounded by the clamor of combat, I am satisfied and I understand that all I have sought in mortal existence has been nothing more than to draw breath from moment to moment.

Summers in Michigan are invariably hot and humid and toward noon the dogs and I would be making our way back home. The only trophies I ever brought from these expeditions were not the result of any prowess with a pole but rather the result of finding a fish attached to the end of the line as we made ready to leave.

For all the familiarity of Monroe, I could not pass by such well-known structures as the church where we were married without experiencing a tearing in my heart. What a day that was! What glory for us, as a couple and as individuals too. When I looked at the church it would all come back to me.

It was something of a miracle because there were many times when marriage between us seemed as remote as anything on earth.

When I returned to the Great War after meeting Judge Bacon at his club I was still forbidden at that time even to write to Libbie. At every free moment I wrote to a third party, a trusted woman friend of ours, who I knew would share every word with my beloved. Though I did not know it then, most of a year would pass before we were married and in that span our togetherness, or lack of such, we had many ups and downs.

There were moments at which I questioned the very rightness of our union. And there were moments when I was disenchanted with its tiresome complications. Sherman has always said that any struggle lacking monumental hardship is a struggle not worth making and in hindsight it is clear to me that the trials to which our courtship was subjected were indispensable to a lasting bond.

There is one instance I well remember. In fact, the instance was so telling that I think it approached some form of art. I have often thought that, were I able to paint, I might try to paint that moment. But if I were able to put such a thing on canvas, patrons would most likely run screaming from the gallery.

In the youthful manner of being bluntly honest I had told Libbie most of my past. I told her freely that I had always loved women and that the feeling had often been mutual. Some of these former liaisons had been with Monroe girls, and though I tried to skim over my romantic history, once the curtain opened the die was cast.

At first Libbie said nothing of it and I naïvely thought the matter was closed. But it was clear from her letters that my admissions were nettlesome in the extreme. Over hundreds of miles and the risky mails I tried to influence her thoughts in a positive way, but no amount of furious writing and explaining on my part seemed able to keep up with developments.

The gossip was extraordinary—it always has been—and for every rumor or disparaging remark extinguished several more instantly popped up to take its place. I was engaged in war with my sword on one front and my pen on another.

The moment I remember with painful clarity occurred on a day so inclement that the light that marks the waking hours remained gray as slate. I was still a captain, but General Pleasanton had put me in command of a large reconnaissance unit. Speed was always paramount with such groups and in this case we pushed to finish our routine mission in hope of beating the rain, which promised to turn every road into a quagmire.

We had just gone into camp for the noon meal when the gray mantle of cloud overhead began to boil and turn black. The skies opened in the most gentle way, and as I sat inside a newly erected tent, which had been pitched under an enormous tree, I marveled at the simple beauty of the even, falling rain.

I had been carrying a letter of Libbie's for twenty-four hours without opening it. Sometimes I gulped down her letters as soon as they came into my hand, sometimes I made it a test of will to see how long I could endure the excruciating torture of carrying one unopened against my chest. On this occasion I had waited for what I tried to guess as the perfect moment. There had been many tensions recently and I was hopeful of a love letter. The tent under the big tree in the rain seemed a promising locale and I was pleased when my orderly laid a plate of cold food before me, then dashed back into the rain from which he had come, allowing me a few moments alone with the letter.

I had held it to my nose many times already and though I knew the scent of her was no longer there I could not resist the ritual of breathing it in again.

I tended to be careful with the envelope, making every effort to keep from tearing it more than was absolutely necessary. If I happened to tear off some little jagged fragment I kept it. I kept everything.

The storm that broke that afternoon was overwhelming, the kind of natural display that humbles everyone and everything. In the few minutes I had been inside the tent the rain had gone from little more than a mist to a deafening deluge. As I pulled the letter out of the envelope I noticed that enough water had accumulated to turn the surface of the earth into a vast pool. Each raindrop could be read clearly as it struck the surface of the water.

I dropped my eyes onto the first page of the letter and my heart dropped with them. There were no words of longing or desperate love. The letter began, "I have met this Mary Kelly and after speaking with her at some length, I can say without reservation that if I am ever to make her acquaintance again it shall be entirely too soon."

Unfortunately I knew only too well what was going to follow. Mary Kelly was a handsome, rather strong-willed young lady whom I had known since my days at the Point. While still in school our knowledge of each other had become quite intimate during visits home on holidays and in the summer.

I had given Mary an oval picture of myself set in a locket, which she frequently wore about her neck. Our relationship never quite caught fire, but Mary was fond of reminding me that she had a claim on my heart, the proof of which hung about her neck.

It was obvious that she had now informed Libbie and I paused in my reading of the letter, certain that it would contain little of the romantic sentiments I craved.

It is likely that I would have paused anyway, for it was impossible now to ignore the tumultuous power of the rain. The water falling from the sky came in cascades and I was no longer able to see more than a few feet in front of the tent. Nothing could be heard but the incessant roar of the downpour.

As I sat wondering how the canvas over my head could withstand this heavenly punishment my eye was drawn to an irregularity that had appeared on the ground close to my shelter. Through the curtains of rain I could see that something was emerging from the watery soil. I let my gaze travel and discovered that the rain was washing the earth away from more objects, also close by.

I had to see what was being revealed and, leaving Libbie's letter under the plate of half-eaten cold cuts, I let my steps carry me out into the flood.

The hammering of the rain made it hard to see. I squatted next to one of the objects and, shielding my brow with an arm, dipped my face close to the ground. At that instant I found myself staring into the smiling, half exposed skull of a soldier whose shallow grave the rain had washed away. The remnants of a uniform jacket gave proof that he had belonged to the ranks of our enemy. By now I was soaked to the skin but I continued to stand in the rain, staring at the other corpses of fallen Confederates who had been hastily buried after some fight of the previous year.

I slogged back into the tent and sat alone in contemplation of the ironies that now seemed to surround me. The letter from my love was somehow devoid of love. My plate was filled with the dead meat that would nourish me so that I could venture forth and turn more of the living into the dead. I was myself perched atop a boneyard. I wondered whether we would have to kill all the Confederates before the war could come to an end. Perhaps everyone would have to die before there could be peace.

All this as the rain poured down as if it would not stop until it had exposed the bones of the earth itself.

I thought of the melancholy Danish prince and his quandary. For a few moments I understood exactly why Hamlet felt overpowered. What purpose could action possibly serve in a world of careening madness?

A rider suddenly appeared out of the rain. He was coming straight for my tent and I could see that his head was bent, taking notice as he rode past the skeletons blooming in my front yard.

He was a young courier who stepped up to the entrance of my tent with the classic white-washed expression of one who has seen the dead. Wordlessly he handed me a dispatch, which I opened and read on the spot. General Pleasanton was ordering my command to report immediately to a sector twenty miles distant.

I looked up and met the openmouthed face of the courier, who was now regarding me as though I might also be one of the dead. I do not believe one muscle of my face moved as I said, "Thank you, soldier . . . you are dismissed. And take care not to step on any of our friends out there."

He and his horse receded into the rain and as they faded from sight I rose from my stool and stretched my stiff, cold limbs.

Prince Hamlet had found himself unable to act. I understood his dilemma and I knew its precise antidote. I walked into the rain, shouting for my orderly and my horse.

This was but one of an inexhaustible stream of memories that would rise like clouds in my head on those hot summer days when the dogs and I paused across the street from the whitewashed church in Monroe.

My canine friends and I would plop down in the shade of an old elm and I could not gaze at the stately steeple or hear the bell that pealed on our wedding day without marveling at the succession of miracles wrought by the purest fate, which had brought us together as man and wife on the evening of February 9, 1864.

I think Libbie would freely admit if asked by anyone that she had no intention of marrying me, primarily because of her father's adamant opposition. Even after I was made general she did not entertain any but the most fleeting ideas concerning matrimony to me. For Libbie it was not only out of the question, it was out of her mind.

Not so for me. I knew that the judge could not fail to take strong heed of my rapid rise through the officer ranks. And I knew that the word must have come to him as national news, making it all the more impressive.

Achieving the rank of general was and probably will remain the pivotal event of my military life. That single moment seemed to stand everything on its head. Whatever confidence or advantage I lacked in life was made whole when that silver star was sewn onto my navy shirt. I believe it made me bold enough, despite so many negative signs, to pursue Libbie.

The drive to have her was not based on anything but blind, overpowering, and I suppose completely irrational need. I had to make Elizabeth Bacon my wife, this despite the fact that I could discourse for many hours on all the qualities of our love and courtship and marriage without revealing a precise explanation of why it had to be.

Several months after receiving my star another horse was killed from under me and I myself was wounded in the thigh by shrapnel from the same bomb. The wound was slight but it was in a position that did now allow me to sit a horse. I raced home to Monroe with a fortnight's worth of leave.

What followed was at the time an ordeal, but in retrospect appears as a succession of comedic scenes, each outdoing its predecessor. The saving grace of it all was that, if I did not obtain everything I wanted, I did take a large enough step to make the prize of marriage to Libbie inevitable.

I forced myself to remain patient through the obligatory reunion with my family and the circle of old friends surrounding it but inwardly all I could think of was the moment when I might see Libbie again.

The day after my arrival I contacted our go-between and discovered to my despair that Libbie and her family were not even in town but were visiting relatives upstate. Just as quickly I discovered that the Bacons were due back the following day, but to my great consternation two more days passed before I was able to see her, an event that came about only after I took the desperate and extraordinary step of attending Sunday services.

I timed my arrival to the last possible moment and was successful in making a dramatic entrance, which turned the heads of the many who were in attendance, including Libbie, her father, and her stepmother. Tossing all caution aside, I nodded at Libbie and fixed my eyes on her for several seconds before her face flushed crimson and she turned away.

I found a seat across the aisle—everyone wanted to make room for a hometown general in full dress uniform—on roughly the same line as the Bacons. The service then commenced and I was forced to sit still through a one-and-a-half-hour sermon on the virtues of neighborliness, which put my immediate neighbor, a white-haired gentlemen of advanced age, into a sound sleep.

As the preacher's words spilled from the pulpit in an unvarying drone I strained the edges of my left eye constantly in an effort to maintain surveillance of the Bacon family. The judge himself was nearest me and whenever we made eye contact he looked quickly away, as if frightened. I only caught sight of Libbie once or twice, and both times I found her pale face staring straight ahead as though in a trance.

When the singing of hymns began I noticed the judge in sudden contemplation of his pocket watch. After a flurry of words spoken to his wife and daughter he suddenly rose and departed the church. For an instant I thought of following him, but I could see Libbie's profile clearly now and decided to stay where I was.

At last mercy prevailed and the services concluded, at which point every person jammed into the church rose as one and, forsaking normal rules of courtesy, streamed for the nearest exit.

As luck would have it, Libbie and her stepmother reached the center aisle ahead of me and I nearly broke an old woman's foot trying to catch up with them. I half-dragged the old lady along with me as I made profuse apologies, a tactic that had the happy result of placing me in close proximity to Libbie's ear.

"I have to see you," I whispered.

Though I knew she had heard me, Libbie stared straight ahead.

"I came all the way from the front just to see you."

Her face reddened again and she sighed in an angry, rather resigned manner.

Near the front of the church she paused, said something to her stepmother that I could not hear, and made a sudden right turn, following several others of the congregation into an adjacent cloakroom. After a few moments' hesitation, which I filled in accepting the well-wishes of those passing by me, I followed.

There were two or three citizens already inside retrieving their overcoats and hats, but I could not see Libbie anywhere. With absently muttered words of innocuous salutation I drifted toward the far end of the long, narrow closet; once there I was startled at the appearance of a female hand that emerged from somewhere in the apparel along the wall and tugged at my sleeve.

Like a player in a child's fantasy I was pulled through the clothing and into a hidden antechamber. The tiny room was illuminated by a shaft of winter sunshine coming from a skylight far overhead.

"I want to marry you," I said.

She pursed her lips in frustration but said nothing.

"Do you want to marry me?" I asked.

"Oh, I don't even know."

"You don't?"

"It's not the issue, Autie. The fact is, I can't even think of marrying you so long as my father disapproves."

"What does he say?"

"He says," she sighed, "that he doesn't want his daughter living a soldier's life."

"It's just not a soldier's life anymore, it's a general's life. Isn't he impressed with that?"

"Oh, he's very impressed."

"Well?"

"Well you have to talk to him about it, Autie, not me."

I knew suddenly that my love was a young, confused girl under a heavy strain. How could she be expected to keep her feelings clear if the future was clouded? Her wet eyes mirrored her distress.

"I have to kiss you," I said.

"Well, hurry up."

She was gone before the magic of her kiss in the cloakroom had worn off. Now it was I who was confused. I stood alone in the shaft of winter light we had so recently shared and wondered how something so simple and natural as falling in love could be so draining and complicated.

For the next week Judge Bacon was as elusive a quarry as I have ever had to track. I waited outside the Governor's Club each afternoon, but the esteemed judge neither came nor went so far as I know. I shadowed his offices but there was no sign of him. Twice I called at the house but was told by servants that the judge was not inside and that the hour of his arrival was unknown.

On the second futile visit I was walking away from the judge's domicile when I happened to glance between houses and saw an individual whom I could swear was him driving away down an alley in a buggy.

The frustrations of these maddening days made for sleepless nights and as the time drew near for my return to the war my outlook became gloomy and my temper ill.

Finally I barged into the judge's office but found only a clerk who was certain that the judge had left town.

I had told myself that I would accept nothing less than a tête-à-tête with my prospective father-in-law but there was no choice for me but to settle for something less. In a hot and hasty scrawl I penned a note and left it in the clerk's hand. He assured me that he would personally pass it on to the judge. The note was nothing more than a plea to meet but it seemed childish to leave a trivial piece of paper to do my fighting for me.

As I was leaving, the clerk plaintively asked for my signature. I almost said no just to spite the judge, but I signed a blank sheet of paper for him anyway and in the end was glad I had done so. The boy's greatest dream had been to serve the Union, but having been lame from birth, he had been rejected. His joy at having acquired my autograph was such that I left the office feeling good about something for the first time in days.

And yet there was no use fooling myself. A morose pall followed me like unhappy weather the last forty-eight hours of my leave. Short of prostrating myself on the judge's walkway I had exhausted every conceivable method of moving my courtship forward. At this point my spirits had dipped so low that I tried to push thoughts of Libbie from my mind, but even at that I was unsuccessful.

Still fully encased in my little cloud of depression, I found myself waiting on the platform for the eastbound train, wishing and dreaming that Libbie would somehow appear as she had before.

Considering the sadness of the moment one can only imagine my surprise at seeing the figure of Judge Bacon suddenly appear on the platform, walking toward me with an outstretched hand and the closest approximation of a smile I had ever seen on his face.

"I only returned this afternoon," he said congenially. "This isn't the best place to meet but I suppose it will have to do for now."

I was too addled to make an immediate reply. I had been so certain that the judge was avoiding me, and now this . . . not the slightest hint of avoidance.

"Let me add my congratulations to everyone else's on your promotion to general," he added happily.

"Thank you, sir," I replied rather dumbly.

The train had rolled in with the judge's appearance and we were now engulfed by the ingress and egress of passengers.

"Was there anything urgent?" the judge asked.

The moment of truth had come at last. I looked the elder Bacon in the eye as my every muscle stiffened with resolve.

"I wish to have the honor of writing to your daughter, sir."

The judge arched an eyebrow, widened his eyes, and shook his head in a most pleasant manner.

"Why, that would be fine, General Custer, absolutely fine."

We said our good-byes and I got on the train as it pulled out.

For the first hour I stared out at the passing countryside in glassy-eyed shock. How could I have been completely wrong about the judge's avoiding me? Had some event or someone's intervention worked the change on his mind? Had Libbie made some dark and desperate threat? Had a piece of the sky fallen and struck him on the head?

As it turned out I never asked the judge about it and he never volunteered an explanation. The mystery went into the grave with him. Anyway, I was too excited to give it much more thought and by the time the train reached the station in Washington I had three letters to post.

In the months that followed Libbie and I kept up a rapid-fire correspondence. I know that many of our letters survive, but they do not capture, in feeling or in quantity, the depth of our writing. The more we wrote the more we became consumed with thoughts of love in the midst of war.

The fighting continued almost without pause. Casualties were enormous and no cavalry unit suffered more than the Third Division, which I now commanded. To be so fully in love in such an atmosphere was shattering. There were moments when the anguish of separation and the thought of our never being together made me want to cry out.

I wrote the judge asking for Libbie's hand in marriage, and after waiting and waiting for a reply to the first letter was at last unable to resist writing a second. I wrote everyone else I could think of asking for news of the judge.

At last I received a reply. The letter was filled with references to his late wife and her wishes as concerned the upbringing of Libbie—which to my mind had been accomplished. His letter went on to speak of my own virtues and the confidence he placed in me as a soldier and a man. But nowhere could I find a clear answer to my request. The only near mention of it was a cryptic line that said he would soon be speaking to Libbie on a matter concerning us all.

I grabbed the first piece of paper I could find and wrote my request again, this time in the boldest terms I could think of: "May I have the honor of marrying your daughter and becoming your son-in-law?" I signed the one-sentence letter, put it in the hands of a reliable man, and directed him personally to ride the letter to the nearest, urban post, all the way to Washington, D.C., if necessary.

The judge's reply had to be affirmative and in the spirit of planning for success I sought out General Pleasanton with a request for leave in order to return home to be married.

Initially he laughed at this, saying that if I could deliver into his hands Jeb Stuart I could have all the leave I desired. I pressed the matter, and though he understood my seriousness, he pointed out two hard facts to me.

The Third Division was filled with green recruits who had to be trained and General Pleasanton had already made plans to be absent through most of the winter, meaning I would have to stay, since we could not both be gone.

Any plans I wanted to make concerning marriage would have to commence at some point beyond his return in early February. And then I would have to be swift, for the spring campaign would practically be upon us. If I was to be married I had a very small window to crawl through.

Frustration marked my every step that winter. Libbie and I wrote each other almost every day, but Christmas 1863 and New Year's Day 1864 came and went without any physical contact. The old, bad feeling that she might slip away crept back into my heart and I felt certain that unless we married soon we might never marry at all. In all aspects of young love, doubt seems to carry a weight equal to faith. Anyway, it did in my case.

In January of 1864 I finally received Judge Bacon's assent, a development that threw me into new theaters of excitement and action, for now that the road was finally clear I was determined to press ahead at full speed. This is precisely what happened, and the results were astounding.

We had long imagined a quiet ceremony without the usual flair and hysteria that drowns the sweet, simple purpose of the ritual in a maelstrom of endless detail. But our heartfelt desires to avoid this were quickly swept aside by the enormous amount of attention our betrothal received.

The mails fairly burned at my headquarters and from what I could gather this effect rippled out from the circle of family and friends in an ever-widening tide that found its way into every corner of every world with which we had ever had contact.

I was inundated with missives, as was Libbie, and we soon realized that, once set in motion, the machinery that would manufacture our marriage had assumed a life of its own. My reputation, it seemed, had acted as a lightning rod for what became a national interest in our nuptials; before the event of our marriage I had not been aware of the extent to which the national imagination had embraced the legend of "the boy general with the golden curls."

This is not to say that everyone in America came to our wedding, but as the fateful day neared it seemed as if everyone in America wanted an invitation.

The Bacon family was a far more prolific one than I realized. Distant, almost unknown, members of the Bacon tribe, some of them living two or three states away, clamored for invitations.

In my own family, relatives whose actual existence had been unknown to me came forward. Some of these people appeared in person on the home doorstep a day or two prior to the ceremony.

Poor Libbie had to put up with much more than I did. I had the very acceptable excuse of being engaged in a war and leaned on that as justification for my spare and tardy participation in the chaotic attempts to exercise even a modicum of control over preparations.

I left for Monroe charged with the sole responsibility of keeping the dress uniform Libbie had asked me to wear unwrinkled and in my possession. My only other obligations were to plan our get-away—which I had done—and arrive punctually at the scene of our vow taking.

There was little time to assemble any kind of military contingent, but I did succeed in bringing along my adjutant, who was also a

Monroe man, Captain Jacob Greene. He was companionable and efficient as always, providing what was needed and retiring to the rear of the train at every opportunity to practice melancholy tunes on his flute . . . thus leaving me to contemplate what lay ahead.

I contemplated mightily, for I have never been as excited as I was then. As it must be with all grooms, I envisioned every detail of what was to come but could never imagine what was actually about to happen.

We arrived in Monroe late on the evening of February 8, 1864. The platform was brightly lit and thronged with people, whom we quickly learned were there in anticipation of my arrival. I had experienced crowds to some degree and would be lying if I said I did not enjoy being at center of attention, but I was already absorbed by pure emotion on the eve of my marriage and did not think I could bear up under the demands of a well-intentioned mob, the majority of whom were bound to be strangers.

A sympathetic porter showed me and Captain Greene out a door on the other side of the train and we slunk into the night like the fugitives we were, dragging our baggage behind us.

The following twenty-four hours are still opaque in my memory. They play out in recall as colorful fragments, a narcoticlike adventure of sight and sound. My mother's incessant weeping through all the excitement. Tom standing by, a bewildered combination of envy and adulation. My father, lurching in and out of shadow with odd questions and childish pronouncements: "I've been married two times." My sister Lydia and her friends scurrying everywhere like nervous birds. Little Autie Reed, my nephew, clinging to some part of my uniform through every waking hour. And I . . . Old Curly at twenty-four, sitting impatiently in the madness, wanting to be married and nothing else.

People from surrounding communities had come to Monroe in droves. I could never understand—I still don't—how so many people could want to be part of an event with which they have so little connection. I know that the most ordinary citizen can possess a weird desire for the magic dust of celebrity, and while I could enumerate the individual causes of such a craving I still cannot account for the phenomenon itself.

Because the town was swollen with strangers I found myself reluctant to appear in public. But on the afternoon of the wedding, when I could stand being shut up in the house no more, Tom hitched a team to a small buggy and we went for a long ride, I hiding under a blanket until we reached the outskirts of town.

Tom knows my needs as well as anyone and on that special day he rightly perceived that I was starved for the oxygen of open space. We didn't talk a lot and when we did it was mostly superficial. Even so, I detected an undercurrent in Tom's remarks that bespoke a strange duality in his attitude toward me that is present even to this day.

Tom would give his life to protect mine. He would do this unconditionally. At the same time he is convinced that I am somehow the "lucky" brother, the one whose star shines brightest, the one who cannot be bested. This attitude seems composed in equal parts of love and hate. His love has dominated the hate but the presence of both emotions in one mind has always made for a confusion that saddens me.

Typically, in reference to the marriage that evening, he said, "You always get the prettiest and smartest, Autie. I don't know how you do it."

I felt so much for my brother at that moment, though there was nothing I could do for him.

"I don't know either, Tom" was the best reply I could make.

Never have I wanted something to become history so badly as I did my wedding. The bizarreness it produced in my family was nearly unbelievable and because of the enormous public attention I had received since my arrival in Monroe I lived like a criminal in a safe house.

Strangest of all was Libbie herself. I had not seen her in months. I had not heard her voice. I was marrying someone I did not know.

The marriage was based almost exclusively on ideals, not practicalities. It was impossible that such a thing was happening, and yet it was. As the hours melted slowly away all my powers of concentration were focused on having the wedding begin so that it could end.

When it came time for me to wash and dress I did so in a dream. I buttoned buttons, moved the brush through my hair, hung the saber at my side, and through it all felt utterly disconnected, as if I were living something out of my imagination.

Tom and Captain Greene drove me to the church. A block away we could see the light from dozens of lamps illuminating hundreds of spectators crowded outside on the street. Tom guided the team up a back alley, which eventually brought us to the rear of the church.

We jumped out of the buggy and dashed through the backdoor. The room I found myself in was filled with people I did not know and there was an unreal silence as they unanimously dropped what they were doing to stare at the famous groom. How many moments passed before this strange suspension ended and animation returned I cannot remember.

Soon after I was shaking the hand of the pastor, a Dr. Boyd. I introduced Tom and Jacob Greene as my best men, Boyd mentioned something about being honored by my presence—a comment that struck me as oddly inappropriate—and then I saw my father coming toward me, his long white beard covering his new black suit like a bib.

He held out his hand, winked mysteriously, and uttered the words "Good luck, Autie."

All I could think was, "What are you doing back here, father?"

Tom suddenly took me by the hand.

"Autie, you gotta see this," he said, pulling me to a crack in a curtain.

I looked through and saw that the church was overflowing with people. The balcony was full and there was not a seat to be had in any of the pews. People were standing two deep against the rear walls. The noise they made was neither too loud nor too soft but just what might be expected from a large crowd waiting for something to happen.

That I was shortly to appear in front of such an assembly seemed preposterous.

Dr. Boyd sent someone back with the message that all was ready and that I should now make my entrance.

Somewhere in the recesses of my heart I heard a faint appeal to break and run, but even if this foolhardy idea had been a strong one it would have gone unheeded. As it was, I was far too shaky to do any running. Walking was a challenge in itself. My legs seemed to have jellied and I could hear my heart beating as I stepped into the church proper with my brother and Captain Greene.

The candles burning about the pulpit mesmerized me until the music of the Wedding March brought me out of my stupor. Like everyone else in the building, I turned my head and looked back up the aisle to glimpse the bride.

She was coming slowly in the company of her candle-carrying bridesmaids. They hovered near her, washing the bride in the soft light of the flames they held as the party moved inexorably forward with solemn, measured steps.

Libbie was clothed in immaculate white silk, which when joined with the effect of candlelight made her seem an ethereal figure, a haunting, angelic vision spanning all time. Points of light were gleaming in her dark eyes and her small mouth was frozen in an ambiguous smile. A tiara of orange blossoms had been woven into her hair, the crowning glory of an image that tripped my heart and put a catch in my breath. Never had I beheld a sight of such beauty.

Even when I turned away, the sight of her would not leave my mind. It flashed on and off like a heavenly sign, one that I knew would sustain me through all the years of my life.

As Libbie took her place next to me, her radiance effectively blotted out all sight and sound. All through the ceremony I was vaguely aware of the preacher's contented face, less so of the torrent of words he was uttering.

I was waiting only for the "Do you take . . ." question. When I could restrain myself no longer I began to look at Libbie and each time I did the same words jumped into my head: "My bride, my wife, my love, my life." I repeated them until I heard the pastor say, "You may kiss the bride." Then I looked at Libbie, said the words that were in my head out loud and kissed her. It was a long, sweet kiss before hundreds in the church that night and when it was over I awoke as from a sleep, ready to begin life anew.

How many people attended the reception at the Bacon home was not calculated but there were hundreds and I cannot recall a happier gathering.

We were fairly drenched with gifts, and although neither Libbie nor I has ever been a "collector," the outpouring of well-wishes in the form of material objects touched us both. I was deeply moved by the presents of silver that came from the men of my former commands as well of those of the current one.

I did not know one third of the people whose hands closed around mine that night and though the chaos was quite merry I wanted to escape with my bride almost as soon as the party began.

The stupefying image she projected at the ceremony somehow gave way, though she was still in her wedding dress, to a more earthly vision at the reception, and I found my desires shifting in the same way . . . from the spiritual to the earthly. I could see the same shift in Libbie's eyes. There was nothing left to hold on to, nothing left to hold back.

At midnight our wedding party boarded a train for Cleveland and though we were able to steal a fevered kiss from time to time, there were eight in our group, and that plus the excitement of the trip kept everyone sleepless.

It was not until very late the next morning that I was able at last to carry Libbie over the threshold and into a hotel suite. Neither of us had slept much in the last few days but the exhaustion we felt in every drop of our blood was easily overcome by our excitement at finally being alone.

Out of modesty, I turned my back as Libbie got out of her clothes and slipped into bed. I too felt shy but decided to meet the matter head on by facing the bed as I undressed.

This moment had apparently been anticipated by a third party, for when I got to my trousers I found that they could not be unbuttoned. By some magical sleight of hand Tom had glued the fly of my pants shut. The waist was too tight to slip over my hips, and while I tugged and pulled in vain, Libbie's head disappeared under the bed covers with a giggle. It was likely that somewhere in the hotel at that moment Tom was giggling too. I had to laugh as well when left with no choice but to use my saber to slice my way out of the trousers. Then I got into bed with my bride.

We kissed and laughed and talked for some minutes before the kisses and the warmth of our touching carried us irresistibly to a glorious lovemaking of effortless beauty and lust, a lovemaking that removed us for a time from all that we knew of the regular world.

Fully entwined we fell asleep, and when we woke we reenacted the lovemaking that had gone before. Then we fell once more into sleepy oblivion.

Sometime in the afternoon a persistent knocking at the door was followed by a muffled reminder that a dinner in our honor was soon to be held. This interruption set a pattern for our honeymoon trip. We were interrupted at Buffalo, at West Point, at New York City, and at Washington, D.C. We made love whenever possible but were constantly being roused from a new bed, where it seemed we could spend the whole of our lives, to answer the incessant call of the outside world.

It was a completely foreign world to Libbie, but no one could have learned to function in it faster than did my bride. She applied herself to learning the ropes with the spirit of an adventurer. Through every strange stop in every strange town, through every first meeting with every new stranger, her spirits could not be dampened. It made me proud that she would invest so much trust in her husband.

In the beginning her confidence was naturally shaky, but I was amazed to see it grow so quickly, this in spite of the fact that she was a newlywed of limited experience whose travels had barely carried her past the boundaries of her home state. And the wifely role she had to play was performed, out of necessity, in the bright light of the public eye. She was now married to a general of the Union Army, a status that was noted at every waking moment.

Though she always maintained a notable strain of independence and has never been shy about exercising her will, on our first trip she earnestly assumed the role of pupil to mine of tutor, applying herself to the lessons so well that by the time we reached Washington, D.C., she was adept at concealing her naïveté from the predators that inhabit that city.

The politicians, made dangerous by their unwavering duplicity and hypocrisy, she handled like a veteran. She measured the reach of dirty old men and young Turks with equal acuity, and at once I realized I had not only enhanced my life with a devoted wife but as well had acquired a formidable ally.

We did not want to separate for any reason, but events forced us to take an apartment in the city for Libbie while I took the field. Even so, she followed whenever she could during the next year, sharing the privations of more camps than can be counted without complaint, subjugating herself to life as the wife of a soldier at war. And she did these things without changing any of the qualities that made her just Libbie, the girl I had married. Hers was as astounding an adaptation as I have ever seen.

The turning points that immediately preceded the surrender of General Lee at Appomattox took place in a tremendous rush. It was a time when she could not be with me. Even Eliza had to be left behind when the army was surging toward final victory. We had thought it within our grasp so many times that the end came almost as a shock to those involved.

Libbie was remembered at that moment by no less than General Sheridan. As soon as the surrender papers were signed he purchased the small table on which General Grant had written the terms and gave it to me to present to Libbie.

I believe it was the most wonderful day of my life and of many thousands of others. I tripped down the stairs of that house at Appomattox as if I would burst from happiness with every step. There can be no greater joy than to have an end to war, particularly in the case of those who have been successful in prosecuting it.

Balancing Libbie's table on my shoulder that day I rode away enraptured at the thought that the Union had been preserved. And I had been preserved. And I had done exceedingly well through four years of bloody toil.

Such were the remembrances I had during that summer of 1868, the summer of my unhappy exile in Monroe.

My morning trips to the Raisin River with the dogs and our meditations under the big tree across the street from the church brought back many cherished memories, but, sadly, they did nothing to lighten my steps as I made my way home. Uncertainty about the future clung to me like a stain.

As the summer dragged on, I went less and less to the river. It seemed apparent now that I could not merely wait and hope for the rest of my life, but that I would have to begin to think about alternatives.

Libbie and I knew that our resolve never to separate was a lofty but unworkable ideal and it was decided at the end of summer that I would travel to New York alone, there to explore possible business opportunities. Without saying it, I think we both knew that, after more than four years of constant company, that a separation of a few weeks would probably improve our marital health and I think our instincts were correct in every way. No matter how devoted or well suited a couple may be, the old saw "Absence makes the heart grow fonder" remains true.

It was a tonic for me to be on the streets of that great city again, to be swept along by its naked energy, to feel anonymous yet vital in the flow and pace of its avenues.

But for the first few days of my visit I admit to a crisis in confidence. Though I was all the way to the marrow the general of popular mind, technically I was no longer in the army and might never be again. I found myself trapped in the no man's land of transition and I was struck frequently with the queasy notion that I was uncomfortable in my own skin.

I had secured a number of business introductions but approached each one without enthusiasm. I had spent my life as a soldier and had absolutely no experience in business.

As it turned out there was no reason to fret. I visited the offices of the firm with which I had contracted for the publication of my memoirs. They had recently received the first fifty pages, which I had produced during the summer, and to my great satisfaction they seemed genuinely impressed by what I had written. The editors insisted that I write and write and write.

The encouragement of the publishing house seemed to break the ice, for after my visit there the whole city opened up to me.

I attended the theater whenever possible and was reunited with many old friends of the stage who were overjoyed to see me again and with whom I spent many agreeable hours in the fabulous restaurants of the city.

I made new friends as well, mostly from artistic circles. I have always been drawn to theatrical beings, perhaps because the world they inhabit is so different from my own. Most probably we share a certain energy for living the fullest possible lives with a verve not found in many quarters. In the theater, where one individual can assume the identity of another, I find a magic exuberance that holds me in rapt attention. I love the darkness and the rising of the curtain and the story being told. I watch every movement, listen to every intonation, and savor every moment, no matter how large or small, with a fulfillment I get from nothing else.

News of my presence in the city seemed to precede my every step and everywhere I went the doors guarding the sanctums of the rich and powerful opened like the fabled entrance to the hiding place of Ali Baba and his Forty Thieves. In fact, I did not even have to say "Open sesame" because in most cases I was invited to enter.

My interviews with these commercial giants of the age were strangely perplexing. They regarded me with great interest and, on hearing that I was considering a career in business, were enthusiastic. Almost all told me that it was a shrewd idea and that they were sure I would be successful, but invariably they went back to business and I went back to the street.

In later years I became involved in a number of different enterprises, none of which have ever yielded much. I am still hoping that some of my initiatives in business will prove out, but it seems that my dalliance with commerce has lacked the spark that makes for abiding love.

I returned to Monroe much refreshed and with much of my confidence restored, but I was still unsure of what to do. In my heart it was a return to army life that I wished for most.

Back in my hometown I tried my best to keep up with events taking place on the frontier, especially in General Sheridan's district. I gleaned all that I could from the newspapers and reports from military people I saw occasionally, but this contact only served to deepen my desire to be involved.

The peace policy had created more friction than it had peace: the Interior Department was essentially pursuing a program of bribery, handing out all kinds of provisions, including weapons and ammunition, to the savages while the War Department stood by and wondered how long it would be until the army had to take the field against an enemy that was being armed by our own government.

Late that summer it came to pass that General Sully was ordered out with most of the Seventh to chase down warriors who could not resist raiding the length and breadth of General Sheridan's district.

The campaign was not successful, but, like any other public entity, the army puts the best face it can manage on its undertakings. I don't believe I have ever read a publicly published report that has offered a true reflection of events. As I was removed from the scene of action, it was necessary to read between the lines of newspaper reports in order to obtain a few kernels of truth. Only in that way was I able to gain any idea of what had happened.

The reports of the summer campaign of 1868, against the Cheyenne, Sioux, Arapaho, and Kiowa, carried many references to "vigorous efforts," "marked vigilance," and "determined pursuit." There were no reports of casualties in any number on either side, and when I read that General Sully had spent most of his field time riding about in an ambulance I surmised the campaign had been a failure.

We were dining at the home of friends when a telegram from General Sheridan reached me on the last day of September 1868. Strangely, I was not surprised at its appearance but in no way did that diminish my joy at reading the words it contained. That telegram is another of the documents I have kept safe through the years and I can quote from it verbatim.

"Generals Sherman, Sully and myself, and nearly all the officers of your regiment have asked for you, and I hope the application will be successful. Can you come at once? Eleven companies of your regiment will move about the 1st of October against the hostile Indians. . . ."

General Sheridan's telegram provided me with the deepest feeling of vindication I have ever experienced and created such overwhelming excitement that Libbie and I excused ourselves in the midst of dinner and hurried home.

There was a midnight train west, and because I had no intention of waiting for orders from Washington, D.C., I threw together two valises of clothing and necessities, took two of the dogs, and was standing on the platform at eleven-thirty, having already telegraphed General Sheridan to tell him I was on my way.

It was an uneasy, confused parting for my wife and me. On the one hand there was literally no time to make arrangements for her to come with me. And on the other, we both knew without speaking of it that our single-minded devotion to each other had helped produce my suspension from duty. This knowledge did not diminish our need to be together, it only meant that we had to be more prudent if I was to continue in the army. We would have to pick our spots more carefully.

All of this was unsaid as I departed that night, for at such times a single unspoken question, the question of whether or not we will ever see each other again, is uppermost in our thoughts.

JUNE 16-17,

1876

We are on the march again and have reached the headwaters of the Powder where it joins with the mighty Yellowstone.

I have seen Captain Marsh, pilot of the steamer *Far West*, and have learned that General Terry has ordered the supply base moved considerably farther west, to the headwaters of the Rosebud. I also learned, to my dismay, that Libbie was unable to inveigle her way onto the steamer and remains at Fort Lincoln.

There is no word from Crook, no word from Reno, and no substantial word from General Terry. All I know is that I am to continue marching west for our long-projected rendezvous on the Rosebud.

The longer it goes on the more I am troubled by the disparate elements of this campaign. With multiple columns and scouting parties wandering about the country, our enemy can easily be stampeded. In my mind it greatly increases chances for escape by the hostiles. If it were left to me, I would force-march west at this moment and have done with it. All this dilly-dallying only fosters indecision, and indecision is the father of catastrophe.

I am not much concerned that I will miss any action because everyone knows that is why I am here. Unless there is a purely accidental engagement I believe it is common knowledge that Custer will go first.

The prospect excites me, for as unwieldy as this campaign has been, I sense that it will reach a climax soon, probably in a few more days. They must feel the pressure, so many of us pushing in from the east, north, and south. The closer we get, the greater my fear that they will find a way to escape. Of all the things that might happen I dread escape the most.

Had this campaign been carried out as originally planned, I would have none of these misgivings for it was to have been a winter campaign. Organization was held up partly because of the Missouri River's being ice-bound far into spring made it impossible for supplies to reach us on time. And of course once the supplies did reach us, they were found to be wanting in a hundred different ways, all of them traceable to the rampaging graft that has so thoroughly corrupted the present government.

In fact, these pathetic conditions necessitated my traveling to Washington, D.C., there to testify before Congress in a protracted round of hearings that further delayed commencement of the campaign and has probably been the ruination of my career.

No longer will I be able to rely on my former allies in government, and those few in the army who support me will be powerless to help except in spirit. There is only one avenue by which I can further ascend in the military and that is by distinguishing myself in the field. And even what I might or might not accomplish there may not be enough to advance further.

I do not question my will or spirit or that of my men in battle, but the winter campaign we all counted on is now a summer one. Our animals are belly-deep in grass as are the ponies of the enemy.

General Terry is the most able of officers but possesses none of the aggressive nature of a fighting commander such as General Sheridan. If Sheridan were in overall command of this campaign I am certain the outcome would have been decided by now . . . perhaps it would have been decided in winter, just as it was on the Washita.

The Washita Campaign was a success from the beginning. I suppose it could be said that I left Michigan with the conviction that given a second chance, I would not be denied some kind of victory. As my train cut through Kansas, every stop at every settlement told a story. Major changes had taken place in the year of my absence.

Everything had grown. The settlements I had known previously had doubled in size and there were others that had seemingly been erected and populated overnight, for I had never seen them before.

Though all the villages evinced a crudeness normally found on the frontier, I could not fail to notice the addition of churches, schools, banks, and other signs of the stability that comes with civilization.

As the West becomes more and more settled, Indian raiding of any kind can no longer be tolerated. No amount of benevolent thinking by citizens in the East can stifle the demands for action in the West. Congress and the President can legislate and proclaim all they want, but unless the raiding is stopped there will always be pressure for war.

These impressions were confirmed as I alighted from the train at Ellsworth, Kansas. I had remained on the train through every stop, for word of my coming preceded my arrival and at every station crowds came to the train at a time when my mood was not inclined toward public encounters.

Ellsworth was then the end of the line, and as I stepped off to meet the escort that would convey me to Fort Hays, a large group of civilians pressed in about me, every voice crying out for action against the Indian menace. So vehement were these sentiments that I was left with no doubt that the people settling the frontiers would eventually be granted the vengeance and lasting security they demanded.

Many words of encouragement were directed to me personally and it was only natural that I found them deeply satisfying after my year in exile. These civilian pats on the back were, to my even greater satisfaction, but a preamble to the outpouring that greeted me at Fort Hays.

General Sheridan and his staff were waiting outside as I was driven up and I have never seen such genuinely hearty grins on the faces of any group of officers. With each day of living it becomes easier to tell the real from the false; though I was not yet thirty I had seen enough of both to tell the difference. The feeling was so real that afternoon that I believe it carried me along on a wave of good-will that lasted through the Washita campaign. Even Captain West, who had curtailed his drinking sufficiently to remain in service, offered me the hand of friendship . . . which I nodded at but did not touch.

It did not take long to discern that a significant factor in the warm—I could say joyous—reception accorded me was the low state of the Seventh Cavalry. The dismal campaign of the previous summer had drained all pride from the command and my arrival was hailed as a sign of deliverance for what had become a nearly hopeless unit.

During my first cursory inspection of the men it was clear to me that the force was unhappy. Even the enlisted troops seemed glad of my presence, but beyond their salutations lay a queer meekness, a kind of sad embarrassment.

The Seventh Cavalry had somehow misplaced its fighting spirit. General Sheridan admitted as much at our first working session during which he reviewed in detail the failure of the summer campaign and laid out his new strategies for bringing the depredations of our Indian foes to a halt.

He told me that we now had complete authority to punish murderers, kidnappers, and thieves hiding in the Indian ranks and because no other approach had been effective, he was now convinced that nothing short of total war would suffice to do the job.

General Sheridan proposed attacking the enemy while he huddled in the warmth of his winter camps: his ponies too thin for long marches, the cold and ice and snow making escape difficult if not impossible. He proposed that we track the enemy to his lair and surprise him by attacking while he slept. The hoped-for result would be to shock all the tribes, to serve notice that they would be safe nowhere and that they must submit if they valued their lives.

I concurred with every aspect of General Sheridan's plan and told him so in plain terms. He leaned back and, as he often did, swiped at both sides of his mustache while he stared intensely at me with his small, dark eyes. He then said flatly that he had missed my ability and my companionship. Then he produced a cigar, which he gazed at fondly while rolling it between his fingers.

"I'm going to smoke this now," he said, "and I'm going to enjoy it knowing that I finally have a field commander who has never failed me."

There was little time to prepare for a winter campaign of total war. Hundreds of troops had been mustered out at the end of summer and were now replaced by green recruits, many of whom had not even handled firearms.

The regimental band had fallen into disarray and I began at once to rebuild it.

With an eye toward shepherding a return of morale I ordered that each troop ride horses of the same color and I directed Lieutenant Cooke to organize an elite troop of sharpshooters.

In a short time every man on post was so weighted down with activity that depression was impossible. The air was turning colder each day and as it did every set of feet in the Seventh Cavalry—horses' and men's alike—stepped smarter. A palpable feeling of purpose drove our preparations, and as the regiment took shape, I and everyone else in the command was infected with the sense that we would not be denied our ultimate goal that winter.

The ordinary—and lamentably predictable—problems with various channels of supply slowed the smallest arrangements. Even the arrival of ammunition was delayed to the extent that regular target practice had to be suspended for more than a week.

While we wrestled with these problems the unusual complication of waiting for a civilian force to arrive further tangled our plans.

Kansas had taken the brunt of Indian attacks the previous summer, having suffered one hundred and fifty people murdered and more than thirty women and children carried off. Understandably the citizenry had pressured federal authorities for the right to defend themselves and after much wrangling had been allowed to raise a volunteer regiment, which would be led by the governor of the state.

I sympathized with the Kansans but I doubted that the soldierly abilities of their farmers and merchants would compare favorably with ours. Yet somehow it had been determined that we would all function as a combined force and as such the Seventh Cavalry was under orders to await the volunteers' arrival before taking the field. For many reasons, only a few of which I was privy to, the Nineteenth Kansas Volunteers took forever to arrive.

As the Seventh reached readiness I chafed against every bureaucratic restraint and was finally able to convince General Sheridan to let us temporarily forsake the Kansans and move south to Fort Dodge, which was much closer to the enemy. In fact, it was situated at the edge of their territory.

This was colorfully confirmed when the post was attacked, practically as we arrived, by a small group of decoys hoping to lure a few fools onto the prairie. We returned sufficient fire to drive them off on this and several subsequent attacks. In essence we paid them no more mind than we would a persistent handful of biting gnats. If all went well we would have our chance to fight back in force.

Two weeks after we came to Fort Dodge the first snow flew. It was nothing more than a dusting but temperatures dropped to below freezing, a turn in the weather that caused excitement in the ranks, for the advent of winter was to mark the advent of the campaign.

Initially there was some confusion over who would command. General Sheridan had told me privately—and it was I believe unofficially understood by every man in the command—that I was to be their leader in the field.

But General Sully was also attached to the expedition. He had an excellent record as a soldier, having distinguished himself in the Great War to a high degree. He had also engaged the Indians of the northern plains, and although he had not won clear-cut victories, neither had he suffered any decisive defeats. Despite these achievements, the summer campaign he had just led was the most miserable of failures, a fact to which he turned a blind eye, carrying on as if he were still in charge.

To put it plainly, General Sully was pretending to be in command, hoping that his recent ineffectiveness would somehow be overlooked. I indulged his self-deception by playing along, though I was certain it could not last.

Our scouts had brought word that hostile camps would most likely be found that winter on the banks of a stream called the Washita and it was decided that the best staging from which to attack the camps would be a point we called Camp Supply, roughly equidistant between Fort Dodge and the hostile villages.

The tardy Kansas volunteers had still not appeared, but General Sully and I, eager to establish a base, secured permission to leave Fort Dodge and make our way down to Camp Supply.

On the march we cut the trail of a war party consisting of seventy-five men riding in a northerly direction, probably intending to terrorize Kansas once more before going into winter camp.

By virtue of his slightly higher rank in the regular army General Sully was technically in command, and I respectfully suggested that we detach a portion of our group, led by myself, to follow and attack the war party.

For some reason General Sully clung stubbornly to the misguided notion that we must somehow wait to be joined by the Kansas Volunteers before taking the offensive.

I was incensed. What were we waiting for? What had been the purpose of a month and a half of training if not to attack the enemy? General Sheridan himself had declared to all that this was to be a campaign of total war. We were to attack and destroy the enemy whenever and however we found him. And we were not doing so.

I held my tongue until we reached Camp Supply. Then, in a barely civil confrontation, I told General Sully that he could not now command because he was out of his assigned district and due to that, brevet rank was supreme. I was a brevet major general, he a brigadier general.

Sully countered that Governor Crawford would on his arrival outrank us both, and after much tense argument it was decided to let General Sheridan sort out the problems of command. This he did several days later when he arrived at Camp Supply with the long-lost Kansas volunteers and their commander, Governor Crawford.

The general made up his mind quickly. He sent General Sully back to division headquarters while instructing Governor Crawford and his regiment to stay put at Camp Supply while the Seventh Cavalry took the field.

He and his staff presented me with a pair of buffalo overshoes and a fur hat with ear flaps. I had already acquired an excellent set of buckskins, a practical improvement on the standard woolen uniforms I had worn during the Hancock campaign. All I needed to complete my winter outfit was a special horse.

The day before our departure Camp Supply was crackling with excitement as final preparations were made for moving out eight hundred men, a like number of horses, and about forty wagons filled with ammunition, rations, and forage for the animals.

The weather had remained cold and quite clear, but great banks of gray snow clouds were making their approach that afternoon as I searched through the horse herd for a suitable mount.

The most likely candidate was standing by himself at a far corner of the pasture: a tall, light-brown animal who seemed content to mind his own business. He raised his head as I came near and, ears forward, stared at me curiously. Then, exuding confidence, he took a step or two toward me.

I asked the herder what the horse's name was and he said, Dandy, adding that I had picked the best of the bunch.

This proved out when Dandy was under saddle and we were coursing over the plains as the first flakes of snow from the oncoming storm fell to earth. We flushed a few antelope on that first ride and Dandy impressed me with his deftness of foot, his capacity for wind, and his adventurous but steady heart.

When I find an outstanding horse my enthusiasm is tempered with morbid thoughts of losing him or her—I have lost so many great ones. I think of loss as a reminder that I must not get too close, lest my eventual heartache be too devastating. I must confess, however, that these attempts at maintaining reserve are never more than partial successes.

I told myself not to get too close to the remarkable animal I found that snowy afternoon at Camp Supply. It is almost eight years later and, happily, he is with me yet, standing only a few feet from this tent nibbling grass in the darkness with his friend Vic. That Dandy has lasted so long, through so many hard campaigns, is perhaps the strongest testimony to his greatness. To think that he is still alive and will probably last through a number of years more gives me the deepest pleasure.

At midnight that evening at Camp Supply I was still working on a letter to Libbie when John Burkman appeared out of a howling wind and suggested I look outside. Snow was at least a foot deep on the ground but I was not in the least disappointed. In fact, the harshness of the weather excited me.

Shortly before reveille at three A.M. I made my way through almost zero visibility to General Sheridan's quarters for a prearranged conference. The wind was still blowing mightily, and huge, dry flakes of snow were flying everywhere like confetti.

The general looked grim and dejected.

"Well," he said, "I would call these blizzard conditions, wouldn't you?"

"Yes sir," I answered, "I could not have ordered better weather."

"You propose to take the column out in this?"

"I do . . . look here, sir."

I opened the general's tent flap and we looked out at the covering storm. Men and horses only a few yards away looked like ghosts.

"Even the wiliest red man could not detect our departure on a morning such as this. If we go now we greatly enhance our prospects for surprise . . . and for victory."

"How will you find your way?"

"I have a compass, sir."

Sheridan looked sternly for a moment at the compass resting in my open hand. Then he shook his head and looked out once more at the storm.

"It is said that the insane are the most brilliant of all," he commented. Then he turned to me with a fondly sarcastic expression. "I suppose you are one of those."

"You should know by now, sir."

The general said nothing. He looked again at the maelstrom of wind and snow and cold.

"If I might add, sir, it is my opinion that if this campaign is to be one of total war we must be willing to make total sacrifices. I believe this blizzard is heaven sent—if you—"

"Yes, yes, yes, yes," he interrupted, "go, go, go, go."

In an hour the column had been formed as planned and we were

marching out of Camp Supply. When I saw him later General Sheridan said the departure had been unsettling as we had not so much faded from sight as we had suddenly disappeared into the gloom of the storm.

It was an apt characterization, but at the time I had little opportunity to think of colorful descriptions. However, the irony of my personal situation crossed my mind a number of times. A celebrated general returns from exile and is placed in command of the single most daring expedition since the close of the Great War. Will the general's tarnished star rise again or will he suffer further blemishes? At that moment the answer did not matter. In fact, the question made me laugh. What mattered was that once again I had the opportunity to risk all for victory. I had dreamed so long of having the chance that I did not bother to think much about the outcome. There would be too many critical decisions to make, hundreds upon hundreds over the duration of the campaign, far too many to leave room for dreams of individual glory.

By necessity I had placed myself at the head of the column when we started out. Normally, the Osage scouts would have occupied that position, but the inability to see a dozen feet ahead effectively rendered their skills ineffective.

Dandy and I rode alone, plowing through the storm with nearly a thousand unseen souls at our back. I remember gazing down at the tiny compass resting in my gloved hand and thinking how slim was our margin for error, how by the merest slip of my hand the compass might fall into the snow and all might be lost. I saw myself and the command circle aimlessly as the blizzard went on for days. I saw the disaster only as an entertaining fantasy, for I knew that of course I would not drop the compass.

We marched fifteen miles that day, going into camp in a small valley dotted with fallen timber. Since late morning the storm had been tapering off. As the clouds rose the flakes fell like huge, wet feathers, which soaked every man, beast, and piece of equipment.

By early afternoon the sun's rays were glaring off the bright, white blanket lying over the land and a number of men were almost at once afflicted with snow blindness.

The camp was practically overrun with rabbits and "hare stew" constituted the special of the day around every fire. The column's dogs had a rollicking time chasing about after the rabbits, none of them giving up until they had bagged their game or were so exhausted that they prostrated themselves and lay panting on the cold snow.

I had dispatched our expert contingent of Osages to reconnoiter and they returned with the pronouncement that all was clear for miles around.

A fair amount of light remained and a hunting party consisting of me, two of my dogs, several Indians, and three of Lieutenant Cooke's sharpshooters was quickly organized.

We could not be gone long for the horses were tired, having marched all day with great clumps of snow balling on their shod feet—Dandy, whose stamina was unrivaled, being a conspicuous exception. We were fortunate to shoot several deer and were returning to camp, pleased with our effort, when the dogs hit a scent and ran baying into a ravine.

With the dogs at its heels, a yearling buffalo bull burst from cover and struggled onto the prairie. In a foot and a half of snow his gigantic bulk worked against him and the dogs soon overtook their quarry. Bluecher, the most fearless dog I have ever known—and the most obedient—went immediately for the great beast's throat. Maida followed suit, clamping on to one of the bull's haunches.

For several moments there was nothing but snarling and snorting as the buffalo circled and backed in the snow, trying to fling off the dogs. But they both held fast with their jaws as their bodies flopped like rag dolls.

Eventually the young bull would trample or gore them. I could not shoot for fear of hitting the dogs. One of the Osage's raised his rifle but I barked at him to stop.

I jumped down, borrowed the same Osage's scalping knife, and circled the three fighting animals, at last being able to get at the buffalo's rear. In a wink I had sliced through both his hamstrings and the big fellow went down. It was a simple matter then to draw my pistol and put a bullet in his brain, thereby ending the conflict.

My slaying of the buffalo made a deep impression on the Osages, who served me through the remainder of the campaign with stellar enthusiasm and respect. This was particularly true of their leaders, Hardrope and Little Beaver, who from that point on took great care to report directly to me. It could be said that for the duration of our expedition—and for some time after—I was a chief of the Osage.

We continued marching west the following day. The sun shone brightly, and despite the slush and mud of quickly melting snow we were able to make eighteen miles. I kept flankers out at all times, and scouts, including myself, ranged far ahead of the column. All precautions were carried out with the supreme hope that we would discover the enemy first and not the other way around.

In our second day's camp rabbits were again plentiful and the dogs made such a racket that I had to order that all but the most obedient have their throats cut. Two of my own animals had to be destroyed.

We had pushed west, deep into the enemy's homeland but were still north of our supposed objective and on the morning of the third day I ordered a turn due south. At the same time I sent Major Elliot farther west with a mixed detachment of white and Indian scouts in the hope they would have the good fortune to cut the trail of some returning war party, which could lead us directly to a winter camp.

The weather turned again as the column pushed toward the Canadian River. The sun shone on and off as the clouds descended and rose. Save for the scream of an occasional hawk and the jangle of the column the land lay silent as we crossed, the white layer of snow smothering all other sound.

It was a strange, treeless country of hidden ravines and swales, so limitless as to produce the feeling that one could march for eternity and not cross it. Occasionally the lonely landscape was broken by a misshapen knob. Now and then the sweep of it would begin a slow rise culminating in the formation of a small hill several hundred feet high. Just as it seemed certain that the country was level as a tabletop some ridge or jagged mesa or conelike blemish would surprise us and I could not help but think that only the hand of God would make such unimaginable shapes on such a magnificent plain.

Coming into the wooded bottoms of the Canadian the column was forced to halt while our scouts searched for a fording place. The river is wide and flat and to the traveler seems made entirely of quicksand. After looking for the better part of two hours a difficult but not impossible ford was located and the column addressed itself to the arduous task of getting across.

Those of us on horseback galloped through the muck and mire so as not to get bogged down. The wagons of course were another matter. Four-horse teams were required to pull the heavy vehicles across with the requisite speed.

There was no way around the tedium and time consumption of such an operation and while the crossing of the wagons was effected I rode with a small group to a nearby hill several hundred feet high for a look around.

On reaching the summit we were suddenly surrounded by a freezing mist, which produced a rare, optical illusion. Shining down on our party was not one but three rainbow-colored suns, which hung just above our heads in the cold winter sky. Though we could see them distinctly, those occupying the temporary bivouac only a few hundred feet below us were completely ignorant of the spectacle. The Osages who had accompanied me to the top of the hill considered these sun dogs as harbingers of bad weather and possible bad luck. I was hoping for bad weather anyway and paid their superstitions little mind.

Still atop the hill, I began a search of the surrounding landscape with a field telescope and almost immediately caught sight of a far-off dark speck moving through the whiteness in our direction. As I watched I could hear cries of alarm from those in the camp below who had also seen the solitary rider.

The horseman was Jack Corbin, a young white scout who had ridden west with Major Elliot, and the news he brought electrified the command. The fresh tracks of a war party one hundred and fifty strong had been discovered at a ford on the Canadian twelve miles to the west of us. The pony prints were less than twenty-four hours old and were headed south. Major Elliot had already crossed the Canadian and was hot on the trail.

I ordered Corbin to find a fresh horse and return as soon as possible to Major Elliot with instructions that he should follow the war party until nightfall, then wait for us.

The remaining wagons were gotten across the river as quickly as possible. I directed that eighty men be detailed to help bring up the bulk of the train while the column itself force-marched to catch up with Major Elliot. One hundred rounds of ammunition were issued to each man and in a short time we set off.

Following Corbin's tracks we reached Elliot's little camp at nine P.M. and found that all was well with them. The scouts told me that we were but a few hours behind the war party, which must have reached the Washita River and their home village by now.

The horses were unsaddled and fed and the troops boiled coffee on what were the last fires they would have for many hours while I convened a final meeting with my officers. I told them there was to be no talking during the next phase of the march, no firearm was to be discharged and there was to be no light of any kind. Tobacco users would have to chew and no utensils would be carried, only overcoats and haversacks.

By ten o'clock that night we were on the trail again. Little Beaver and Hardrope went ahead on foot, myself and the remaining scouts coming a half mile behind and the column not far to the rear of us.

I remember it as an eerie night. There was no precipitation, but the atmosphere seemed caught in transition. The moon was up but its light was made murky by high, thick clouds. Temperatures quickly dropped past the freezing mark and the snow beneath our horse's feet developed a brittle, noisy crust which put my nerves on edge. Surprise was our greatest weapon but also the easiest to lose.

At midnight Little Beaver and Hardrope emerged from the darkness in front of us in a state of high agitation. They had smelled wood smoke and felt sure it was coming from an enemy village.

I reiterated the orders I had issued before—no talking, no fires, et cetera—and taking one of the interpreters with me, slipped into the blackness with Little Beaver and Hardrope for a look at what they had found.

The four of us picked our way carefully over the frozen snow for twenty minutes before reaching the area where the Osages had smelled smoke. A few yards later we came upon a campfire, which had probably been tended until very recently by boys guarding the pony herd.

We crept on and though the moon was still out, visibility was poor. At a critical moment the overcast parted and the moon's light splashed on us just as Little Beaver and Hardrope went prone in the snow. For those few seconds I could make out an outcropping only a few feet in front of us, which I imagined looked over an expanse below . . . perhaps the Washita River Valley.

The interpreter and I dropped on our bellies and snaked up to the Osages. Little Beaver encouraged me to look down into the valley but squint as I might I could see nothing. The overcast parted again and I was able to make out a curving band of silver, which I assumed was the Washita and beyond that a large, indistinct group of objects in varying shades of black, which could have been hostile lodges or trees or horses or buffalo, for all I could tell. Little Beaver assured me that there were "many Indians" camped just across the river and though there was no reason to doubt his veracity I could not bring the column up until I was certain of what lay before us.

We sat in silence for ten minutes more before we all heard the clear bark of a dog followed moments later by the light tinkling of a bell probably worn by the pony herd's lead mare.

We strained forward, trying to pick up the slightest nuance of sound, when something startlingly familiar flooded up to us in the midnight. The sound was so perfect that I could have sworn the Indian baby cried no more than a few paces away.

I retraced my steps to the column, and after having the officers remove their sabers, I brought them in a group to the short ridge that lay above the river valley. We listened for a time to the sounds emanating from the village and the nearby horse herd.

With patience and determination it is extraordinary how much one can, as the Indian might put it, see with the ears. Twenty minutes of silent listening presented a reasonable floor plan of the target area and there in the freezing blackness I whispered my strategy of attack to the officers on whom I was depending.

The column would be split into four units. Two would attack from the near side of the river while the remaining two would cross the stream under cover of darkness and attack the hostile camp from behind.

At my signal, which would come just after first light, all four detachments were to converge simultaneously on the village from four separate directions.

As per General Sheridan's instructions I restated the orders of total war. All combatants were to be destroyed, women and children to be taken captive when possible. The village itself, once cleared of warriors, was to be formally destroyed, the destruction to include all private property of the inhabitants. "If you find yourself in doubt," I said, "give no quarter. Our mission is not one of mercy."

We waited until the hour before dawn, at which time I deployed the men, first ordering them to pile their overcoats and haversacks behind our lines.

For me the battle is somehow easier than the waiting, and as I watched the other three parts of my command disappear into the predawn darkness, I began to count off the minutes in the hope that nothing would go wrong until the moment of our attack.

I had gone so far as to give strict orders that the men refrain from stomping the ground to keep warm and I know the biting cold made the wait excruciating for every troop. But I had not returned from exile and marched nearly a thousand soldiers across many miles of hostile, foreboding territory to be discovered when victory was within our reach. The orders stood and were obeyed.

I fully expected to reach the village first, if for no other reason than the presence of Dandy, who, like all great horses, could feel my excitement running along his back. He became harder to hold as the minutes melted away and I knew he was as eager as I to fly down the slope ahead and into the enemy camp.

Instructing Lieutenant Cooke to bring on his sharpshooters, I had them line up in a column of fours directly behind me. I ordered the musicians to assemble just behind them. They were to strike the notes of "Garry Owen" at the instant of my signal and at the first sound of music all units were to charge the village.

These well-laid plans never came to pass. Shortly after the first streaks of color appeared in the eastern sky a shot from the village rent the air about our heads. Instinctively I laid my heel against Dandy's flank and he leaped forward as a Thoroughbred bursts from the gate. I could feel the sharpshooters coming behind me and the opening notes of the "Garry Owen" soared overhead for a few seconds before the music literally froze in the air.

The little valley filled with battle cries as the various troops bore down on the village. Every sound carried on that morning and I especially remember the horses' hooves, rumbling from four different directions like four enormous trains coming together.

As we tore down the incline leading to the valley I could see the ribbon of the Washita in the halflight. There were high walls on the other side of the stream but in a heartbeat I also saw a pony trail cutting up the bank and laid rein on Dandy's neck, guiding him in that direction.

We took the ice-bound river in two leaps and were up the pony trail and over the lip of the cut bank in what seemed like one. As we spurred into the village I cast a quick glance over my shoulder and saw Lieutenant Cooke and his sharpshooters following close behind.

Ahead loomed dozens of tipis scattered through leafless trees. Warriors were emerging now, many of them taking position behind their lodges or fallen timbers or the slightest depressions offered by the frozen ground.

Suddenly Dandy and I collided with a warrior who had rushed blindly into our path. The man was knocked flat beneath us and Dandy leaped into the air to clear him. On landing, he stumbled slightly and I dipped my head to one side, coming face to face with a rifle barrel poking out of a lodge flap. I fired two rounds from my revolver and a warrior pitched forward through the opening.

When we reached the center of the Cheyenne town, rifle fire seemed to come from every direction. Dandy and I wheeled around and around, returning fire that was coming from several of the lodges. This flushed a number of women and children and several warriors, all fleeing desperately. I rode down one of the men and shot him in the back.

A pronounced lull came over the position I presently occupied and, as there seemed to be much firing coming from the vicinity of the river, we galloped back in that direction, shooting all the way.

Everywhere there were women and children fleeing or taking cover in the brush. And everywhere there was combat. Some warriors had managed to mount their ponies and in the chaos of fighting and screaming and firing they were putting up a tenacious defense, trying to buy what time they could for their women and children and elderly.

There were many scenes of action up and down the river and it was my misfortune to witness one of the most heartbreaking. A squaw had crossed the river with an emaciated, nearly naked white boy in tow. I doubt if he was more than ten years old. Several troopers on horseback were bearing down on her in an attempt to rescue the boy, but as they came near a butcher knife glinted in the squaw's hand, and as I and the pursuing troopers watched help-lessly, she disemboweled the boy.

She then pointed the knife at her attackers but before she could use it was driven to her knees by a number of rounds. She keeled onto her head and lay still. Her captive knelt next to her, holding his intestines in disbelief as his life drained away.

I rode back through the village, which had already been emptied except for a few noncombatants whom we later found huddled in several different lodges.

On a patch of high ground a few hundred feet behind the village I established a command post from which to direct operations. This vantage point gave me an excellent view of the village, the river, and the valley they both occupied. Everywhere there were pockets of fighting being carried on against the backdrop of strange, swirling mists, undoubtedly the result of the warming sun and the action that seemed to be in progress everywhere I looked.

Though I was now beginning to receive a flood of reports I could not help but watch a curious engagement taking place near the river between Captain Benteen and a warrior who was obviously a boy—later found to be the son of a chief. Three times the boy charged in on his pony and three times Benteen parried his thrusts in a purely defensive manner. By his gesticulations I judged that Benteen was trying to make the boy stop and surrender. But when he charged a fourth time Benteen brought his revolver up and fired, emptying the pony's back.

Though there would be spirited resistance from different groups of hopelessly trapped warriors I felt assured of victory before the fighting was an hour old. But there were still a plethora of duties large and small to be carried out deftly and quickly in order to seal the victory.

While surgeons scurried about setting up a field hospital near my command post, I inwardly fretted about the fate of Lieutenant Bell, the young officer to whom I had given the task of bringing up several wagons of ammunition as soon as he heard the battle commence.

At the same moment I began to receive reports of dwindling ammunition I glanced across the river and ran my eyes up the incline from which our charge into the village had begun.

Here came Lieutenant Bell and the precious wagons surrounded by a detail of mounted men. Surrounding them were a band of Cheyenne, firing rapidly at the wagons as they rode down the slope. Lieutenant Bell and his men returned the fire in a running fight, a romantic image that could not be exceeded by a schoolboy's daydream.

Lieutenant Bell had made the mistake of attempting to pick up the overcoats and haversacks we had discarded before the fight. Though it was a considerate gesture, the foolhardiness of it nearly cost him his life and could have cost many others. But I could not be angry at his timely arrival without a single man lost.

Our casualties were not severe in number. In the whole battle we had less than forty men killed or wounded. But with so few losses each is felt more keenly and I was deeply dismayed to see the chalk-faced corpse of Captain Louis Hamilton laid out not a dozen feet from where I stood. The youngest and I thought most promising captain in the army had been shot through the heart on the initial charge.

Another captain, Alfred Barnitz, was brought in with a severe wound suffered in hand-to-hand combat. He was placed under several buffalo robes in hope of making him warm and comfortable for what little time he had left.

A number of enlisted men were brought in, three of whom I believe died shortly afterward.

Mercifully, most of our men were merely nicked, including Tom, whose hand was grazed by an arrow.

When it was apparent that the only fighting that remained was of the mop-up variety I rode into the village, ordering that an inventory be made of all the goods we had captured. I gave strict orders that there was to be no looting. When a complete listing of the village's contents had been made all would be destroyed.

I made a visit to our makeshift hospital and encountered one of the buglers, no more than a boy, sitting on a pile of buffalo robes while a surgeon tended his wounds. He had been struck in the head by a metal-tipped arrow and though the projectile had not penetrated his skull, it had split the skin from forehead to ear and covered the front of his face in a sheet of blood.

I enquired of the boy how his adversary had fared and he responded by saying, "Here's how he made out." He then reached deep into one of his pockets and pulled out a large hank of Indian hair caked with blood.

Personally, I find the practice of scalping and the taking of any human trophy repugnant in the extreme and I have been largely successful in dissuading the men of my commands from mutilating or dismembering the enemy. Scalping, however, particularly in the heat of battle, is practically unpreventable. In my experience I have known few who kept these grisly souvenirs for very long after taking them. In the case of the bugler I was told that he discarded the scalp after his ire cooled.

I then turned my attention to the women and children who had been captured. These survivors were ushered into a number of lodges at one end of the village and held there under guard. They were certain they would be executed and no amount of reassurance could convince them otherwise.

While Lieutenant Cooke's sharpshooters cleaned out the last suicidal defenders of the village I noticed riders on a low hill nearby and, sighting through my field glass, was surprised to see a number of fresh warriors in full war regalia. I knew that some of the Cheyenne had escaped, but they had done so with little in the way of clothing or arms. Who could these people be and where had they come from?

The answer was provided when Lieutenant Godfrey returned with most of the enemy pony herd and a startling new report. Hostiles, apparently from other villages in the neighborhood, were swarming up the river valley. He had not made a count but it appeared that fresh warriors were coming by the hundreds.

Immediately we interrogated several captives, who confirmed Godfrey's report. Camped downriver were large villages of Kiowa, Sioux, and Arapaho.

We also learned more about the village we had invaded. A war party had returned from the settlements only the night before and the attendant festivities greeting their arrival had helped to mask our approach.

At the end of the interview, most of which had been conducted with a single individual, a curious event took place that seemed incongruous in light of the carnage all about us. Our interviewee, a woman of high standing, introduced a girl in her late teens whom she seemed eager to foist on me. After some confusion it was at last ascertained that the girl was being offered in marriage to me.

This offer was made despite the fact that my appearance was not the best. A horse I had been testing a week before had reared suddenly, cracking his head against the bone over my left eye. The swelling, which had just lately begun to recede, gave me the appearance of a slightly built ghoul and I suspected immediately that this oddly timed proposal was based more on political considerations than it was on true love.

It took some lengthy explaining to impress upon the captives that, under the law of the white man, it would be impossible to consider such an attractive proposal. I was already married and could not take another wife.

I emerged from the lodge in which the interrogation took place to find even more warriors occupying the surrounding hills. Two troops of cavalry were formed near the river and made a charge up the slope, scattering a portion of warriors before them. But like birds fluttering off only to return, they soon resumed their original positions and it seemed that more were joining them every minute.

I ordered the captives assembled outside in full view of our unwelcome voyeurs, so as to make them think twice before opening fire.

By midafternoon the inventory of the village was complete, yielding in addition to many other items more than a thousand buffalo robes, five hundred pounds of powder, a thousand pounds of lead, four thousand arrows, and uncounted thousands of pounds of winter food reserves. All of this, plus miscellaneous equipment and personal property, I had consigned to flame.

The pony herd was suddenly a terrible problem. Most of the nearly nine hundred animals which had been rounded up were too wild to effectively herd, especially if we were being threatened on all sides by fighting men from downstream. At the same time we could not let them fall back into the hands of the enemy.

We had fifty-three captives and they were allowed to select mounts for the trek back to Camp Supply. Officers were given the option of selecting any two animals they desired as spoils of war and the Osage scouts were given the same privilege. The remainder I ordered destroyed.

Cutting the ponies' throats would have been preferable but they would not tolerate the smell of our men; at last picking up a rifle myself, I ordered the execution squad surrounding the herd to follow my lead. I further instructed them to make every shot count in an effort to minimize the suffering of the ponies.

As the first shots were fired and the first animals went down a screaming as real as any human misery rose from the herd. It took hours to kill them all, a procedure that caused grief among the men and despair on the part of the warriors who threatened us from the surrounding hills. The destruction of the herd that afternoon was but one of the necessary cruelties of total war. I fired until I could stomach no more and retired from the slaughtering ground.

An hour before twilight I ordered the village set on fire and a huge conflagration ensued in which virtually every stick of Indian property was reduced to ash.

The hundreds of warriors who had now formed a ring around

ourselves and the doomed camp were greatly disturbed but neither attacked or withdrew.

Though I had hoped the shooting of the ponies and the firing of the village would drive the hundreds of warriors who now surrounded us away I was not surprised to see them remain, for they now had several strategic advantages.

Having watched us all afternoon they were well informed as to our overall strength. Unbeknownst to them we were entirely cut off from our supply wagons and I was constantly concerned that some of their far-ranging scouts would discover the train and its eighty defenders and destroy it. If they overwhelmed the train it would greatly reduce our chances of ever getting out of hostile country.

At present the entire command was encircled, and though the enemy showed no inclination to attack, it seemed certain that they would eventually try to retrieve the captives.

Complicating everything was the fact that Major Elliot and eighteen men could not be accounted for. They had last been seen many hours before, pursuing a band of mounted Cheyenne downriver. To search for them would jeopardize the entire command and privately I was sure they had been lost.

Faced with innumerable options I chose the one I perceived to be our best chance for escaping. If the option proved unworkable it could result in our annihilation for its success depended on the enemy's reaction.

Instead of retiring from the field we pretended to take it again. I ordered the column to form and march downriver on a course aimed directly at the home villages of our present tormentors.

The command started out in a column of fours, guidons to the breeze, and the band playing "Ain't I Glad to Get Out of the Wilderness." Our skirmishers were out in full force and our prisoners marched at the rear under a heavy guard.

For a time the hundreds of Indian warriors on our flanks followed us with what must have been great curiosity. I think they must have found our movements difficult to believe.

At last light the column reached a series of rises, and with a strong escort, Lieutenant Godfrey and I rode to the crest of one for a last look down the valley. The light was not very good but far down-river I could see clusters of distinctive, conelike dwellings everywhere.

Being so near the other villages caused a flurry of action amongst the warriors who were trailing us. They scattered toward their homes and families, fully convinced that more attacks were imminent.

Quietly, our skirmishers were brought in, the entire column was about-faced and we countermarched in the direction we had come. On reaching the bluffs above the burned-out village we found to our dismay that the enemy had run off with the overcoats and haversacks.

The men were marched in shirtsleeves through freezing temperatures and we did not bivouac until after two A.M. Great fires were built and the troops were able to brew coffee, eat what remained of the rations, and rest for the first time in almost twenty-four hours.

We maintained the temporary bivouac until daybreak, at which time we resumed the march, hoping our course would result in a reunion with the supply train—which, to the joy of all, it did at late morning. Fresh rations and fresh clothing were issued and I cannot recall a happier camp in the field than that one. Even the weather had changed dramatically for the better.

With camp established and evening mess finished I called the officers together and listened to each of their reports before writing my official account. After careful checking and rechecking we arrived at a figure of one hundred and three enemy dead, these dead to be characterized officially as "warriors" though a number of them included women, children, and the elderly.

Of course it could not be reported that the Seventh Cavalry had shot squaws and twelve-year-olds. I have never instructed any man of my command to kill noncombatants, although in war it is inevitable that some will die. What the public does not realize—or wishes not to—is that in combat a mature woman or a resolute boy can kill just as effectively as a seasoned warrior. The battle of Washita has already been argued to death, but I will always have pride in what was accomplished there. The one hundred and three Cheyenne who died did so in the midst of battle as did the twenty-three of the Seventh Cavalry who were killed.

I hurriedly wrote my report concerning the campaign and sent it along with our two best white scouts to General Sheridan, who was still at Camp Supply.

It seemed that for the remainder of the return march the sun turned brighter and warmer with every mile. The command had experienced privation and had fought with distinction and that all of nature appeared to smile on them was, I thought, well deserved.

When we awoke for our last day's march the weather was almost springlike and at noontime we met the two scouts I had sent ahead. They carried with them General Sheridan's effusive congratulations, which I read aloud to the regiment.

Not far from Camp Supply we halted to form the column for a victory review. I was to lead, followed in turn by the Osage scouts, the white scouts, the captives, the band, Lieutenant Cooke's sharp-shooters, the regiment in a column of platoons, and the wagon train.

To the casual observer such a demonstration might seem more elaborate than suited the occasion. We were not a mass of ancient legions preparing to pass through the gates of Rome, nor was I Napoleon, returning to the seat of empire. We were merely a regiment that had waged a campaign lasting less than a week on a distant frontier and were returning in victory, not to a sparkling capital thronged with thankful citizens but to a rude outpost of civilization peopled by military men, a regiment of civilian volunteers, and the foragers, mule skinners, and scouts who comprised rough, border elements.

I insisted on a review of triumph because it was all the men would get in the way of thanks. The Washita was the first victory of any kind for an army that had been engaged on the plains for almost two years. Long before we took the field I had predicted—in the company of General Sheridan and his staff—that whether we were victorious or not, the winter campaign would set off a national explosion of controversy. There would be no parade in the capital, no editorials of thanks from big-city newspapers, no citizens hanging out of windows waving flags.

Our moment to drink from the clear, inimitably sweet waters of victory was now and I wanted the men to take as deep a draught as possible. So we marched into Camp Supply that afternoon as if we were passing through the gates of Rome.

Dandy, who had an uncanny ability to sense occasion, was fairly prancing. The Osages were singing and firing their rifles. The prisoners, plucked whole from a time long past, were all eyes and ears. The band, their instruments thawed, played the "Garry Owen" with a spirit reserved only for the brightest occasions. Best yet the rank and file, passing with arms shouldered, received a salute of sincere gratitude from their chief, General Sheridan, and I knew that none of them would soon forget their commander's coming out to greet them.

That same afternoon, around twilight, we laid young Captain Hamilton in the ground. General Sheridan, I, and Tom were among the pallbearers.

JUNE 18,

1876

We have reached the mouth of the Tongue River and are now marching along the Yellowstone, angling downriver for a rendezvous with Generals Terry and Gibbon at the mouth of the Rosebud.

I spent some pleasant hours last night in the company of Grant Marsh, captain of the steamer *Far West*. He is an urbane, well-spoken man of much experience and, most happily for me, the possessor of a dry and biting wit that often has me in stitches.

He was in rare form last night, taking some of the edge off my disappointment at learning that Libbie was not aboard the steamer. There was but one chance in a hundred that she would be there but my spirits sank like a stone anyway. For reasons I myself do not fully understand I practically lost heart when informed that she had not made the trip, this in spite of our long time together, in spite of all we have experienced and endured in twelve years of marriage.

So shaken was I that I had to excuse myself from my company. I walked to the bow of the boat and stared at the dark eddies of the Yellowstone until my composure came back. But I felt out of sorts all evening and might have soured completely were it not for the brilliant companionship of Captain Marsh.

Perhaps I crave her because I feel a strange aloneness. I feel disconnected from all that I know. Even the presence of almost all my family on this campaign cannot alleviate the sense of isolation that has been growing larger in me each day. There were letters from Libbie but it is her that I want. I want the touch of her. Perhaps I want to see her and feel her because I have written so much these last few days about the Washita, a subject that cannot help but stir other memories, deep and vivid, which, though many years old, are still unresolved and probably always will be.

I believe Libbie knew what happened in the months following the Washita. Without revealing everything, I told her about Monah-setah. I suppose I told her in the tangled hope that she would enquire further, thus forcing the whole story and somehow assuaging the guilt I still feel.

But she did not inquire further and I think it was a conscious decision, for she must have been curious. All I know is that Libbie's willingness to let it all lie turned out to be the correct manoeuver at what I failed to see was a crossroads in our married life. It is now part of our history—or I should say nonhistory—for the winter of 1868–69 is a period we do not discuss . . . they are blank, nonexistent months out of our years together.

Why is this so difficult? Am I in love with someone else? Was I ever in love with someone else? Did I forget myself completely? Did she have a hidden power over me? I know the answers to nothing.

In the days after our return to Camp Supply it was decided to push the considerable advantages we had won at the Washita. The speed, surprise, and totality of the victory had profoundly shaken the plains tribes. They had long held superior attitudes as regarded military affairs and the tremendous setback they had suffered caused much confusion and anxiety among them.

We were now in custody of fifty-three Cheyenne women and children, a fact that unsettled wild Indians everywhere. More than any other element, the hostages we held were directly responsible for the successes we experienced that winter.

Two weeks after our return we were again in the field, this time in the company of General Sheridan and the volunteer regiment, the Nineteenth Kansas, commanded by Governor Crawford. Our avowed aim was to strike more blows against the enemy while he still shivered in winter.

We revisited the Washita and several miles downstream discovered what fate had befallen Major Elliot and his small command. They lay in a rough circle, doubtless the configuration they chose for a hopeless defense of their lives. The bodies were in an advanced state of decomposition but most yet showed the obscene marks of many mutilations. It is a widely held belief among the warriors of the plains that an enemy hacked to pieces will have difficulties finding his way in the afterlife. If that is true Major Elliot and every member of his doomed party should be lost for eternity. We buried all but the major, whose body we brought back with us.

Not long after we broke off our campaign. The various tribes had scattered and the weather was such that it would be almost impossible to track them. Instead of returning to Camp Supply we proceeded to Fort Cobb, on the Washita, which General Sheridan had recently decided to make his headquarters for the remainder of the campaign. Fort Cobb was also better suited for housing our captives.

Once there, we concocted a new strategy. Our victory on the Washita had as I predicted provoked a storm of controversy in the East, a development that made more prudent approaches necessary. Before General Sheridan's departure for division headquarters, we concluded a change of mission was in order. No longer would we seek total war. Rather, we would pursue a new single-minded and unobjectionable policy: that of obtaining the release of all white captives.

No congressman would rise in opposition to such a quest. At the same time our mission would keep us in close contact with hostile groups, thereby maintaining pressure on them.

Our captives from the Washita would play a pivotal role in the campaign. Not only were they excellent leverage in ongoing negotiations but they proved to be immensely useful as intermediaries in dealing with the wild tribes.

It was a largely successful campaign. We were able to effect the release of several white women and children and my memory is filled with exciting moments. Riding virtually alone into hostile villages. Parleying with extraordinary leaders like Satanta and Medicine Arrow and Little Wolf. Marching hundreds of miles through untrodden country. Matching wits and nerve with formidable savage opponents and winning. I learned more about the Indian and his environs in one winter than the ordinary settler learns in a lifetime and it has served me well every day since.

But all of these events are pale shadows when placed next to the single seminal experience of that winter. Nothing compared with entering the orb of one who defines the term "unique," one whom I do not believe any man could resist.

Her name would be roughly translated as "Young Grass That Shoots in the Spring," but I did not call her that. I cannot remember myself or anyone else calling her by other than her Indian name . . . Monahsetah.

I have described her before in my writings but only in a superficial manner. At this moment my pen hesitates, intimidated at the prospect of making an accurate description.

Though made of flesh and blood she was not of this world, not of the civilized world governed by rules of protocol and etiquette and the trends of the time.

The world she inhabited was her own. In her worship of freedom and independent action she stood out, even from members of her own highly independent race. Nothing could be forced on Monahsetah, whether it be made of thought or action, and anyone who dared do so ran the risk of incurring her magnificent wrath.

Her father was a leading chief of the Cheyenne and being descended from aboriginal royalty suited her well. She was alone in the world, as we had killed her father at the Washita and all other members of her family had escaped.

I have no doubt that Monahsetah would also have escaped had she not been knocked from her horse during the battle and struck her head on a stone. Had she not been rendered unconscious and if escape proved impossible, I am certain she would have died fighting.

I met Monahsetah in the process of screening potential go-betweens at Fort Cobb. Three women were selected for this duty; picking Monahsetah was one of the easiest decisions I have ever made. After thirty seconds of conversation it was clear that she possessed a superior intelligence which was perfectly married to her lack of trepidation, ideal qualities for an intermediary.

Rising above her outstanding intellect was her special beauty. The fact that she was almost nine months pregnant with her first child only seemed to enhance the loveliness that inspired everyone who saw her.

Her hair was the longest, richest, and blackest I had ever seen and no matter what conditions we found ourselves in it always seemed to shine. Her hands and feet were elegant, her shape was delicate and beautifully proportioned. Her skin was unblemished and silky to the touch.

The expressions on her face were wide-ranging. Melancholy and womanly warmth and aggression seemed to be present in varying degrees at the same time and the physical structure of these expressions was comely in the extreme. When animated, her upper lip would curl from time to time, whether in a sneer or a crooked smile it was impossible to discern.

Perhaps her greatest attribute was that there was no circumstance in which she could be ignored. No matter the make up of her audience, no matter the levity or gravity of the situation, Monahsetah never failed to captivate those with whom she came in contact . . . myself included.

The many aspects of her beauty held me so rapt during the initial stages of our interview that I was caught dreaming at one point and blustered out something about her pregnancy, a feeble enquiry to which she did not reply.

"Is you husband living?" I continued.

"I am not married," she answered stoically. "I am divorced."

This was not a subject she wanted to pursue, but as I came to know her, the full story of her background was revealed, a story already well known amongst the wild tribes of the region. Monahsetah was as unique amongst them as she was to us. Everyone knew her or knew of her.

Her marriage had not been one of her choosing, and that, as might have been predicted, was where the trouble started. Whereas one or two horses are usually ample payment to secure a wife, Monahsetah, as also might have been predicted, was much sought after by eligible Cheyenne men both young and old, and her price was high.

When a youthful and highly thought of warrior offered eleven ponies for her hand the payment proved irresistible to her father. Temporarily blinded by the richness of the offer he made the mistake of assuming that things would somehow work out between the potential couple and accepted the swain's ponies, thereby ordaining the marriage.

Monahsetah refused to take up the duties of a wife. She refused to cook, sew, or do any of the work that was taken for granted by Indian women. She also refused to share the marriage bed. Naturally, this frustrated and embarrassed her unlucky husband, and apparently many hours of discussion and argument did nothing to change Monahsetah's attitude.

Oftentimes, I am told, an Indian husband considers saving face more important than saving his marriage. In this case, however, the young man was so obsessed with his wife that he sought redress in council with his family, her family, and several tribal elders. The Indian is loath to force any member of his group to do anything and the distraught husband was unable, despite all his efforts, to activate the marriage.

In a fit of pique he tried to physically force Monahsetah to follow his will, at which point she grabbed up a pistol and shot the unfortunate man in the kneecap, laming him for life.

This tragedy resulted in the instant return of the eleven ponies and the rapid dissolution of the ill-starred marriage.

I never learned who was the father of the child she gave birth to in early January of 1869 at Fort Cobb, but I would wager that it was someone she chose and not the other way around. That was simply the way Monahsetah was made. The choices were hers and God have mercy on any foolish soul who tried to make it otherwise.

At our first interview I asked why she had come forward and without hesitation she said, "I want to return to my people. You have the power to make that so. I don't think anyone can rescue us here."

"No, they cannot," I assured her, "and you will not be able to go back to your people unless they agree to be at peace with the white man."

"Do the whites want peace?" she asked, her lip rising in the trademark sneer and smile.

"We are here for peace," I said. "That is all we seek."

"And if there is peace, I and the others will be free to return to our families?"

"Absolutely."

"Then I will help you all I can." She fixed me with a knowing look and added, "What choice do I have?"

A little laugh flew from her mouth. I chuckled too and from that moment on until midspring we were constantly together, a condition that made deeper attachment inevitable.

In the beginning I had no such notion of deeper bonds. I respected Monahsetah as an original person whose youth and beauty was inspiring and whose unshakable pragmatism made for excellent working relations.

Many of the officers and some of the men obtained companions that winter from the pool of captives. I would have picked Monahsetah if I could, but it was not that way . . . it was she who picked me.

We spent much of that winter in and out of the field and each time we departed Fort Cobb, Monahsetah placed her infant son in care of a wet nurse among the captives. On returning, her first order of business was always her baby and when we were on post I never saw her without him. Like Indian mothers I have observed, Monahsetah did her child rearing without hearts and flowers, without public exclamations of joy, with no declarations of pride. Her dedication was quiet but total. A finely honed instinct seemed to guide her every move in caring for the child. No race on earth places a higher premium on its offspring than does the North American Indian.

It did not take long for me to realize that her skills were indispensable in the field and it was fortunate because that winter our mission had to be carried out with great delicacy.

President Grant's administration had quickly put to bed all lingering notions of total war, embracing instead the policy of total peace. We were still charged, however, with rescuing captives and cajoling or intimidating hostile bands into the controlling mechanism of a reservation system. Active engagement was something reserved only as a last resort and any armed clash would have to be built on a mountain of justification.

The policy was still muddled—as always—but I now had the benefit of experience and the positive repercussions of the Washita in my arsenal. Still it was a tricky proposition; leading one regiment of regular cavalry and another of volunteer infantry over every hill and dale in the wilderness, attempting to pressure concessions from hostile factions of thoroughly wild Indians without engaging them. At best, the campaign's success relied on achieving the most tenuous of balances.

Were it not for the presence of Monahsetah I believe such a balance could not have been created, much less maintained. She was at my side always, a magical weapon that brought many difficult contacts to satisfactory conclusions.

Monahsetah knew when to travel and when to remain in camp. She knew when to speak and when to keep quiet and she taught me the same. Where our scouts spent hours tracking and reading sign, Monahsetah had only to glance at a jumble of pony prints to provide a clear indication of tribe, numbers, destination, and even disposition. How she did any of this was a mystery, but we were able to follow several bands simultaneously, much to the irritation and puzzlement of Indian groups that were doing everything they could to avoid us.

After the Washita, the Indians, though they might not have cared for me as a member of the white race, proffered a grudging respect for me as a soldier. The women and children in captivity demonstrated a reverence and outward good nature befitting a conqueror, which in their view I certainly was. On the plains I found that my reputation preceded me wherever I went, opening some doors that would otherwise have remained closed. I even learned that I had acquired a new nickname, being most often referred to by my Indian counterparts as Creeping Panther.

None of our advantages would have amounted to much that winter without Monahsetah. She told me in detail the backgrounds of men before I met them. I followed her lead through many negotiations, avoiding the numerous potentially lethal pitfalls that seemed to surround our every effort. Whether on the march or at the council fire she made a difference.

Twice we fell out, once when I entered Medicine Arrow's village without an escort and once when I took a peace delegation hostage and threatened to hang them within twenty-four hours unless my terms were met. Both cases ended with favorable results and though she would never admit it, my successes made a good and lasting impression.

There are times when I cannot help but be weak, and in writing these events down I have indulged in weakness, for I have danced all around the point. I have not written what is in my heart, partially because the remembrances bring me pain both sweet and sour. But there is no reason not to be truthful. I have espoused the truth thus far. I must continue to write it down.

For a time there was nothing between us. Being on the march, seeing to the command, and endeavoring to devise strategies for dealing with the wild tribes required more hours than there were in each day. But as the campaign progressed and she became more and more integral to it we fell into a kind of rhythm that bore the earmarks of a smooth-functioning, necessarily intimate team of two.

Gradually we began to share more and more of the common details of life: food and talk and the warmth of a fire after a long day's march or tedious negotiation or both. There had been no one on whom I depended more for advice and soon I found myself depending on her for simple company as well.

My personal code of conduct has been inflexible virtually all of my life. Among many other tenets it demanded absolute fidelity to the woman I loved, the woman to whom I had pledged heart and soul. Other men might intend or pretend to maintain a code but rarely did they adhere. While others might fall by the wayside, Autie Custer remained true to his highest convictions and that he did so in the face of every temptation was a deep source of pride. Yet I knew I was slipping.

I found myself thinking constantly about Monahsetah. When she was absent I was unable to concentrate on anything but her return. I began to think of what it would be like to kiss her, how her lips would feel against mine, how her body would feel against mine. I thought little about the right or wrong of such daydreams for when they were in my head—and they were there constantly—I could think of nothing else.

I wrote a regular stream of letters to Libbie and attended to all of my duties, but each spare moment was devoted to Monahsetah and I only felt fully satisfied when we were together.

There were times when I would look at her and be convinced that a consummation of what I felt was inevitable. At other times I would be just as certain that our relations would remain chaste.

Cheyenne women are known for their modesty and Monahsetah in particular seemed to have little overt interest in the carnal. She had amazingly little awareness of her splendorous beauty and went about the day's business without showing the slightest personal vanity. This, of course, only served to heighten the overall effect, making her even more attractive.

I invented scenario after scenario in which we shared a look or a kiss or an embrace. I could conceive them but I could not fathom a way to make them real. It would be impossible to force any affection on Monahsetah, and though we had grown quite close, she gave no sign that she desired anything deeper.

Finally there came a reckoning. It occurred on an evening in February. After almost two weeks in the field we had returned to Fort Cobb during blizzard conditions. The weather made all activity impossible and every man hunkered down in quarters to wait out the storm.

Monahsetah had as always disappeared to locate her baby son while I tried to make the rude log cabin that served as my quarters warm and comfortable. As it was, I did not have to do much. John Burkman not only had lit a fire but had started a kettle of buffalo stew, which was already simmering as I arrived. I had seated myself and was just beginning to eat when Monahsetah came to the door, her baby in her arms.

I had learned quite a number of Cheyenne words from her and easily understood that she sought to borrow some item that would keep her child warm through the freezing night. I told her to select anything she might find useful, at the same time inviting her to stay and take some food. We had shared many meals by then and the invitation and her acceptance were nothing out of the ordinary.

For ten minutes she spooned the rich broth into her baby's mouth, stopping when the infant fell asleep. Laying him down on a robe, she took a bowl for herself and we ate mostly in silence, watching the fire and listening to the wind outside.

After eating our fill, we engaged in a review of the day's events before lapsing once more into silence. At some point we gazed at each other in a familiar, friendly way and I almost kissed her then but courage failed me.

At last, she yawned and turned away to lift up her child. I laid a hand on her arm and she stopped, looking mildly surprised. I suppose that was understandable because of the earnest expression I was no doubt wearing at that moment.

"I want so much to kiss you," I said in English.

Monahsetah knew precisely my meaning and her reaction was so vivid that I can see every nuance of it now. A look made entirely of sweetness and warmth washed over her face. She smiled the softest smile I have ever seen and suddenly my lips were against hers.

Everything that followed remains locked in a wonderful, warm haze of memory. We made love but I remember little of our encounter that could be called material. I only remember that it was exquisitely easy, that its gentleness and its glow seemed to transcend every quality that might be associated with this kind of meeting between two people.

Monahsetah and her baby boy left before dawn the next morning and our parting was as sweet as our lovemaking had been. It also carried a subtle but definitive finality. I might have continued but Monahsetah made it clear with utmost delicacy that the previous night was the only one we would ever spend together as lovers.

Curiously, this knowledge made me neither sad nor anxious. In fact, it was a great relief. All the good things between us had been celebrated without any of the pressure that attends such a coming together.

It was Monahsetah's native wisdom that made this so. I have never known anyone with as well-developed sensibilities for all that matters in life. Monahsetah knew where to put her heart as surely as she knew where to put her feet. She brought me the simple inspiration of her being and by way of some mysterious miracle, left the inspiration inside me when she departed my life.

In a sense her legacy is a curse. That the Indian can be wise is connected directly to the simple free life he lives. The way of Monahsetah is the way of perfection but while I salute and admire and even revere the view she held of life it is one that is wholly inapplicable to myself. There are times when I have imagined myself as a child of nature, but the trappings of such a life cannot be for me. I am a general of the United States Army and as such my own life is fraught with all the complications, and entanglements, and excesses white civilization has to offer.

I cannot judge what I am or how I was born. I only count myself lucky that I have escaped a life spent in some large building of many corridors and countless offices, in one of which would be found myself, staring up from behind a desk identical to a thousand others save for the little nameplate resting on its surface.

Libbie came out in April. We had enjoyed five years of blessed matrimony, were as devoted and loyal to one another as always, and despite what had happened, my heart frequently jumped for joy at the thought of her arrival. But the joy I felt echoed with guilt, guilt that was now a permanent part of my soul. Neither circumstance nor reason held sway over the fact of my infidelity. I did not know what would happen. Would my wife sense my unfaithfulness? Would I tell her of it? Could I tell her? What would happen to us if I did?

Two weeks before her projected arrival I discovered through the pain of passing water that I had somehow recontracted a disease I thought had been cured years before.

During the Great War I had indulged myself, as had many other young soldiers, in the fleshpots of Washington, D.C. Then, I had taken the cure and all seemed well. Though Libbie knew something of my past indiscretions, she did not know that I had once been infected. That Monahsetah had been unclean seemed impossible, and I could only think that our lovemaking had somehow awakened a long dormant affliction.

Some of the other officers, including Tom, had indiscriminately traded Indian lovers over the winter and now they too had the clap. We all journeyed to new Fort Sill for treatment, and though my body responded well to the medicine, I waited out the last days before Libbie's arrival feeling sick in my heart.

As if all of this were not enough I had to face the terrible chore of breaking to Libbie the news of Custis Lee. He was the only horse she ever loved, having carried her safely across the swollen rivers of Virginia and the muddy roads of Maryland during the Great War. She adored him and never failed to mention him in her letters from Michigan. Now he was dead and it was up to me to tell her for he had died by my own hand, shot in a freakish hunting accident for which I was entirely to blame.

I no longer saw Monahsetah. Many of the hostile groups had finally begun to come onto the reservations and it appeared as if all the captives from the Washita would soon be returned. There was nothing left for her to do but tend her baby as she waited with the other hostages for freedom.

It rained every day for a week before Libbie's coming and Fort Cobb was a muddy swamp on the day of her arrival. Up until the very moment of seeing her face I was praying to be delivered from all these miseries.

Behind the smiles and kisses of our reunion I could tell from the washed-out expression on her face that she was suffering from some inner depression. That night she told me that her Monroe physician had diagnosed her as having a disease that could only have come from me. It was, of course, the same that I had so recently been treated for at Fort Sill.

She asked then if I had been with others since our marriage. I said no, adding that it must have been a holdover from my youth.

I never told her about Monahsetah. The damage was already done and there did not seem to be any reason to deepen the wound, although I have thought from time to time that she has never believed me. Strangely, I feel like telling her now, though I will not do that in a letter.

I think the hardest thing we have ever done has been to reconcile our magically romantic union with the repugnant reality of conditions. This has happened to other military couples, but that it could happen to the golden couple, to Autie and Libbie, is still hard to accept. For a long time it was a grave threat to our marriage.

Eventually, we were able to restore our sexual lives, at the same time accepting the unacceptable: that we would probably not have children. In time, we realized that the only way to carry on was to redouble our mutual devotion, that the only way to live with the past was to sweeten every present moment. This we have done and though we both carry scars, I do not see how we could be happier.

Those weeks we spent in the mud of Fort Cobb, however, were not very happy. They were nothing but agony and torture, the worst being that we were too distressed to touch each other.

In the meantime, the world continued to turn. Implementing the policy of peace, President Grant had made the bold move of replacing corrupt Indian agents with many of the Quaker faith, who, while inclined to gullibility were at least not cheaters. Their presence reduced tensions immediately, and though there would be serious conflicts in years to come, the beginning of the end of the free life was upon the tribes of the southern plains.

The day before the Cheyenne captives were repatriated Libbie and I made a last visit to them. Monahsetah was squatting in a corner of the stockade suckling her little boy. She looked up and, seeing me, offered her funny smile that was half a sneer. It was the last time I saw her.

Several days later we passed through Fort Sill on the first leg of our journey east, where we were to enjoy an open-ended leave from the army as a reward for my service.

A large band of Cheyenne was camping near the post in order to draw rations and as I watched them mill about, I happened to notice a group of children playing in the dirt. One of the youngsters was drawing on the earth with the blade of a jackknife. It was Milton, bouncing once again into the white man's world. He did not look up and I did not have it in me to say hello. I never saw Milton again either.

JUNE 19,

1876

Major Reno has returned from his scout, and as it always seems to be with that officer, the news is mixed. He completed his reconnaissance of the Powder River country, but then, instead of returning straightaway to our camp on the Tongue, he crossed over to the Rosebud River, this in total disregard of specific orders that forbade such a movement.

They were General Terry's orders—generated mainly by myself—and we are both furious at Reno. If it were more convenient, charges would be preferred against him now, for his movements, if detected by the enemy, may have compromised the entire campaign. But there is no time for that now.

Reno's limp excuse for disobeying his orders was that fresh signs induced him to cut across country to the Rosebud. He had not gone far up that river before striking a recently abandoned camp of free roamers. That is the only good to have come from his blundering scout. We have found them at last and it seems certain that they are headed for the valley of the Big Horn.

We have just gone into camp here at the mouth of the Rosebud. General Terry was waiting for us, the *Far West* is moored along the Yellowstone, and with Reno's return it is a large camp indeed. It will grow even larger once Gibbon's force finally arrives, hopefully in the morning. If Crook's column were here it would be a gigantic bivouac, but nothing has been heard from him or his men, who must yet be toiling in the wilderness somewhere to the south. I hope they have not taken leave!

The next twenty-four hours should produce a plan of action. Now that the cat is out of the bag, I suspect that we will all vote for contacting the enemy as soon as possible. It is unquestionably a unanimous fear among the commanders present that the enemy, especially if we have been discovered, might slip away before we can engage him. That is the one result that every man dreads: to come so far only to end up empty-handed.

Camp is unusually quiet tonight for all the men know that pursuit of the hostiles is imminent and most have withdrawn to their tents in order to pen a last, hasty letter to loved ones left behind. Tomorrow there may be no time, as every commander and every member of every troop will be preparing for what will probably be a frantic chase and a spirited engagement with the best fighters the Sioux have.

Alas, it means that I must also hurry through the last of this ongoing testament, the same that has given me so many hours of stimulation and satisfaction on this long march.

I will miss filling each day with so many written words but I shall be relieved as well. I was born to wage war, and as I will always be a better fighter than I am a writer—at least until I am too old to fight—it is a good feeling to point myself once again toward the path of combat. Every sense will come fully awake and my blood will run until the final battle is fought and won.

For the moment I am again in my tent. Tattoo has just been sounded but here at the junction of the Rosebud and the mighty Yellowstone there is little serenity, for the rushing water of both streams create a cacophony equal to that of a storm-tossed sea.

I too have been tossing the last few nights, my sleep coming in fitful snatches. Perhaps I am reliving the past too deeply for it now occurs to me that sleepless nights are a close approximation of what married life was like for us in the two or three years after Fort Cobb. I wish with all my heart that there were some way to change the past. I wish.

When on active duty we lived in the West, mostly at Fort Leavenworth, in Kansas, which was the scene of constant entertainments as we received a heavier than ever flow of visitors from the east.

We traveled often, particularly to New York City where we spent night after night at the theater—I love the theater, so much so that I have actively imagined a life on the stage—and we saw everything that was playing. At farces I laughed so loud as to draw the attention of the audience, though it was certainly not my intention to do so. We sobbed our way through the tragedies. Libbie's handkerchief was never up to the job and when she invariably turned to borrow mine found that it was already well soaked too.

Judge Bacon died, another terrible blow to Libbie, for she was now completely alone in the world, except of course for her loving betrayer and his family.

Though never better than shaky, the peace policy was firmly in place, and somehow it held, leaving the Seventh Cavalry to rust from boredom and inactivity. I made several more overtures to the business world with what were by now predictable results.

As a couple Libbie and I sleepwalked through it all, presenting the outside world with the well-known image of a model marriage while inside we suffered through what seemed an incessant winter of the heart.

Libbie did not suddenly become a different person. Her indomitable spirit was unvanquished and she continued to look after her husband, his family, and our widening circle of friends with the tireless enthusiasm she had always exhibited. But deep inside she was hardening and much of the calcification had to do with family, or I should say the lack of it. I believe it was more than a year before we made love again, and though it was as impassioned as always, a dream that could not be replaced had been lost. For this I blame myself. It was I who deceived the naïve seminary girl from the Midwest into thinking we were a couple who could achieve anything, a couple who could touch the stars if we wished and it was I who had robbed her of that sweetest dream.

We resolved at last to make a supreme effort, but after trying very hard were unable to conceive a child and our every disappointment could not fail to remind us of the source. How could we touch the stars if we could not create a family?

Through the years I have tried at every turn to extol the virtues of a childless life but each time the words come from my mouth I regret them. And yet I cannot stop. I mentioned the subject in a letter to Libbie just a week ago. I wanted to cross out the lines but I could not. I am addicted to trying to make right something that will always be wrong.

And yet through all these tribulations, I do not believe there is a couple on earth who has gotten more out of life than we have. Today we are more like the best of friends than we are breathless lovers, but our mutual attachment could not go deeper. There is no one on earth I love more than Libbie and I believe she feels the same about me. We live for each other.

The army at last decided to divide up the Seventh Cavalry and send its various components on detached duty overseeing Reconstruction in the Deep South. I could not turn down the assignment and we found ourselves at a new post in Elizabethtown, Kentucky.

I would have liked nothing better than to stay in New York to pursue my career as a writer but my income from the written word at that time would barely have covered expenses. The army had been sending subtle messages that it was growing weary of paying full wages to a commander on leave and we had to go for financial considerations if none other.

How we loved New York, though. A city always alive, it treated both of us as its own and we enjoyed the benefits of celebrity there as we did in no other place.

By 1871, however, I was earning some debits as well. I was no longer just the "boy general with the golden curls." Conflicts over the Indian question had split the country and many had raised their voices in vehement opposition to the army's role in general and my own in particular.

A well-dressed matron stopped at my table in Delmonico's one evening just as I was cutting a steak and wondered aloud whether "that was how you butchered your meat at the Washita." She quickly added that the least I could do was demonstrate a little humility by not eating in public places.

With that she turned on her heel. I shrugged at my dinner partners and for a few moments our table was silent. My friends consoled me then, saying among other things that they were sorry I had to be a target of anyone's frustration and assuring me that they empathized with my position as a celebrity. This led to quite a long discussion of the intricacies of the public persona, a lively topic to which I contributed little. The woman's words had shaken me and I walked home alone that night, purposely taking a roundabout line of march through the rainy streets in order to be with my thoughts.

Even tonight, all these years later, remembering the incident at Delmonico's still provokes thought. Everyone wants to be right, and with few exceptions, a dictator lies hidden in every human soul, ready to rise when given the chance. It is the blessing and the curse of the race, driving us forward as it holds us back.

As a soldier I have spent my entire life in struggle with other hearts and minds that seek to dominate my own. If I were a philosopher I might seek better ways to live but the struggle to dominate or deflect domination has taken the sum of my earthly energies.

I cannot say I have regrets. In fact, there is little I would change were I given the chance. In my life, reward has been ever present, reward in the form of triumph, which to my mind is the child of domination. Each triumph is a delicious feast, a moment of love, an odd elixir that once tasted leaves a thirst for more. And the higher the stakes, the greater the triumph. Victory born of dust and sweat and muscle and blood creates celebrity and celebrity is the headiest brew of all, for it is neither real nor unreal but rather a state unto itself that cannot be understood by those who haven't achieved it. Once one achieves it, the discovery is made that this unique status cannot be understood through firsthand experience, either.

Those who consider themselves anonymous dream of being known, but are oblivious of the troubles that celebrity can bring. I am no different from other celebrities. There are times when it is a distinctly disagreeable thing to be, but I have known many who would do anything to keep fame and perhaps I am among them.

The advantages far outweigh the drawbacks . . . the reason, I suppose, why so many give so much to dreams of glory and recognition. If humility were truly worshiped, the world would be a different place, but humility is one of those qualities that receives much attention but is rarely practiced. Certainly not by me. There is no such thing as a humble general.

Kentucky was a sort of purgatory, being neither pleasant nor unpleasant. Aside from my sister Maggie's marriage to Jimmie Calhoun, I would nominate the disappearance of my horse Vic as the only other event of note that took place in our year and a half there.

My only diversion was the magnificent horses which are a tradition in that state, and in a brief time I had acquired a stableful, of which Vic was the most outstanding.

One afternoon I returned from an outing and after a brief inspection of the barns discovered that Vic was gone. Men were out all night searching for him but all returned without a trace. The search continued through much of the following day, with the same result.

There is nothing that disturbs me more than a lost animal, a trusted friend who is suddenly prey to the world's every misfortune while at the same time his or her custodian is left helpless. Tortured with images of what might be Vic's fate I returned to the barn after the noon meal the next day hoping that I might discover some clue that had been overlooked.

I carefully inspected his stall and stepped into the barn's alleyway, looking in each direction as I tried, without much luck, to determine which way my horse might have gone. The front of the barn opened onto a road that in less than a quarter mile split into a number of different routes. The rear of the barn opened onto a gentle, tree-covered rise. In the flat foreground was the circle of one of our shallow wells, which had recently been undergoing repairs. I started toward it thinking, "He could not possibly be in the well."

I peered over and there he was, standing on all fours in water to his chest, quiet as a mouse. As if embarrassed, he stared straight ahead at the wall of the well, ears pinned back in irritation. When I called his name he rolled one eyeball up in my direction, then sighed unhappily.

With a dozen men and a heavy block and tackle we were able to haul him out that same afternoon. He had lost a few pounds but was otherwise unhurt. How he fell into the well is a mystery that is still unsolved. I believe to this day that he made no sound because of his acute embarrassment. He is a true athlete with as much pride as I have ever seen in an animal.

JUNE 20,

1876

Vic the wonder horse is standing outside now, picketed in the darkness with Dandy. I cannot see them but know that they are alternately browsing new grass along the river's banks or standing head to tail as they sleep standing up. Though there are always dangers in this country I am comforted in knowing that there is no well for them to fall into.

They know the Yellowstone country, for they were with me on the expedition of 1873. In many ways it was a carefree summer of exploration, enlivened by occasional skirmishes with bands of Sioux warriors who harassed us whenever they thought they had an advantage. The casualties we suffered were light, and though our clashes with the Sioux featured real bullets, there was an unmistakable flavor of boyish gamboling in our fights. Looking back, I am reminded more of Hide and Seek or Capture the Flag than of mortal combat.

We were entrusted with protecting surveying parties who were establishing one of the great rail routes that would span the northern recesses of the continent. The Sioux made it warm for them from time to time, but on balance our expedition was something of a lark.

My only significant difficulties that summer were with my commander, General Stanley. He was a staunch devotee of the bottle, and after repeated disagreements brought on by liquor, matters reached a head when I was placed under arrest by an inebriated General Stanley—I had incurred his anger by running a whiskey peddler out of camp.

The incarceration—in quarters—lasted only twenty-four hours before the general regained his sobriety and set me free. It was ironic that during my brief period of arrest, I should experience one of my happiest reunions of my life.

I was alone inside my tent when I heard a voice outside enquire as to where might be found "General Custer's abode."

Curious, I poked my head out. The man I saw was the Union Pacific's chief surveyor, but I did not know him as that. I knew him as Thomas Rosser, general of Confederate cavalry, and previous to that, Cadet Thomas Rosser, a valued friend and classmate from my days at West Point.

I had not spoken with him since our time together at the Academy but had opposed him in open battle during the Great War on a number of occasions, the most memorable—for me, at least—being our engagement at Tom's Brook on October 9, 1864.

Not long before, I had been promoted to the rank of major general, a move that meant I would have to assume a larger command. Leaving my beloved Wolverines, I assumed command of the cavalry's Third Division, to my mind the most distinguished division of horse to serve in the war. It was a unit that captured every piece of artillery turned upon it, seized scores of enemy battle flags, and achieved victory upon victory without once being defeated.

Shortly before Tom's Brook the division had been covering the withdrawal of General Sheridan's Army of the Shenandoah. During this operation we had been pestered to distraction by a division of Invincibles that, as I soon discovered, included a brigade under the command of my old friend from Texas, General Rosser.

While we were busy with other duties, General Rosser cleverly deployed his troops across Tom's Brook, placing his artillery on high ground overlooking the stream and effectively blocking our path.

He clearly had an advantage in position and numbers, having nearly four thousand fighters to our twenty-five hundred. But the Third Division had been outnumbered many times before, and knowing that other friendly forces would soon arrive in support, I deployed our artillery in the best positions possible and made ready to fight.

As final preparations were being made to "begin the show" it came to my attention that the Invincibles across the creek were under the command of my old friend.

The day was very clear and the battlefield was distinct in every detail. The picture of the opposing forces was one of beautiful perfection, like line after line of toy soldiers arranged with great care. In moments these pristine images would melt into the grime and fury and discord of battle.

Suddenly my heart swelled with sentiment for all the upturned faces I had seen, the young friends who had breathed their last at my side and for the living who experience the horror of combat over and over with such bravery.

The thought that all of this was about to happen because of a political disagreement between the two opposing commanders, who otherwise loved each other as brothers, was incomprehensible.

As I looked upon the scene I was overcome with images of beauty, and though I alone could not still the inexorable march of war, I alone could make some gesture that might acknowledge the honor and respect and even the love each side shared.

I was mounted on a black stallion named Coal and without knowing precisely what I was about to do, guided him onto the flat no man's land separating the two forces. At a prancing walk we traveled several hundred yards before coming to a stop in full view of the enemy.

High on a bluff, near the artillery, I saw the commander's guidons. Taking my hat from my head, I swept it across my knee and bowed in the direction of General Rosser and his staff. Then I called out as loudly as I could "Let's have a fair fight . . . no malice."

Coal carried me back to our lines at a gallop and on reaching them I ordered our own batteries to open fire on General Rosser's men.

Ironically, it was the Michigan Brigade who came up in support that day and we not only won that battle, we made it a rout, chasing the rebel cavalry twenty miles in what was known afterward as the Woodstock Races.

General Rosser's men fought hard, but I doubt that any army on earth could have whipped us that day. We captured their battle flags, almost all the artillery, and most of their train, including General Rosser's headquarters wagon.

I appropriated his long dress coat and hat and made a promenade through our bivouac that evening to the uproarious delight of the whole division; later I penned a note to General Rosser himself, thanking him for all the beautiful gifts but asking that he instruct the tailor to shorten the coattails next time.

And now, after all these years, he was with me again as a friend. We lay in my tent all afternoon, both of us stretched out on our stomachs like schoolboys, reminiscing hour after hour on Tom's Brook and many other episodes that colored our lives for all time.

Having lived among strangers so much of my life and having so many of the friends of my youth dead, I deeply relish every contact with those who are left like Tom Rosser. Now and again I receive a letter from him but I have not seen him since that summer of the Yellowstone in 1873.

I miss him and I miss many others from the period of the Great War. I miss the war itself. For all its heart-breaking carnage it demanded my best. And I gave my best, as did my men.

For the Third Division the war did not stop until that final grand review in the capital. When the parade was over, we formed up for the last time in a fallow field not far from the heart of the city.

I had meant to deliver a farewell address, but as I looked out over the ranks of surviving veterans who had fought so bravely and endured every hardship of body and spirit that can be imagined, I could not find my voice. It had turned to liquid in my eyes.

Don Juan and I then walked every line of horseman. Tears filled to the brim of my lids and spilled down each cheek during that last inspection of my valiant troops. I held my head up as they did theirs but I saw not a single man whose face was dry. We all knew that we had seen the last of the Great War and were seeing the last of one another. Two thousand men in tears.

❧

Cannot sleep tonight. Too many details of preparations running through my mind. I can only catnap, but that will do. All I have ever needed on the march is ten minutes in a muddy ditch or on a hardscrabble road and I have been refreshed, ready to ride all day or night.

We will soon be going after the Sioux. Precisely how we will go after them is to be determined at a meeting on the *Far West* set for tomorrow night. Then General Terry will reveal his plans. It is already a hard wait, probably the reason for my sleepless condition.

❧

Libbie and I came to the Dakota Territory early in 1873 when the army regathered the Seventh, elements of which were scattered throughout the Deep South, and made it a single unit again, sending the whole outfit to Fort Abraham Lincoln. The new post was situated in the most desolate, uninhabited country I had ever seen and it is still much the same, despite the subsequent establishment of a number of towns in the area.

We made a wonderful life for ourselves at Fort Lincoln. It was almost as if we had established a society all our own, a world apart from any other. This was particularly true during the subzero winters, when it seemed that the entire universe was frozen.

Guests made their way back and forth across the icy landscape and every moment of our lives was filled with some entertainment: amateur theatricals, living-room recitals, endless charades, afternoon sleigh rides, and long, happy dinners.

Eliza had found a husband, and Mary, who cooks just as well and is equally unafraid of expressing her opinion, has become a member of the family.

Other members of my family have found their way into our world. My sister Maggie is a year-round resident at Fort Lincoln. Brothers Boston and Nevin and nephew Autie have all been out, in addition to a large number of Libbie's lady friends from Monroe.

Tom has been there from the first day. I love him and I know the affection is mutual but sometimes I wonder what will become of my dearest, nearest brother. He is able to enjoy periods of sobriety but always seems to fall off the wagon at the worst possible times. He should be married by now but is somehow unable to summon any charm when making contact with the opposite sex. He has a sweetheart, a friend of a friend of another friend from Monroe. She wears his medals all day but as a couple they seem strangely sparkless and I am skeptical that anything will come of their romance.

He has not been promoted since the close of the war and I doubt he will receive any promotion for a long time to come—for that matter, it's doubtful that I will, either.

In February of 1874, our big house at Fort Lincoln burned to the ground, a total loss. The smoke that disappeared into the winter sky that night carried a lifetime of memories with it. Losing all that we owned was staggering. We nearly collapsed from the loss, but like a surrogate son, Tom came to the fore and we both leaned on him. Then we leaned on each other.

Strange as it may seem, the firing of our home had a purifying effect on our lives. The past was burned away, leaving us no choice but to begin with a clean slate, rebuilding our home and our spirits at the same time. After the fire, all that was left standing was us. We alone were the source of renewal and necessarily we made ourselves strong, regaining in the process some of the luster that had faded from our marriage in the years immediately preceding the loss that winter. Today, I thank God for that fire, for it brought Libbie back to me in many ways.

As a new house rose from the ashes of the old I was preoccupied with organizing a new expedition which was to spend the summer of 1874 exploring a mysterious and enchanting region known as the Black Hills.

The Sioux had long claimed the region as their own. It was sacred to them, and they, along with other tribes, defended it vigorously, punishing most trespassers with death.

But the need for an expedition to the Black Hills was compelling at that time for many reasons. The rumor had long persisted that gold was to be found there in large quantities and if gold could be discovered it would give all of America new financial hope as the country was still recovering from the near bankruptcy brought on by the Panic of 1873.

No mapping of the region had ever been carried out and in 1874 it remained an undiscovered country in the midst of civilization. In the minds of every citizen it was a place to be explored.

Perhaps the strongest reason for going into the Black Hills that summer was one that I have never heard fully articulated. The machinery and mechanics of the reservation system had been in place for some time but it had little effect on the free roamers. The Indians who lived without restraint were a model of temptation to those who had conformed and I believe that the hoped-for result of the Black

Hills expedition was to demonstrate to the free roamers the supreme power of our government. I believe the government wanted to show that it could penetrate any country, no matter how wild or inviolate, that there was no place to hide as no place was forbidden to us.

The expedition was a magnificent success. Gold was discovered, the topographic engineers mapped the entire region, and though they watched us constantly, the free roamers never challenged us.

The only Indian trouble we experienced was in keeping Bloody Knife and the Ree scouts from murdering and scalping a small band of impoverished Sioux.

Personally, it was a great privilege to lead such a grand expedition. In our company was a small army of geologists, biologists, botanists, writers, and geographers. To be among such distinguished personages for an entire summer while exploring a country in which only a handful of white men had ever set foot was the experience of a lifetime.

Game was everywhere. Cool, clear mountain water flowed in profusion. Every valley was a limitless meadow, blanketed with flowers of every color and description that tickled the horses' bellies and had the men picking bouquets. No army in the field ever had better duty. The summer was a long, happy picnic.

The demonstration of our supreme power did not have the desired effect on the free roamers. The Black Hills expedition only shook the hornet's nest. Instead of conforming, the free roamers' defiance hardened. That is why we are hunting them now.

It is inevitable that their free lives will end, but only by being defeated in battle can they fully realize this fact. The sooner they are run down and defeated the more lives and expense will be saved.

I often think that if I were one of them, I too would be defiant. I too would fight for my freedom. Like them, I am every inch a warrior. The difference is that I fight for the other side.

JUNE 21,

1876

I am confused by my own anxiety. My emotions are like stirred soup, swirling in every direction. My every nerve is bristling. Perhaps it is from lack of sleep, but I do not feel tired despite tossing and turning all night.

Even taking a ride with Tom this morning did little to calm my inner turmoil. It did, however, provide one funny distraction.

As we neared camp we gained a wooded ridge above a deep, overgrown gully and looking down we spied a sight ripe for merriment.

Our younger brother Boston, apparently out for a ride of his own, had stopped to answer nature's call. At present he was squatting over the earth, trousers draped about his ankles, in the midst of evacuating his bowel.

Tom whispered in my ear as he unholstered his pistol.

"Shouldn't do that in Indian country, should he, Autie?"

"Certainly not," I whispered back.

Splitting the air with our best imitation of the Indian war whoop we fired several rounds over Bos's head.

The boy leaped straight into the air, came back to earth on his stomach, scrambled to his feet, and with his trousers clinging to his knees managed to take hold of his horse and climb onto the animal's back.

Tom and I were reeling in our saddles as Bos sped away. While overcome with laughter we realized we would have to catch him if we wanted to prevent several thousand soldiers' being put on alert.

We were able to ride him down before he reached camp; when we told him how rudely he had been deceived, he became highly mortified. He is not speaking to us now, but on the basis of past experience, I expect Tom and I will be forgiven in a day or two.

The noon meal has been eaten and I am alone in my tent with pen poised to write what is the most difficult part of this narrative, for it will necessarily sprinkle salt on recent wounds, wounds that have yet to close and may never.

I know that my anxiety today is intertwined with many different threads reaching far back into my life. At the moment I do not know precisely what role I and the Seventh Cavalry will play in this campaign. For all my confidence, it is uncertain even now whether we will be out front where we belong or whether we will be relegated to the sidelines, a place where we will be wasted.

It is all up to General Terry or, more accurately, to the whims of the masters whom General Terry serves. Will he dare to send me out at the head of the army's supreme fighting unit or will he not? I feel today as I did when waiting for a verdict to be returned at the court-martial. I can guess the outcome but I am not absolutely positive, so I must wait.

Whether or not I lead the Seventh Cavalry to another victory on this campaign will probably have little effect on my military career, which, if the unvarnished truth be known, is over. I entered West Point at seventeen, and, as I will be thirty-seven in December, the total years in uniform come to twenty . . . all in service to my country.

But even though I have been positive all my life, I know that it is over. I have not received a regular army promotion for nine years but that is merely the point of the iceberg when compared to events of the last six months.

Though I did not know it at the time, the sun began to set on the military career of George Armstrong Custer when Secretary of War Belknap visited Fort Lincoln last September, setting into motion a long string of fateful events.

During all of 1875, action assignments had been given to others; left with virtually nothing to do, I turned my attention to writing. *My Life on the Plains* was published and, to the delight of a first-timer, was well received by both readers and critics. The remainder of that year I spent every spare moment writing articles for leading magazines and newspapers, all of whom wanted more than I could produce.

Under cover of a pen name I criticized our government's cruel treatment of the defeated South and frequently scolded President Grant's administration. Libbie often warned me about involving myself in politics but my ire was such that I could not resist.

What everyone in the army knew but would not say was that the runaway graft and corruption of the Grant Administration, already implicated in many civilian frauds, had constantly compromised the army's ability to carry out its mission. Post and reservation trader-ships were bought and sold like franchises. Indian agents stole everything that could be stolen. In short, falsifying on every front was standard practice.

I had devoted a good portion of the spring of 1875 to solving a long series of grain thefts. The stealing was so widespread that I had to take over the entire town of Bismarck to apprehend the conspirators, which included the mayor.

Secretary Belknap was a prime architect of this virtual government of crime and when he visited Fort Lincoln, I snubbed him at every turn. Only Libbie's charm and goodwill kept him from realizing how deeply he had been insulted.

Two weeks later the powers that be decided to organize an initiative against the Sioux. Runners were sent to the villages of the free roamers to inform them that the government expected them to report to previously assigned reservations by mid-January.

The Indians must have laughed heartily at this directive for they consider themselves sovereign. If they were going to travel anywhere it would be of their own free will and certainly not in winter when movement of entire tribes was all but impossible.

That a campaign would be mounted against them was a foregone conclusion, and General Terry himself told me that he intended to have a base camp established on the Yellowstone by February. From there I would march against the hostiles, attacking them in their winter camps.

But this was not to be. The winter was uncooperative. Both river and rail travel were dependent on the melting of ice which was very late in coming.

I visited General Terry at his headquarters in Saint Paul, Minnesota, and found that no resources had yet been organized for the so-called winter campaign. My heart sank. Everything would have to be delayed until spring at the earliest, which would make the enemy harder to catch. At last, a date of April 6, 1876, was set for the beginning of the campaign.

The main culprit of this chaos was the Grant Administration. The Democrats had gained control of the Congress and had succeeded in revealing great cracks in Grant's regime, cracks that threatened to bring down even the President.

Unbeknownst to me, a Democratic committee had opened hearings on the War Department and the heat had proved too great for Belknap, who resigned on the second of March. The committee decided to keep probing, however, and to my surprise I received a summons on March 15th to travel back to Washington and testify before Congress.

Perhaps I was the architect of my own demise, for I was naïve, unbelievably naïve. Darker elements of the human spirit have always fooled me and in the world of political intrigue I have functioned as a smiling, unknowing lamb among the wolves . . . a lamb to the slaughter.

I know now that I should never have gone to Washington, but all I could think of at the time was to strike a blow against the corruption that had enraged me for so many years.

The Democrats treated me like a hero. I told what I knew on March 29th and again on April 4th, never dreaming how deeply my testimony would provoke the already wounded Republicans. I was asked to stay on in Washington in the event Belknap was impeached, at which time more testimony might be needed. I stayed on reluctantly and fretted impatiently as several more weeks passed before I finally received another summons to testify.

All the while I was attacked. The Republican forces had selected me as a target of retaliation and suddenly the newspapers were full of charges against my military standing, ability, and character. As if that were not enough the army was now taking sides and many former supporters, among them some of my oldest friends, lined up with Belknap and Grant.

I pleaded with the committee chairman, a Democrat, to let me go back to my regiment, but just as I secured permission to return to Fort Lincoln, I was informed that President Grant had relieved me of command and had designated General Terry to take the field as head of the campaign against the Sioux.

Furthermore, I was now informed that every word of my testimony before Congress had suddenly been judged heresay and ruled inadmissible, a development that some newspapers used to intensify their attacks on me.

How can I describe my feelings then, except to say that the culmination of these events had an explosive effect, as if a bomb had burst in my face.

I sat alone for several hours in my hotel room on the morning I received the President's order, unable to believe that politics were interfering, perhaps ruining, a major military effort on the northern plains. And yet it was true.

When I had sufficiently recovered my senses I went straight to General Sherman's office for advice and counsel—this I did, despite the knowledge that Sherman had suddenly become a stolid defender of the President and his disgraced secretary of war.

Twice before during my stay in the capital I had attempted to see the President, hoping to make clear that my testimony in no way reflected an unwillingness to serve him or to cast any intentional negative light on him personally. Both times he refused to see me.

Now, I sat in the office of the army's commanding general, and was told by Sherman himself that I should try once more to see the President, advising me to wait out the weekend and present myself at the White House first thing Monday morning.

I did just that, arriving at the very minute the gates were opened and settling myself in the reception room while my card was carried inside. I waited an hour and was told to return at one P.M. Returning at one I waited till almost three before being told to return at five P.M., which I did. At six-thirty I was told that President Grant had left for the day.

I went immediately back to Sherman's office, only to find he had left town for New York City and was not expected back for several days.

That night I boarded a train for the West. I wired General Sheridan at his headquarters in Chicago, expressing my desire to meet with him on my arrival concerning matters of utmost urgency.

Before I could get off the train in Chicago an aide to General Sheridan came aboard and handed me a telegram that had just been sent from General Sherman to General Sheridan. The wire said that I was to be detained and that the campaign against the Sioux was to proceed without me. I was told to stay where I was and await further orders.

I asked the aide who had brought the telegram if I was under arrest. He told me I was not.

"Then take me to General Sheridan," I commanded.

Almost an hour went by before I was allowed to see Sheridan, and when I was finally ushered into his office he did not rise from his desk to greet me.

"Sit down, Custer," he said flatly.

"Sir," I stammered, "sir, I don't know where to begin. I don't know what has happened to me."

"What has happened," the general said coldly, "is that you have shot off your mouth against the President and his friends and family. You have gotten yourself in so far over your head that even I cannot help you."

Overcome at these words, I dropped my head and held it in my hands as Sheridan continued.

"Don't you realize that they set you up, that you were set up all through your stay in Washington?"

I listened openmouthed.

"They're like wounded bears. They were looking for revenge long before you became involved. In coming to Washington you made yourself a perfect target for everyone with an ax to grind. Didn't you realize that?"

Still in disbelief, I shook my head. "No," I said.

"You're a fool, then. We all want you in the field, but you have lost every friend in every high place you ever had. What are we to do with you, Custer?"

To hear this coming from a friend of such long standing, a man I had fought with and suffered with and rejoiced with, a man I loved . . . to hear the words "What are we to do with you, Custer?"—all of it threw me into a tangle of emotion that spun like a top, spun me to the point where I could not determine what was real and what was not. The whole of me tumbled in agony.

I could only think of somehow making a direct appeal to the President, and when General Sheridan said he would not stop me from doing so I composed a brief telegram, the meat of which pleaded, "I appeal to you as a soldier to spare me the humiliation of seeing my regiment march to meet the enemy and I not to share its dangers."

Too depressed and embarrassed to remain at General Sheridan's headquarters, I requested and received permission to travel north to General Terry's headquarters, there to await President Grant's reply.

For the first time in my life I wished I were invisible. I knew that disgrace must be etched on my face for all to see. I endured the train ride not as commander of the elite Seventh Cavalry but as a pariah so wretched he seeks to be shunned.

My emotions hung on tenterhooks as I was showed into General Terry's office, and on seeing the face of that honest and gentle officer I began to cry. I had not cried so helplessly since childhood, but I was too shaken to care any longer.

Through my tears I begged him to do what he could to secure my reinstatement. The general had me sit, gave me a cup of coffee to steady my nerves, and said he would do what he could.

He left the office and I sat alone for a time trying to dry my eyes in hope of returning to some kind of normalcy. Libbie knew nothing, nor did Tom or any other of my loyal officers. I realized that I could count on their sympathy and that they would stand firm no matter how far I fell. What I could not abide was being left behind on the campaign. Any punishment would be preferable to being left behind. I could not be left behind.

General Terry returned to say he had wired the President, asking that I be allowed to return to duty as my services were vital to the campaign. He told me that General Sheridan had sent a similar telegram.

Mercifully, the wait for a reply was short. The President relented, allowing me to assume command of the regiment while insisting that I take all orders from General Terry, who was still to be in overall charge of the campaign. At almost the same time a wire arrived from General Sherman advising General Terry to make sure that I was prudent and not allow any reporters to accompany me.

I boarded the train to Fort Lincoln with General Terry as one who has received an eleventh-hour reprieve. There can be no finer feeling.

Ten days later we began our march, and now I await General Terry's penultimate meeting on the *Far West* this evening, the meeting that will at last decide what role I will play in this campaign. Will I be held back, punished like a delinquent child, or will I be free to run the enemy to ground?

I have done everything I can think of, going so far as to have John Burkman make a final trim of my hair this noon. Libbie had a recurrent dream this spring that I would be scalped, and the only thing I could do to allay her fears was promise to keep my hair short. So fearful was she that I was made to swear that I would have Burkman trim it in the field. No one can say that I do not keep my end of a bargain.

ᘉᘉ

The meeting has been concluded and the results are the best I could hope to have. No longer am I standing at the door of a politician's office, no longer do my words mean anything beyond an order. Now it is going after the enemy—catching him, fighting him, crushing him. Public or private relations have no standing. Everything is action now.

It is one of the ironies of life that we devote worry to circumstances that in no way warrant anxiety. Who did I think would be picked to go after the hostiles? General Terry is the administrator of the campaign and has no experience in fighting Indians. Colonel Gibbon is so decrepit that he would not even be in the field were it not for the uselessness of his second-in-command, Major Brisbin. Crook has disappeared. Who then would President Grant and Generals Sherman and Sheridan have? Major Reno, who cannot follow the simplest instruction? Captain Benteen, the bitter grump?

No, there is no one but the Seventh Cavalry and its rightful commander. We will get on the hostiles' trail, and if any cavalry on earth can catch them it will be us.

Reno thinks they might have eight hundred fighting men. General Terry believes there might be as many as fifteen hundred warriors, if the reports of the reservation agents are to be believed. But even if the odds are four or five to one it will be no disadvantage. Odds mean nothing. Preparedness and willingness to fight are everything, and the Seventh Cavalry has both in abundance.

Gibbon has offered me the use of his Gatling guns, which I have declined. Better not to drag cannons over a rough, unknown country. He has also offered me the use of his Crow scouts, and that I have accepted.

The Crows know every inch of the alien country we are about to enter. They are marvelous-looking men and they look like royalty compared to the Rees. They will be a vital asset in finding the Sioux, punishing them, and putting them to flight.

General Terry's plan is simple—in my opinion, the best we could ask for in light of the impossibility of communications and the little we know of recent enemy movements.

I will take the Seventh up the Rosebud, following the river in a direction roughly southwest. Once we strike the trail Major Reno discovered we will move at the brisk pace of pursuit.

General Terry and Colonel Gibbon will march west along the Yellowstone and turn south on reaching the Little Bighorn country, the region where it seems most likely that the savages will be found.

If the trail I am following turns west I shall go ahead, taking care not to let the enemy escape either south or east. We shall then drive north and strike them the hardest blow possible. Most likely they will flee north, where they will find themselves blocked by the Terry-Gibbon column. If they flee west we shall all chase them down.

I have just received my written instructions from General Terry and after reading them could not resist dashing off a quick letter to Libbie, who has been greatly distressed by all these events of the last few months. I quoted her the following from General Terry's instructions:

"It is of course impossible to give you any definite instructions in regard to this movement; and were it not impossible to do so, the Department Commander places too much confidence in your zeal, energy, and ability to wish to impose upon you precise orders, which might hamper your action when nearly in contact with the enemy."

Oh, it is Christmas in June for Custer. I have an opportunity to make a great victory, which will go miles toward restoring my standing. The public will demand it. The chiefs of government and army alike will have no recourse but to bow to public demand if I succeed. And success is all that I am thinking of.

Christmas in June for General Custer!

JUNE 22,

1876

By design we made only twelve miles today, going into camp long before sundown. I am happy. I have broken out. So many of the officers left behind half-joking about saving some of the fighting for them. I sympathize but doubt whether they will get their wish.

Still happy about General Terry's decision but have been beset by morose thoughts all day. Sometimes it seems that I am the bad boy, called forth only when exploitation of my abilities might suit the aims of others.

Always I have held my tongue when it came to casting aspersions on others, always championed charity over cruelty, and even gone so far as to think the best of my enemies. I have minded my own business and what has it got me?

Practically nothing. That is the answer.

In 1867 the regular army approved my promotion to lieutenant colonel, a promotion I can only conclude came about from a desire to install me as commander of the then new Seventh Cavalry. Since that time I have given nine years of continuous and devoted service and what have I received in return? While the whole country knows me as general the army's rolls say that I remain a lieutenant colonel. Nine years without promotion. The most well known officer in the army?

Perhaps they do not want fighters to assume such power. Perhaps they fear that the tigers they create today will turn and devour them tomorrow.

Perhaps it is because I have always been an odd boy, a stuttering boy with a high voice, standing off to one side.

Perhaps I have worshiped my superiors too well with not enough thought of myself. Libbie says I have always been too hasty in putting the needs of others ahead of my own.

I cannot understand any of this. I think I understand more as I grow older but I only become more confused. What can I do anyway? And what does it matter? I have never been a thinker or a schemer. A doer is what I have been. The world is run by thinkers and schemers, not doers.

I always performed without complaint for my masters—McClellan and Pleasanton and Sherman and Sheridan and even Grant—and what, in the end, do I get in return? A pat on the head for being their boy. I suppose that is what I have always been. Always a boy, never a man. Have I brought this upon myself or have I been singled out? Is it I myself who has resisted taking my place as a man among the society of men? Perhaps I am an eternal boy? I have always loved being a boy.

I love a cavalry camp. Every sight and sound and smell do I love.

The men grooming their friends the horses, their partners and life-lines in battle. The pickets at night. Officer's call and a hand or two of cards. I love it.

This Rosebud River valley is a strange country. Lonely. And silent. For so long the exclusive domain of Stone Age people. For centuries.

I have delegated to each officer full responsibility for each of the twelve companies. There is fighting ahead and I want the command to act independently if need be. I determine when to move and when to halt but that is all for now.

Fighting ahead. Unless they escape somehow. But I do not think they will.

Why do I give each officer so much leeway? Can it be that I will not be there to command? I feel odd; calm and quiet and a little afraid. I cannot seem to raise my voice.

Can it be that my time has come? Perhaps God is finished with me. The only thing I can think of that I have yet to experience in this life is old age.

The Crows are excellent, tireless and alert and eager to find the Sioux.

We all are.

JUNE 23,

1876

Marched twenty-three miles today. Have picked up the trail where Reno found it, a large trail headed southwest.

Why do I feel as though I am dying? My head is clear, my thoughts are lucid, my body is strong and lean and suffers no complaint.

But I have a knowledge, knowledge defying definition . . . one that resides beyond mortal boundaries. It is a maddening knowledge, elusive as it is distinct.

There are trails of smoke about my head that hold the answers, yet each time I reach for one, my hand passes straight through. It seems that I am dying, yet I feel nothing. I have not felt this peculiar in all my life. I am watching myself from outside in complete calm.

Perhaps I am merely experiencing what has been recorded throughout time as a premonition of death. Perhaps my time is coming and somehow I know it.

At the noon halt Captain Keough mentioned casually that a number of his men had become jittery and that he overheard one wondering aloud if we were not all "marching to Valhalla."

At the time I told Captain Keough that at least we knew from this comment that the men were not falling asleep, but the remark stuck in my head all afternoon and into this evening because I believe Valhalla is the one thing I have truly wished for in my life.

When I was five or six I would accompany my father to gatherings of the rural militia of New Rumley, Ohio. So insistent was I about attending these Saturday sessions that my mother sewed for me a tiny uniform.

I drilled alongside the men and was adopted as a kind of mascot. The talk was always of armed conflict, and it was during a lull or at the end of one of these Saturday sessions that I was first made aware of the warrior's heaven . . . Valhalla.

What a grand place to go—to be carried up from the earth by ravishing women warriors; to be transported to a heavenly kingdom where food and drink and joy are limitless; to wander such a place for eternity in perfect satisfaction.

Valhalla has always been the only heaven I wanted . . . my heaven . . . my fondest, undying wish.

Early in our marriage I told Libbie about Valhalla, but she, being a thoroughly trained Protestant, judged it "too heathen a concept" to embrace. She did not like the idea and I did not pursue it.

But I did make a pact with my wife on the first night, in the first camp she slept in during the Great War. I made her promise that if I were to depart the earth in battle she would pray for my deliverance to the halls of Valhalla as soon as she knew I was gone. We have not spoken of it in a dozen years, but I am sure she will keep her promise.

I am sure that I will get in there. If I have earned nothing else in my life I have earned the right to a place in warrior's heaven. I have always faced the enemy and have never run from battle. I have never commanded from the rear—which is popular these days—but from the front, leading my men into no place that I would not enter first. I have never feared a warrior's death, not once in my life.

A mental list of what I shall miss should I leave this earth behind: Libbie and Tom and all our family; my books, my pen, and the precious comradeship of men in arms. There must be horses in Valhalla, so I will not list them.

JUNE 24,

〜

1876

This morning we passed the farthest boundary of Major Reno's late scout and a short while after discovered the remains of a large and puzzling Indian camp. The valley is filled with sign—so filled with layer after layer of travois scratchings and pony droppings that it was impossible to tell how many people had been there. Some of the droppings were but two days old, meaning the enemy could be as close as thirty miles.

It was an eerie scene. Apparently, a Sun Dance of some duration had been held there.

Inside a dilapidated lodge we found a white scalp.

The Crows were highly agitated, saying that the Sioux had made powerful medicine. I told them to watch the medicine that six hundred Seventh Calvary men will make.

It is now nine P.M. and to no one's surprise the Crows have discovered that the hostile trail has turned sharply west, for the valley of the Little Bighorn.

I have just called the officers together to inform them of a change in plan. In about an hour we will make a night march across the divide, find a place where we can remain in seclusion for most of the day and attack on the morning of the 26th.

JUNE 25,

1876

Went into camp at two A.M. and, bareback on Dandy, have just completed a tour of our bivouac. Men are weary but anxious to engage the enemy. Bloody Knife says there are enough warriors ahead to keep us fighting for two or three days. I say one.

&

At eight A.M. Crows report that they had discovered our objective. I rode forward and climbed to a place called the Crow's Nest, from which I could see nothing, though I have been assured a large village is there, fifteen miles ahead.

The scouts are certain we have been discovered and I have just given the order . . . we cannot wait until tomorrow . . . we attack now.

Have sent Dandy with John Burkman to the wagon train in the rear. In moments I will be on Vic and we will be moving up the valley to fight them where we find them.

I shall be in front, bugler on one side, color bearer on the other, facing the enemy.

AFTERWORD

George Armstrong Custer, age thirty-six, and 210 men of his immediate command died on the ridges above the Little Bighorn River on the afternoon of June 25, 1876. Killed with him were his brothers Tom and Boston, his nephew and namesake, Autie Reed, and his brother-in-law James Calhoun.

After the disaster his widow, Elizabeth, moved to New York City where she lived marginally until her death in 1933, having survived her famous husband by fifty-three years. She never remarried.

The devoted couple lie buried side by side in a small graveyard at West Point.

About the Author

MICHAEL BLAKE's previous books include *Airman Mortensen* and *Dances With Wolves*. He began writing professionally while enlisted in the U.S. Air Force from 1964 to 1968. In addition to writing, he is also devoted to public service and has received many honors for his efforts, including the Animal Protection Institute's Humanitarian of the Year Award. He lives with his wife on a ranch in southern Arizona.